Julia has always made up stories in her head, and until recently she thought everyone else did too. She grew up in London, one of eight children, including a twin sister. She married Dave, a dentist, in 1989, and they have four daughters. After the birth of the second, Julia went freelance and decided to try her hand at writing. Ten bestselling books later, it's safe to say the gamble paid off! Her books have sold across Europe, and she has sold half a million copies of her novels to date.

To find out more about Julia go to her website at www.juliawilliamsauthor.com or follow Julia on Twitter @JCCWilliams.

By the same author:

It's a Wonderful Life

JULIA WILLIAMS

This novel is entirely a work of fiction.
The names, characters and incidents portrayed in it are the work of
the author's imagination. Any resemblance to actual persons,
living or dead, events or localities is entirely coincidental.

AVON

A division of HarperCollins*Publishers*
1 London Bridge Street,
London SE1 9GF

www.harpercollins.co.uk

A Paperback Original 2016
1

Copyright © Julia Williams

Julia Williams asserts the moral right to be identified as the author of this work

A catalogue record for this book is available from the British Library

ISBN 978-1-84756-360-6

Typeset in Minion by Palimpsest Book Production Ltd, Falkirk, Stirlingshire

Printed and bound in Great Britain by Clays Ltd, St Ives plc

MIX
Paper from
responsible sources
FSC **FSC™ C007454**
www.fsc.org

FSC™ is a non-profit international organisation established to promote
the responsible management of the world's forests. Products carrying the
FSC label are independently certified to assure consumers that they come
from forests that are managed to meet the social, economic and
ecological needs of present and future generations,
and other controlled sources.

Find out more about HarperCollins and the environment at
www.harpercollins.co.uk/green

To my family, who light up my life

Beth

I don't know what's wrong with me lately. I have a wonderful life. No, really I do. I'm very lucky. I am pretty healthy, I have a lovely husband and two kids who, if no longer at the adorable stage, still make me laugh on a regular basis, as well as giving me the usual frustrations teenagers do. I have a good career as a picture-book artist, and a family that loves me. Why can't I be satisfied with my lot? I know my sister, Lou, would never understand, but sometimes I feel as if life is passing me by. Is this all there is? It feels so ungrateful, and yet I can't stop myself from feeling like this. If my life is so damned brilliant, why do I feel there's something missing?

Prologue

August

Beth

It's a gorgeously hot afternoon in August. I am sitting in my kitchen with the patio doors wide open, to let the little breeze there is in, staring at an email I've received this morning from my editor, Karen. I've been looking at it for several hours, in between trying to get a sketch right for my new picture book. Inspiration isn't flowing, and several pieces of paper are scattered on the floor.

The Littlest Angel synopsis
By Beth King

This is the story of a little angel, whose job it is to find the baby Jesus. She sets out with a band of angels and gets lost. All she knows is a special baby is being born in Bethlehem, and she has to follow a magic star which has risen in the East in order to get to him.

3

On her journey she meets a young shepherd boy, a page, a camel, a donkey and finally some sheep, who lead her to where the baby Jesus is. She is the first angel there and sings him the first ever carol.

Beth, I just love this story. And the spreads you've worked up are really wonderful. I know we'll get a lot of interest in this one, I'm only sorry that I won't be able to take you all the way through, but as you know, my own little arrival is about to put in an entrance. It's been great working with you, and I'm sure you'll be in good hands with Vanessa.

I'm wishing you great success for your little angel. You deserve it so much.

Much love

Karen x

It's great that Karen likes my new idea, not so great that she's gone on maternity leave during the biggest crisis of my career. Just as I pick up another version of the spread, and decide it's as rubbish as the rest, I'm sidelined by my mother ringing.

'So, what are your plans for Christmas?'

Typical Mum, straight to the point as usual.

I swear she asks this question earlier and earlier every year. Just in case Daniel and I have made devious plans to escape the Holroyd Family Christmas and booked a week away somewhere. As if we would. As if we could.

'Mum, it's August!' I protest. I scrumple up the sketch and throw it on the floor, where it joins all the other discarded pieces of paper. I honestly don't know what's wrong with me, I don't normally find it this hard to get my ideas down.

'And soon it will be September and you'll be too busy to talk to me.' My mum does *such* a good line in passive aggression. I not only speak to her every other day, I'm usually round her house once a week. I am after all the dutiful one of the family. This is my job, while my erstwhile brother, Ged, takes gap years aged thirty-six and at thirty-eight my sister Lou lurches from one disastrous love affair to another. I'm the one who did things right: had a family, moved close to Mum and Dad.

They still live in the cosy cottage where I grew up in the small Surrey town of Abinger Lea. Our house is about a mile away from them. Initially we stayed nearer to London, in the house Daniel's mum left him, but then when the children came along I needed some help and it seemed like a no-brainer to come here. We like being close to the countryside while having good train links with London, which has been useful for my work. Daniel used to work in an inner-London comprehensive, but he's just about to start a job in the slightly larger town of Wottonleigh, which is only three miles away. That's going to make life a lot easier.

It's not as though I don't like being near my parents, it's just that sometimes I wish I wasn't the 'good' sibling. It's a feeling I've had more often than not lately. Mum and Dad are perfectly capable, but I seem to always be doing them little favours, like dropping Mum off into Wottonleigh when Dad's busy playing golf, or going to the art classes I finally persuaded him to take (he's always had a creative side, but he keeps it under wraps). And I seem to be on constant call to help them sort out their computer problems. I feel rubbish for being so resentful, particularly as they were always so great about babysitting when the kids were small, but sometimes I feel stifled by the fact that I've never quite managed to move away from my family.

Belatedly I realise Mum is still in full flow.

'Anyway, as I always like to say, fail to prepare—'

'Prepare to fail. I know, Mum,' I say. 'Anyway, we'll do exactly what we do every year and come to you. I don't know why you feel you have to ask.'

I've occasionally tried to change the 'Christmas Plan' by suggesting that I take the slack for Mum and have them all over here, as it's not as though we don't have the room. But she always knocks me back, and I've given up trying, even though the kids get more and more stroppy about it each year. Sam is going to be eighteen next year and Megan's fifteen. They're not little kids any more, and I think Mum forgets that sometimes, and doesn't quite get that they have other things going on in their lives, particularly around Christmas time. The trouble is, Mum loves doing Christmas, so even though I have a family of my own, I don't get a look in. The only time I was allowed remotely near the turkey was the year Mum had had a hysterectomy, and even then she sat directing operations from the lounge. Nightmare.

'I just wanted to check, dear,' Mum says, 'in case you might have had other plans.'

I refrain from snorting. I know far, far better than to make other plans.

'You've no need to worry, Mum, we'll be there,' I say, and put the phone down.

'Who was that?' Daniel wanders in from the garden, where he's been working hard cutting the grass. Sweat is pouring off his brow, and he's taken his T-shirt off. I take a minute to enjoy the view. At forty-two my husband bears a distinct resemblance to Adrian Lester, and is still pretty trim and sexy for his age. Sure we argue like all couples do, and in term time when he's busy I sometimes wish we saw more of him. The great thing though is that despite the ups and downs of married life, I still fancy the pants off him, and that's dead lucky at my age. I know so many women who moan constantly about their husbands. While we have our disagreements, Daniel and I still get on pretty well, and at *this* particular moment I am rather wishing we were alone in the house. Shame the kids are upstairs.

'Mum,' I say, in answer to his question. 'I'd put your shirt back on before the kids see you, they'll be horrified.'

Daniel looks upwards to their bedrooms.

'I doubt they're going to be downstairs in a hurry,' is his wry response, and I laugh. It's the summer holidays. They're teenagers, it would probably take a bomb to get them up before lunchtime. He comes and gives me a kiss. I feel a little lurch of desire, and regret even more that the kids haven't gone out for the day.

'Ugh, you're all sweaty,' I say jokingly, pushing him away.

'Just the way you like me,' he teases. 'What did your mum want?'

I roll my eyes. 'To ask about Christmas. Honestly, it's only August.'

'Oh, come on, you love it,' says Daniel, 'the Holroyd Family Christmas is legendary. Christmas wouldn't be Christmas if we didn't go to your mum and dad's.'

This is true. There was the year Dad accidentally set fire to his beard when he dressed up as Santa, and the year that Mum cooked the turkey with the giblets in by mistake, not to mention the year when Lou and Ged had a massive row and Lou ended up in floods of tears in the kitchen with me and Mum comforting her. Oh wait. That happens nearly every year. Perhaps Daniel is right. I suppose it wouldn't be the same if we didn't go.

The Christmas Day routine in our family never varies. Mum and Dad come back from church at 10.30 – some years if I've been nagged enough I join them – and we go round for drinks at eleven – Dad always believes in opening the bubbly early. Mum has usually been up since 6 a.m. slaving over the turkey so we can eat promptly at 1 p.m., making sure we have plenty of time for lunch before the Queen's Speech, after which Dad makes us all sing the National Anthem. Depending on the levels of drunkenness (in which Mum disapprovingly doesn't take part) this is either hilarious or excruciating. After that it's a free-for-all with presents, and we collapse in front of the TV till Mum starts producing turkey sandwiches and Christmas cake. By this time Dad, Daniel and my brother Ged will have usually managed to demolish a bottle of port between them before Dad insists it's time for Christmas charades, the bit of Christmas Day which I absolutely loathe. Everyone else always gets into the swing of it, but I've always hated it, ever since I was little. Dad gets really involved: I blame the fact that his job in insurance always suppressed his creativity, so he insists on letting rip at home. I hate standing up in front of other people and performing; I always find charades a massive trial. Maybe that's why I'm an artist. I prefer to channel my creativity from behind an easel. Growing up hasn't made it any more fun. I long for a charades-free Christmas, but I won't be getting it any time soon.

'It would just be nice to be at home one year, don't you

think?' I say half-heartedly, but I know Daniel doesn't really get it. His family are so different from mine. He was very close to his mum, who died shortly after we met, but he doesn't get on well with his dad. They're barely in touch. He very rarely talks about it, though I do know his dad was pretty useless when he was little. It makes me sad, because Daniel has so much love to give, and as an only child he has no family of his own since he lost his mum. From what he's told me he had very quiet Christmases growing up, so he's always loved being part of our family celebrations.

'Nah, that means we'd have to do all the hard work. Come on, Beth, it will be fine.' He comes over and gives me a big hug. 'You'll enjoy it – promise.'

Lou

I'm lying in bed with Jo one Saturday morning in August when Mum rings up.

'Hi,' I say, suddenly feeling immensely guilty. She doesn't know about me, or about Jo. As ever, when I speak to her on the phone if Jo's about I feel like there's a big red sign on my head saying 'Your daughter's a lesbian!' which she can somehow see. Which is ridiculous. One day I'll tell her. One day. When I'm sure she won't flip out and I won't be cast from the family home. She and Dad are so old-fashioned I have no idea how they would take it. So I'm not going to be telling them any time soon.

'Who's that?' says Jo, tickling my feet.

'Mum,' I mouth, trying not to giggle. I get up out of bed, not wanting to be distracted, not wanting to feel that I have to behave myself. Oh God, I wish it wasn't like this. I wish

I could tell my parents and my family who I really am. I haven't even told my sister Beth. I want to, and she keeps hinting that Jo and I should come round, but I've let her think 'Joe' is a boy, and now I don't know how to get out of it.

Jo of course doesn't understand this. Her parents are perfectly relaxed with her being gay, in a way I can't imagine mine ever being. So much so that it took me till my late twenties to really admit to myself that I was into women not men. At school being a lesbian was pretty much a dirty word, and I thought I was odd for being attracted to girls. So I continued to have awkward sex and fumbled encounters with men I didn't fancy, until one day I realised I couldn't go on with it.

But I still haven't told my family, and now I don't know how to. It's pathetic to have got to thirty-eight and not come out to my parents, and I know Jo doesn't understand it, but I can't see a way to get around it.

I tune into what Mum is saying. Oh. Christmas. Of course. We have to have the Christmas conversation in August in my family. It's bloody nuts.

'Yes of course I'm coming for Christmas, Mum. Where else would I go?'

'And you haven't got anyone you want to bring?' She dangles the question. Christ – does she know? Has she guessed by some kind of telepathic Mum power?

'No, no one,' I say. 'But don't worry – I'll be there.'

'Jolly good,' she says. 'And how are things at work now? Any better?'

I sigh. 'Not really. We're all still in limbo, just waiting to hear.'

I work in credit control and the company I've just joined is in trouble. They've told us there might be redundancies but, surprise surprise, no decisions have been made yet. The waiting isn't fun at all.

'Well, you keep me posted,' Mum says, and I promise I will.

I get off the phone and get back into bed with Jo, lovely Jo, with whom I've spent a blissful spring and summer. I put my arms around her, trying not to think about work. I'll cross that bridge if I come to it. For now, Jo is all that matters. We've had such a good summer; we've even spent a fabulous week in Greece together. I still can't believe someone like her would be interested in me, and have to keep pinching myself because I feel so lucky.

'What did your mum want?' she asks.

'She just wanted to know about my Christmas plans,' I say.

'Christmas? Now?'

'I know,' I say. 'Mad innit?'

'So what *are* your Christmas plans?' she asks. 'We could do something together if you want.'

Woah. I wasn't expecting that. I'm completely nuts about Jo, but I can't seem to shake the feeling that she's too good for me. Maybe it's just because I've had so many disappointments in the past. I don't want to jump in head first when it could still all go down the pan.

'Maybe,' I say. 'I have great difficulties getting out of my family Christmas.'

'Oh, go on Lou Lou, it will be fun.' She seems a bit disappointed, which gives me a secret thrill. Much as I want to commit to it, I am too afraid to jinx what so far has been my most successful relationship yet. I prevaricate instead.

'Christmas is ages away. Let's not think about it now.'

So we don't, and I put it to the back of my mind. If by

11

any chance I'm lucky enough to still be with Jo at Christmas, I'll worry about it then.

Daniel

'Good luck.' Beth kissed Daniel as he left the house at 8 a.m. for the first day at his new school. There was a lot riding on this new job for him.

'I think I'm going to need it,' he grimaced.

'Oh ye of little faith,' said Beth, 'you'll have them eating out of the palm of your hand by the end of the day.'

Touched as he was by her belief in him, Daniel wasn't entirely sure whether that were true. Moving from the big inner-city comprehensive which he'd run for the last five years to a much smaller Academy in leafy Wottonleigh was a big leap. In many ways, it should be easier: the results were better, the majority of students spoke English as a first language, and the parents, by all accounts, were committed to both the school and their children's education, which had been far from the case for so many of his former pupils. Daniel had loved working in London, but the stress of commuting and the strain of the job was becoming untenable. He and Beth hadn't seen nearly enough of each other in the last few years, and he was uneasily conscious that he sometimes spent more time thinking about other people's children than he did about his own. So the chance to work locally seemed too good to be true.

But . . . it was one thing being that rare beast – a black Head Teacher – in the inner city; it was quite another out in the sticks. Daniel was used to being one of the few black faces he saw every day in Abinger Lea, but would the parents at his new school accept him? And would the staff? The governors had given him the heads-up that his deputy, Jim Ferguson, had been certain Daniel's job would be his. There was bound to be resentment, particularly if they disagreed on the running of the school, which after a couple of short meetings with his staff team, Daniel felt sure was likely. From what little he'd seen, Jim Ferguson was a yes-man, who liked to keep wheels well oiled. He was a capable administrator, but an uncharismatic teacher. People respected him, but they didn't like him. It was why he hadn't got the job.

'This school needs new blood,' Sarah Bellows, the Chair of Governors, had told him. 'It's doing well, but it could do better. It needs strong leadership and an inspiring educator in charge. We believe that's what you can offer us.'

That, and the chance to bring the school up from Good to Outstanding in their next Ofsted report, which was due to happen some time in the spring term. Daniel was under no illusions that inspiring educator or not, the bottom line was they wanted better results. If he failed to deliver, they'd probably revert to Plan B and Jim Ferguson would get the job he craved. In the meantime, Daniel had to find a way of trying to bring him onside. He had a feeling it wasn't going to be easy, a feeling that was confirmed when Jim arrived late at the staff meeting. It was a getting-to-know-you session, which Jim was supposed to be chairing. The fact that he couldn't be bothered to turn up on time didn't bode well. He didn't seem impressed when Daniel outlined a few of his ideas about how to improve staff morale by using their freedom as an Academy to invest in proper pay structures, and allow younger teachers to see that there'd be opportunities for advancement if they worked hard. He also rolled his eyes when Daniel began to talk about setting higher standards of uniform conformity. He'd been horrified on a visit in the summer to see how lax the staff had been in implementing many of the school rules. He wanted to use his new role to ensure the students took the greatest pride in themselves and their school by giving them more responsibility for helping keep it tidy.

'With all due respect, Head Teacher,' said Jim, managing to make his title sound like an insult while smiling at him, 'I think you'll find morale at this school is very high, and that the students already take pride in their environment. I'm afraid you'll find there's very little to improve in that regard.'

'It can't hurt to take a look at it though, can it, Jim?' Daniel said. 'And please, no formalities, do call me Daniel.'

If there was one thing Daniel hated it was unnecessary bowing down to hierarchies. He had a feeling that Jim would see it differently.

'Of course, Daniel,' said Jim, with a smirk, managing again to make it sound sarcastic.

Unwilling to get into an awkward discussion on his first day, Daniel moved on, and by the end of the meeting felt he hadn't acquitted himself too badly. It was clear that one or two members of staff were definitely Team Ferguson, but Carrie Woodall, Head of Maths, sidled up to him after the meeting and muttered, 'Welcome on board, and don't take any notice of Jim – he always likes to throw his weight around.' Daniel smiled politely, but didn't comment. It was good to know he had supporters though. Determined not to let Jim's negative attitude ruin his day, he spent the rest of it trying to get a handle on what the job entailed. It was busy and exhausting, but by the end of it he felt exhilarated. The kids were nice and polite, the teachers, in the main, friendly, and even if he worked late, he lived a mere twenty minutes from home. More time with Beth. More time with the kids. Despite any difficulties that might lie ahead, this had been a good move.

*

Christmas Day

Beth

'Merry Christmas.'

'Bleugh.' I awake gingerly, my head hammering from a combination of too much wine and not enough sleep, to see Daniel enter our bedroom bearing a tray with two glasses of fizz, and scrambled egg and salmon for breakfast. 'Is it time to get up already?'

'Afraid so, but I thought after the night you've had you deserved breakfast in bed.'

Although I could really do with staying in bed several hours longer, I'm touched by his thoughtfulness. I had hoped to be up and about early on Christmas morning, but thanks to Sam choosing last night to get spectacularly drunk I've barely slept. He's started going out a lot more recently, and I'm struggling to get used to the nights of sitting up worrying where he is. Daniel tells me not to fret so much and tells me he's just being a teenager, but it's not easy. And last night, despite promising to be in by midnight, Sam finally staggered home at 3 a.m., having lost his iPhone in a nightclub, and promptly threw up everywhere. I hadn't been able to sleep for worrying, and

I came downstairs to find him lying with his arms wrapped round the base of the toilet bowl. I couldn't get him upstairs so I ended up sitting up for the rest of the night, checking on him intermittently. I've only been back in bed for a couple of hours.

'And this is for you,' Daniel says with a flourish, handing me a present.

'This doesn't look much like a puppy,' I say in mock disappointment. I've always wanted a dog, thinking it would be romantic to go for long walks together in the country, but Daniel can't stand the idea. It's been a standing joke with us for years that he's going to buy me a puppy for Christmas. I know he never will.

'Next year,' he grins, giving me a kiss. 'Anyway, I think you'll like this more.'

I do like it. Daniel has thoughtfully bought me a set of paints and paper, and some lovely new pencils. He knows I'm still struggling with the book I've been working on all year.

'Thought they might help boost the creativity,' he says, as I lean over to kiss him.

'Thank you, they're perfect,' I say. 'And so are you.'

We stay together for several minutes in a cosy embrace, before Daniel says, 'Breakfast?' and I tuck into the scrambled eggs. The bed is so warm and comfy. I sigh, wishing once again we could stay at home this year. But no chance of that of course, so after breakfast, I go to call Megan and Sam, neither of whom want to move. They're still not out of bed by the time Daniel and I have showered and dressed. We look at each other wryly. Time was when they'd have been up for hours by now, and we would be at the end of our tether. How life has changed.

Eventually we manage to bully them to get up, and we

have just enough time to open a few presents, before chivvy-ing them off to get ready to go to my parents'. Relaxing it's not. One day I'll manage to get the Christmas I want. One day . . .

Finally we load ourselves and several bags of presents into the car, with Megan whinging about wanting a lie-in, and Sam sitting in moody silence. His eyes are red and bloodshot from whatever poisons he thrust down his throat last night. I'm beyond cross with him, but it's Christmas, so I'm determined to be cheerful. I put some Christmassy tunes on, but Sam moans that they're making his head hurt. I heroically manage to restrain myself from snapping *whose fault is that then?* I feel that would be distinctly lacking in Christmas cheer.

Fortunately the drive is a short one, and while Daniel parks the car, the rest of us stagger into the house with the presents.

'We're here!' I shout, pushing open the front door. 'Merry Christmas!'

'Merry Christmas, Merry Christmas!' Dad comes bounding into the hall, which as usual is strung with horrible paper decorations we probably made in infant school. He's dressed in his usual Santa Claus outfit; he insists on wearing it every year, even though it gets more and more threadbare. I can hear Christmas carols playing in the background, and begin to relax a bit. As usual, Mum will be chopping vegetables in the kitchen, warbling away to them. I take a deep breath. It is Christmas after all; I need to let go of my lack of sleep induced grumpi-ness.

Dad is waving a bottle of Prosecco around and looks rather red in the face. It's unlike him to start drinking before we arrive, but never mind.

'Still not got rid of that ghastly costume, Dad?' I laugh. It's a running joke every year.

'Never!' he says. 'Bubbly anyone?'

I accept a glass, but Daniel says no as he's being generous and driving this year. Sam looks like he might throw up at the thought, but I let Megan have a small one.

'Where's Mum?'

Is it my imagination, or does Dad suddenly look shifty? 'Kitchen,' he says.

Dad is in full *mein host* mode and ushers Daniel and the kids through to the lounge. Honestly, it makes me laugh how well he and Daniel get along now. To think of the grief I got when I first brought him home to meet them. It's not that my parents are racist exactly, but I guess when imagining a much longed-for son-in-law, a black one hadn't really featured, and Dad was quite sniffy at first. I can remember an excruciating occasion when he'd quizzed Daniel endlessly about his prospects. I wouldn't have blamed Daniel for not giving my parents a second chance, especially as his own mum, in the short time I knew her, proved to be much less intolerant. But after she died, Mum forgot all about any prejudices she had and said, 'That poor boy needs a mother.' After that she really took him under her wing, and Dad quickly followed suit. Now they're the best of friends, and you'd never know there had been a problem. Daniel is a forgiving sort, so he saw the best in them, and I have always loved him for it.

I wander into the kitchen to see if Mum needs any help. I always offer, even though I know her response will be to shoo me away, but to my surprise she's barely made a start on the vegetables. She looks a bit pale and wan, and I feel guilty. I've barely seen her in the last month as I've been so wrapped up in my book. I have a sudden stab of worry that she might be ill.

'Is everything OK, Mum?' I ask.

'Of course it is, why shouldn't it be?' she says, picking up a carrot ready to chop. 'If you're going to stand around in here, you may as well be useful.' She hands me a knife.

Something's a bit off here, but I can't quite work out what, and there's no point asking again. It's not that I don't get on with my mum. I do, and I love her very much, but we don't have that cosy mother–daughter relationship that so many of my girlfriends enjoy. My mum doesn't do cosy, and wouldn't understand at all if I suddenly launched into a litany of my woes. She's very good at practical advice, but go to her for help in emotional matters and you may as well howl at the moon.

We chop vegetables companionably, with carols playing in the background while Mum starts her annual moan about why Ged and Lou can't ever get here on time, which is the main reason Daniel and I always come early, just to keep her from feeling totally unloved. Although it pisses me off too. Why is it always up to me to be the sensible one?

'You know they have further to come,' I say, trying to be diplomatic. 'And Ged only just flew in from Oz yesterday, so he's probably really jet-lagged.'

Ged has been taking a year off to 'discover himself'. If I were to do such a thing, Mum and Dad would both think it's ridiculous, but Golden Boy Ged, as the baby of the family, always does what he wants and gets away with it too. I love my younger brother dearly, but it's sometimes very hard not to get fed up with the way he gets treated so differently just because he's a boy.

'He's bringing Rachel,' says Mum. 'Did I say?'

'Only about a hundred times,' I laugh. Rachel is Ged's new girlfriend. It will be interesting to see if she lasts longer that the rest. 'Do stop trying to marry them off. Ged will run a mile if he thinks you've already bought your hat. You've already been on enough at Lou about Joe. You need to give them both some space.'

The doorbell rings.

'That'll be them now,' says Mum, her face brightening.

Dad has got to the door first and we all troop out to say hello.

It's Ged, with a very beautiful blonde girl in tow.

'Oh,' says Mum, her jaw dropping.

Oh indeed. Ged's beautiful blonde appears to be pregnant.

Lou

I'm running late. As usual. Christmas has started with a very unpleasant bang. I had been so looking forward to it: my first Christmas as part of a proper couple. Jo and I had agreed to spend the day apart with our families, as I still hadn't got round to breaking the news about our relationship to mine, but we'd planned to have breakfast together at the flat I share in Kentish Town, and make Boxing Day our Christmas. I had prepared stockings for her, and gone to town on the decorations. My Christmas tree was as sparkly as I could make it, much to the amusement of my flatmate, Kate, who had left three days earlier to spend the festive season with her family. I had spent hours making mince pies, mulled wine and eggnog. I'd even hung mistletoe over the door. I had everything planned down to a T. I so wanted it all to be perfect. I might have known it wouldn't work out like that: Lou

Holroyd and her spectacularly pathetic love life triumphs once again. Instead of a lovely evening in with a bottle of bubbly cuddled up on the sofa, Jo has dropped a bombshell, standing in the doorway of the lounge, underneath the sodding mistletoe, barely noticing the efforts I'd gone to.

'It's not you, it's me, babe.' She actually said that, and I know it's not true, because her initial, 'I'm a free spirit and I can't give you what you want,' quickly descended into, 'You're so clingy and need to sort your shit out.' Which, given that I was wailing pathetically in a corner, probably wasn't too far off the mark.

I suppose I should have seen it coming. We'd both been so busy in the run-up to Christmas, and I'd had to blow her out a couple of times because I was working late – is it my fault that after a while where I looked safe jobwise, things are looking decidedly dodgy again? – and I suppose she'd been more distant recently, but I'd just put that down to the hectic nature of both our lives. She's a nurse in a busy medical practice, and I'm obviously working hard to try and reduce my chances of being made redundant. We both take our work seriously; it was one of the things that attracted me to her. That and the fact that she's bloody gorgeous and I feel so lucky that someone as fabulous as Jo could have chosen me. But now . . .

'It's definitely over,' was her parting shot to my pathetic plea for us to take a break and have a rethink in the New Year. And with that she was off, swanning out to join her friends, her other life, the one she barely let me get involved in, leaving me cold and lonely by the Christmas tree, which now looked gaudy and overdone in her absence. I guess now I look at it in the cold light of day, she was always a little bit ashamed of me. There were the times when she pulled away from me if I was being too affectionate in public, and the times she would put me down in front of our friends if she thought I was too loud. She'd stopped mentioning Christmas, which should have been a clue. I should have seen this coming. But then, I never bloody do.

So I spent last night in a drunken sobbing haze, barely slept at all and then missed my alarm. Now I'm driving like a maniac, feeling heartsick and hungover, to get over to Mum and Dad's before 1 p.m. so I can prove to them that I'm not their most useless child. Poor old childless single Lou, turning up at Christmas on her own – *again*.

The drive from London down to Surrey is depressing beyond belief. The roads are mainly empty – everyone is clearly already with their families – and the sight of everyone's Christmas trees and garden lights makes me feel miserable. It feels like everybody else is celebrating and having a good time, whereas my world has just collapsed.

My phone has been buzzing furiously the whole time I've been driving across London – so when I pull in at a traffic light, I stop to look at it. Three messages from Beth.

OMG!!! Ged's girlfriend is pregnant, says the first.

Followed by, *Mum's crying in the kitchen and Dad's ignoring it all.*

The last one says *GET YOUR BUTT HERE NOW. I CAN'T COPE.*

Great. All I bloody need. A new baby in the family, and not one provided by me. I know by the time I get there, Mum will have come round to the good news and turned it into a positive. Ged can do no wrong in her eyes; Mum doesn't half cut him some slack. And while she won't be ecstatic about having a grandchild out of wedlock, I don't doubt that within seconds she'll be talking about knitting cardigans. After the grief I've heard over the years about her only having two grandchildren, I can't see her being put out for long. Great. She's given that one up of late; this will give her another excuse to pressurise me about babies.

The lights go green but my foot on the accelerator doesn't move; I'm lost in a world of my own. I didn't want to go today anyway. I'd much rather be curled up under the duvet in a miserable state, but if I missed Christmas I'd never have heard the end of it. But now? I've always wanted children. Ged never has, and Beth always says that domesticity and family life isn't all it's cracked up to be – which seems damned ungrateful to me. She's so lucky to have her kids. It's not bloody fair. Why do I have to be the one on my own? I might never get to have babies.

Tears start spilling down my cheeks, and suddenly I'm sobbing on the wheel, my car engine off. This is terrible. I can't turn up like this.

There's a knock on my car window, and I look up to see a policeman.

'Are you all right, madam?' he asks as I roll my window down. 'Only you seem to be causing a bit of an obstruction.'

I look behind me. Oh shit, somehow I've caused a mini traffic jam out of the only ten cars driving in London today, and got the attention of the one policeman who seems to be at work.

'Sorry, officer,' I say through my sniffles, and turn the engine back on.

'Cheer up,' he says, 'it's Christmas.'

I wipe the tears from my cheeks.

'Yeah, that's the problem,' I say as I drive away.

Christmas. The time to be happy and jolly. The time to be with your friends and family. The time to have that special someone in your life and hold them close. I've never felt less like celebrating in my life.

Daniel was sitting on the sofa, making polite conversation with Ged's new girlfriend, Rachel. She'd been introduced to the family and ushered into the lounge, while his mother-in-law, Mary, had called Ged into the kitchen for a not very subtle conflab. Beth had been dragged in too, but her dad, Fred, seemed determined to rise above the drama. He was sitting next to the Christmas tree, knocking back the Prosecco like it was going out of fashion. He seemed in a very strange mood. Daniel might have expected some reaction to the news of an impending grandchild, but he seemed to be totally oblivious to it.

The kids, meanwhile, found it hilarious. They were keeping a lid on it, but he could tell they were Snapchatting the odd comment to each other by the way that every so often they'd both burst into fits of giggles for no apparent reason. He shot them a warning look, but luckily, Rachel didn't seem to notice.

She was very beautiful and at least ten years younger than Ged. Daniel hoped she knew what she was getting into. Ged didn't exactly have a good track record with women. He had left a string of broken hearts behind him, and Daniel had lost count of the hours Beth had spent counselling Ged's ex-girlfriends over the years.

'So where did you two meet?' he asked politely, trying to put Rachel at ease. The poor girl understandably looked a bit shell-shocked. Ged presumably hadn't warned her that his parents might not be too thrilled to discover they were going to be grandparents straight away.

'Oh.' Her face lit up. 'It was at the Full Moon party in Thailand. It was full of utter losers, and then there was Ged being the perfect gentleman.'

I bet he was, thought Daniel, but smiled and said, 'That sounds great.'

Rachel carried on about what a wonderful time they'd had together, first in Thailand, then going on to Singapore and Bali before visiting her parents in Australia. 'I fell pregnant in Bali,' she confided. 'So romantic.'

'Well, congratulations,' said Daniel. 'I bet your parents are pleased?'

'Oh, they're thrilled,' said Rachel. 'Mum's a bit annoyed with me for coming over here to have the baby, but I just want to be wherever Ged is, and he wanted to come home. He was so excited about the baby, he wanted to tell everyone.'

Really? Daniel wondered if Ged had changed his mind on that one. But knowing Ged, he wouldn't have thought any of this through.

It was getting on for 1 p.m. and for once it didn't look like the turkey would be ready in time. Daniel could hear slightly raised voices in the kitchen, and wondered whether he should go and smooth over troubled waters. He was about to get up when the doorbell rang and in rushed Lou: breathless, late, and looking suspiciously like she'd been crying. Oh no, poor Lou, what had happened now? Daniel was fond of his sister-in-law, but she always seemed to pick the wrong men when it came to her love life. This time he'd thought she and Joe, the mysterious new partner she'd met in the spring, were really going places. She'd been so happy last time she'd been over to see Beth and Daniel, and they'd both hoped it would work out for her. They'd asked to meet Joe several times, but Lou had always put them off. Now it looked like another one had bitten the dust, and they'd never get that chance.

'Sorry I'm late,' she burst out, 'traffic was mayhem.'

'Are you late?' Fred looked up, seemingly a bit befuddled.

He stood up to greet his daughter, and staggered a bit, nearly falling back into his seat. Daniel frowned. Fred normally liked a drink on Christmas Day, but Daniel had never known him to be pissed before.

There was a shriek from the kitchen, followed by a massive crash.

Daniel and Lou immediately leapt up and ran into the kitchen to see what was going on, the kids following on close behind, only to find Mary in hysterics with the turkey lying on the floor. Ged and Beth were looking a little dumb-founded.

'It's not a problem, Mary,' said Daniel, stepping forward to put a hand on her shoulder. 'Come on, we can pick it up, a little bit of dirt won't kill us.'

'I don't care about the bloody turkey,' shouted Mary, her crying stopping as abruptly as it started. Daniel was shocked. He couldn't recall ever hearing his mother-in-law shout. She turned round to face them just as Fred wandered in, looking confused.

'Is everything all right in here?'

'What do you care?' said Mary with a surprising bitterness.

'Mary, not today,' warned Fred.

'Why the bloody hell not?' she said. 'Just because it's Christmas?'

'Yes, because it's Christmas,' said Fred. His voice was rising too, and he was looking decidedly red around the gills. 'You know, family time and all that.'

'Could someone kindly tell me what's going on?' said Lou.

'I'll tell you what's going on,' said Mary. There was a brief pause, and Daniel found himself holding his breath; he had never seen his mother-in-law behave this way. What on earth was the matter? Mary looked around the room, her hands on her hips. 'Your dad is a cheat and a liar and is having an affair with Lilian Mountjoy. And I've had just about enough.'

You could have heard a pin drop. The entire Holroyd family stood in total shock. At which point, Rachel wandered in and said innocently, 'Can I do anything to help?'

Part One

The Journey Begins . . .

January–March

The Littlest Angel

The Littlest Angel was very excited. The whole Heavenly Host were preparing for a Big Event.

'*The* Big Event,' Gabriel said.

There had already been a buzz around <u>a baby</u> who had been born a few months earlier, but Gabriel said this baby was going to be even more important. *This* baby was going to save the world.

<u>The Heavenly Host</u> was going to go and tell people, and <u>for the first time</u> the Littlest Angel was going to be allowed to come too.

'Is it today?' the Littlest Angel asked her mother.

'Not today,' said her mother.

'Is it today?' asked the Littlest Angel the next day.

'Not today,' said her mother. 'But soon.'

The days went by and still it wasn't the right day, until finally the Littlest Angel asked, 'Is it *today*?'

And her mother said, 'Yes, it's today.'

'Yippee!' cried the Littlest Angel. And she got <u>ready to go</u>.

Vanessa Marlow: What baby?

Beth King: Um, John the Baptist.

Vanessa Marlow: What's the Heavenly Host?
Beth King: The angels.

Vanessa Marlow: What stops her from going? How does she get lost? Who does she visit on the way?
Beth King: Vanessa, I'm trying to work this out.

Vanessa Marlow: Can't she go round the world visiting different people?
Beth King: Why would she do that?

Chapter One

Beth

The Littlest Angel set out on her journey, and soon she was very lost . . .

I am sitting staring into space. I've been working on these same two double-page spreads for months. I've promised my publishers something new for the Bologna Book Fair in April, where they'd be keen to show it to foreign agents, but it's rapidly approaching and nothing is forthcoming. I've never hit a wall like this before. Light-years ago when my original editor, Karen, had suggested this idea, we'd both been dead excited. We had a wonderful brainstorming meeting with the art department followed by a boozy lunch, and I came home completely fired up. This was going to be my biggest book yet – I just knew it.

At first it went great guns. I developed a rough draft which Karen loved, and the first couple of spreads which I did for Bologna last year just drew themselves. The next lot were a bit trickier, but then I hit a stone wall, and I had nothing new for the Frankfurt Book Fair in October. By then Karen was on maternity leave, and her replacement, Vanessa, had been inundated with work. I didn't want to overwhelm her with my problems, and I thought my lack of enthusiasm was just a blip. But as the weeks disappeared, and my self-imposed deadlines kept slipping away, I knew I had to do something. So I bit the bullet in late November and rang her up.

Whereas Karen would have laughed and teased and said something comforting, Vanessa just sat on the other end of the phone in silence.

'So how much have you done?' she said eventually. She can only be in her mid-twenties, but her tone was so severe, I felt like I was up before the Head for not having done my homework.

'I've got some roughs,' I said, knowing it sounded lame.

'Roughs?' she said, so disapprovingly that my heart sank. 'I was expecting some finished spreads by now. We do want *The Littlest Angel* out for next Christmas.'

Me too, I thought, me too. This was not going well at all. I could really have done with some reassurance. Karen would have known exactly what to say, but all Vanessa came up with was, 'Do you think you can get them worked up by the other side of the New Year?'

She sounded tetchy and cross, which made me feel worse. I felt bad enough about being late as it was, I didn't need lecturing.

'I honestly don't know,' I said. 'I'll do my best.'

With Karen I would have told her the truth, said nothing was working, and that my work was in the doldrums in a way I hadn't encountered before. But Vanessa was still an unknown quantity. I wasn't sure how she'd react, so I couldn't face telling her the truth. Particularly if it meant a telling-off.

There was another pause on the other end of the line, followed by an exasperated sigh.

'Well, I suppose we'll have to hope your best is good enough.'

'I suppose we will,' I said. Vanessa was making me feel completely dispirited, and it wasn't helping at all. 'It's all I can do.'

'Good,' she said briskly. 'I look forward to seeing what you've done in January. I hope by then you'll have something to show me.'

'Right,' I said, putting the phone down. I felt like banging my head against the wall.

Since that call I've tried really hard, but something is missing. The special spark of whatever it is that marks out a Beth King picture book (*Sunday Times* bestseller, don't you know?) just isn't there. And I don't know what to do.

I'd deliberately not worked over the Christmas period, thinking the break would do me good. And then all the stuff with Mum and Dad happened. I'm still reeling from their news. I know my parents have never been particularly lovey-dovey, but they've always seemed to get along, and I assumed they always would. This has come like a bolt from the blue.

As families go, despite our differences we are as happy as the next one. Or I've always thought so anyway. When I was in my teens I used to worry Mum and Dad might split up – I seem to remember a lot of arguments back then. But now? I'm about to hit forty, my mum is about to hit seventy. This should have been a year of happy family celebrations, particularly with Sam turning eighteen and a new baby being thrown into the mix. Instead Mum and Dad are barely speaking. Mum is spending all her time indoors, and won't be coaxed out, while Dad is being silently sullen about the whole thing. That's the thing that kills me. I've always worshipped my dad – to be honest I get on better with him than with Mum. When I was little he was always the cuddly one, the one I went to when I was feeling low. Mum's always been a more of a pull-yourself-together kind of parent. Dad always propped me up at those times when I felt I couldn't cope. The thought of him having had an affair makes me feel sick. And I feel partly to blame too. If only I hadn't encouraged him to go to art classes, he'd never have met this damned Lilian woman.

But then, how could I have foreseen what would happen? I find it so hard to believe that my lovely, funny, kind dad could have behaved so badly. I'm furious with him, and I hate feeling like that, but he's made me angrier than I've ever been in my life. I don't know where it's all going to end, but I expect I'll have to pick up the pieces. I usually do in this family.

On top of this, I feel so pressurised by the book. The deadline is looming over my head, and I've been so distracted that the creativity I so desperately need just isn't happening.

Normally, I'd try and thrash this out with Daniel. Although he never tends to be very critical, it's always lovely to hear his supportive comments. But at the moment he's really preoccupied with work stuff. He's still finding his feet at his new school, and some days I know it's a struggle for him. They're expecting an Ofsted inspection this term, and he's already fretting about it. As the first black Head Teacher in a white, middle-class school, there's an awful lot riding on it. Even though said school was woefully mismanaged before he turned up.

I know he's feeling the pressure, and I don't want to burden him with my worries. Besides, I think he's taken the Mum and Dad thing pretty hard too – he's always loved my parents, especially because of his own situation, and now they've thrown us all a huge curveball.

This is not good. I squeeze my eyes shut, trying to focus on the work in front of me.

So – the Littlest Angel – where is she and where is she going next?

I get up to make coffee. I just can't concentrate. My little angel is very lost. And so, I fear, am I . . .

Daniel

'Don't run in the corridors!' Daniel admonished two Year Seven boys who were doing skids down the corridor, blissfully unaware of his presence. They stood up, startled, automatically tucking their shirts into their trousers and adjusting their ties with a 'Yes, sir, sorry, sir,' before scooting away.

Daniel grinned to himself, remembering Sam at that age. He'd been so easy to deal with back then. But now? Now he was a closed book. He didn't appear to be doing any work for his A Levels at all, and any attempts to talk about his future were met with hostility. Years of experience dealing with teenagers had given Daniel the knowledge that a hands-off approach was probably the best; he'd come round in his own good time. But it was much harder doing it yourself than advising other parents. Beth fretted so much. She always wanted to know what Sam was up to, when to Daniel it was clear he didn't always want to say. It was the source of most of their arguments. Beth was a great mum, but sometimes Daniel felt she wanted to interfere too much with the children, and she'd be better off just letting them be. On the other hand, Beth thought Daniel was too laid-back and should be more assertive with them. It was a conundrum they didn't look likely to solve any time soon.

Having dispatched the boys down the corridor, Daniel headed for his office to catch up on some paperwork. He loved his job, enjoyed the cut and thrust of running a school, and the interactions with the kids. He'd gone into education to make a difference, just as long ago a couple of teachers had made a difference for him. After his dad had left home when Daniel was ten, there'd been a time when he had been so angry and bitter, he had become quite self-destructive. Without the support of an English teacher when he was in Year Seven and a maths teacher in Year Nine, Daniel might never have found his calling. He could so easily have gone off the rails. As it was, those two teachers had changed his life, and it had fired him up to do the same for others.

He had never regretted his decision to be a teacher, and he was really enjoying working in the new school, where there was a good ethos and the kids, in the main, wanted to study. But it wasn't the world he'd entered all those years ago, and the pressure to succeed was immense. The thought of the Ofsted inspection was giving him sleepless nights. He knew he had a good management team in place, though he could have done with a couple more senior figures on it; the governors kept going for money over experience. It was cheaper to pay a twenty-eight-year-old to be head of department than a forty-five-year-old. And with the way the budget was looking – a big headache to address this term – saving money was paramount. He was grateful for the enthusiasm and energy his new staff members brought to the school, but he did worry that there was a lack of experience too. Something else he needed to sort out.

Daniel's phone buzzed. A message from Beth. He loved the way she still texted him in the day. Though they had married young – too young some of their friends had thought, especially with a baby on the way – theirs was a good marriage, and he was more contented than most people he knew in his position.

Having a slow day. Any chance of lunch?

He smiled. Eighteen years married and he still was just as much in love with Beth as when they'd first met. He really wished he did have time for lunch.

Sorry, no can do. Meeting. But let's do dinner tonight.

And with the thought of that playing happily on his mind, he strode down the corridor with renewed purpose. As long as Beth was beside him, he could cope with anything.

Lou

'Can I get you anything, Mum?'

I've come into the kitchen to find Mum staring into the garden. She's still wearing her dressing gown and looks like she hasn't slept.

'A different life?' asks Mum bitterly.

Oh God. Here we go. Every day since I've moved back in she's been like this. Never mind that my own life has spectacularly imploded since Jo left. To top it off, I finally got made redundant just after Christmas. My manager blamed cutbacks, told me it was nothing personal, but it was the last thing I needed after the blow of Jo leaving. I can't afford the rent on my flat without a job. If I'd still been with Jo, I could have gone to stay with her. But I had nowhere else to go, hence why I've ended up back home. I may as well be miserable with Mum and Dad rather than be on my own.

I'd thought maybe there might be a silver lining to moving back home, that my being here might help Mum, and help me too in a funny way. I thought it might take my mind off my own misery. But she barely acknowledges me, and I'm not sure if I'm making any difference. I mean, I get how she feels. I've had my fair share of heartache and I'm no stranger to being dumped and cheated on (Jo said there's no one else, but I'm not sure I believe her. But that might be my insecurity talking). Finding out your husband of over forty years has been cheating must be horrendous. But I hadn't expected this. This shadow of a person, not moving, inert, just accepting her fate. The Mum I know would never give up like this. Why can't she be angry any more, the way Beth and I are? It's like all the fight's gone out of her.

I want to shake her and say, *Do something*. Fight for him. But she doesn't. Beth thinks she needs time, but I'm not sure my sister realises how bad the situation is. Sam and Megan, of course, think it's hilarious that Grandpa could even be having an affair. The idea of seventy-somethings having a sex life is completely incomprehensible to them. But this is serious. Mum and Dad have had their ups and downs, but they've always been *together*. And the situation is further complicated by the fact that Dad seems to be spending a lot of time with this Lilian woman, but he still hasn't officially left Mum's house. He's sleeping in the spare room and sneaking out to see *her* every day. He never says where he's going, or what his plans are. Presumably because the first time I asked him about it we had a stand-up row; it was horrible. Dad isn't the rowing sort, and since then he's refused to discuss the situation with me.

I don't know what to do. I've spent my whole life being regarded as the pathetic one in the family: poor Lou stuffed up her A Levels, poor Lou can't get a decent job, poor Lou hasn't got a man – and now here I am having to act like the responsible one. I really haven't the faintest idea how to do it.

'I was thinking more on the lines of a cup of tea?' I say as cheerfully as I can, but Mum looks at me blankly.

'I suppose,' she says. Her eyes look dull and lifeless. It's a bit scary how quickly my energetic mum has morphed into a zombie. She's barely been out of the house since Christmas, and I keep being bombarded with messages from her friends, checking up on her because she refuses to speak to them.

'How about we go out for a coffee at the garden centre?' I say.

I'd like to suggest going shopping, but I know I'll get nowhere with that. I've been doing the shopping for the last two weeks, Dad being incapable of doing any domestic tasks. Lucky Lilian.

'What's the point?' says Mum.

'The point,' I say firmly, 'is you need to get out of the house. Trust me, I know.'

I think of all the times people have done this for me, stopped me drowning in self-pity when all I wanted to do was sit in my PJs eating chocolate and drinking too much wine. I've only coped this time because Mum needs me so much I haven't had time to wallow in it. But when I've been heartbroken in the past, I've always been lucky enough to have someone there to kick me into shape and get me out of my despondency. I know it works.

'So come on,' I say. 'Time to have a bath and pull your-self together. Dad's never going to take you back if you wander round looking like a wet weekend in November.'

'Don't be rude,' says Mum, with a flash of her old self, which gives me some hope. Slowly but surely, she does start to get ready.

First steps, but maybe I'm getting there . . .

Chapter Two

Beth

I'm on a train to London to meet my new editor, Vanessa, in person for the first time. Normally I enjoy my trips to see my publishers. It's always been a chance to catch up with Karen, talk shop and thrash out new ideas – it's creative, energising and fun. Plus it gets me out of the house.

But today is different. If Karen were still around, I'd at least be able to discuss things, but I barely know Vanessa. I've been trying to give her the benefit of the doubt, but so far have found her to be annoyingly patronising, and often quite rude. I know I should be open-minded but I'm finding it increasingly difficult to take suggestions from a woman young enough to be my daughter, who always approaches every conversation as if I'm a problem that needs solving and keeps saying things like, 'Well, it's not that I don't like it, exactly, it's just there's a spark missing.'

I know there's a spark missing. She's the editor, I was rather hoping she'd help me find it, but her latest solution to send my little angel on a journey round the whole world feels overcomplicated to me. 'It'll help give it that international feel that's so vital to the picture-book market,' she gushed down the phone last week.

'Yeah, I know how it works,' I said, biting my lip. I've been doing this for twenty years, and I understand the importance of foreign editions; they help increase the print run and bring down the production costs. Without them, it's much harder to get a book off the ground. One or two of my early projects foundered as a result of too few foreign publishers coming on board. I don't need Vanessa to lecture me on how important it is. I feel she's treating me like an idiot, and it's making me resent her even more.

Anyway, whatever I'm doing isn't working, so I found myself agreeing to take my angel on a journey that involves London, Paris, New York, Berlin and Rome, even though apart from Rome none of these places even existed in Jesus' time.

When I pointed this out, I was given an airy, 'Oh, that doesn't matter, it's symbolic.' Though of what, I'm not quite sure.

So I've done as she's asked and drawn up some spreads of the Littlest Angel making friends with a pigeon on top of Nelson's Column and asking the Mona Lisa for directions. In Berlin she's getting a view of the city from the Reichstag, and in Rome she's at the Vatican.

It doesn't make any sense to me at all. Every time I draw the angel, I can't seem to help myself giving her a puzzled and despairing look. It's just how I feel. Though I know the book wasn't working, I don't think Vanessa's solution is any better.

I get to the office in plenty of time for our meeting, feeling sick to the pit of my stomach. What am I doing? Why am I allowing my gut instincts to be overridden by someone like Vanessa? If only I had a clear view of my story I'd be able to fight back, but the trouble is, I don't, and I know this book is going to end up being a disaster.

Vanessa doesn't keep me waiting long. As I anticipated, she's a pretty, bright young thing, all gushing enthusiasm. Suddenly it occurs to me that she might be as nervous as I am.

'I just can't believe I'm working with you, Beth,' she says. 'I loved your books when I was little.'

Great, now I feel really old, but then, my first picture book did come out seventeen years ago.

'Thanks,' I say, attempting a smile. It's the first vaguely positive thing she's said to me.

'Come on in.' She ushers me into a bright, airy room. 'I've asked our new art director to join us, I hope that's all right.'

'I didn't know you had a new art director,' I say.

'Oh yes, Andrea left just after Christmas, didn't anyone tell you?'

'No,' I say, my heart sinking. Damn. The previous incumbent, Andrea, was with the company for five years. She, Karen and I had made such a good team. Now I'll have another new face to contend with and win over. I'm not sure I'm really up to the challenge at the moment; I'm beginning to feel hemmed in and slightly panicky.

The door flings open and a good-looking man in his late thirties strides through it. I look into his eyes and I'm stunned – it can't be. My legs nearly buckle from the shock.

'Beth, can I introduce you to Jack—'

'Stevens,' I stammer in confusion, and my face flares red. 'Yes, we – know – knew each other . . .' My voice stutters and drops away.

The years melt away and I am eighteen again, standing in the college bar, seeing Jack Stevens for the very first time. He is beautiful. Every head in the room turns as he walks through the door. I long for him to look at me, but of course he doesn't. Not that first time anyway . . .

How can Jack Stevens be here? I haven't seen him in over twenty years. And now he's standing right in front of me, every bit as gorgeous as the last time I saw him. Oh, God.

'Lizzie Holroyd!' Jack throws his arms around me with delight. 'I'm such an idiot, I didn't make the connection when I saw your name.'

I return his embrace in stunned silence. *Jack Stevens* is the new art director? Jack Stevens who I loved so unrewardingly through art school, Jack Stevens who I haven't seen for years, Jack Stevens who is standing here in front of me with his still mesmerising blue eyes, which annoyingly are still working their old magic. I feel faint and dizzy, as if I've just walked out of the dark into the sunlight.

Jack Stevens, a blast from my past. The one who got away. And he's working on my new book.

Lou

'Mum, when are you going to tell Dad to leave?' I say as we mooch our way round Sainsbury's on a grey wintry day. We've managed a step forward this week, I've actually got her out of the house a few times, but it's a huge effort. She always has an excuse not to go – mainly blaming the weather. But today the sun shone for about five minutes, which was enough of a reason for me to drag her out. It's gone back behind the clouds now, of course.

'But where will he go?' she says.

'Mum,' I say as gently as I can, 'he can go to Lilian's or one of his mates, or even a hotel for all I care. It doesn't matter. But he has to go. You can't carry on like this.'

And to be honest, neither can I. Living with the two of them is horrendous. The atmosphere in the house is either glacial, with the pair of them passing icy requests to the other through me, or explosive when they have a massive row. Or to be more accurate, Mum occasionally remembers she's angry with Dad and stirs herself to shout at him, and he looks crestfallen and says nothing. It drives me mad that he won't even try to justify his behaviour. He just looks mournful and says things like, 'I never meant for this to happen.'

'You just fell into Lilian's arms by magic?' I snarled at him last time he said it, and he looked even more sorry for himself, and said, 'I don't expect you to understand.'

Which is true, I don't. I cannot comprehend what he is playing at, especially at his age.

'How will he manage?' Mum says now. 'You know what he's like, he can't even boil an egg.'

And whose fault is that? I think. Mum has never ever let Dad do anything in the domestic sphere. It's her fault as much as his that he's so incapable.

'I know, he's utterly hopeless,' I say, 'but Mum, you can't worry about that. For your sanity you have to let him go. He cheated on you. He's betrayed all of us.'

As I say this, I realise just how angry I am with Dad for what he's done. It's like he's blown apart my whole world view; I have always clung on to the certainty of their relationship amidst the multiple wreckages of my own. How can I survive if theirs has been a lie this whole time?

I know their marriage wasn't perfect, but whose is? Mum and Dad had always lived separate but parallel lives, but they'd always seemed happy enough, even though Mum drove Beth and I mad with the way she'd always run round after Dad. She might be a child of the sixties, but feminism completely passed her by. Which also explains her appalling favouritism of Ged, who can do no wrong in her eyes. Typically, we have barely heard hide nor hair from Golden

Boy since Christmas, even though he and Rachel have moved into a flat in south London, which isn't a million miles away. Mum lets him off, because, 'He must be so busy, what with the baby coming and everything,' but it drives me up the wall. It wouldn't hurt him to ring Mum up occasionally, just to find out how she is.

'You don't understand,' says Mum. 'You can't just throw forty-two years of marriage away like that. If you'd managed to keep a relationship together for longer than a year, you'd know that.'

Dammit. She can be cruel sometimes.

'Thanks for reminding me of my failings in that department,' I say.

'Oh, I didn't mean it like that,' says Mum, looking a little shamefaced. 'Sorry, love, I'm a bit tetchy these days.'

'I didn't think you did,' I say, sighing. 'But still, you and Dad: it's not working, is it?'

The tension between them at the moment is unbearable. They either don't speak or are at each other's throats. I sit for long evenings with them both in silence, or I have to make excuses to leave the house when they start bitching at each other about who hasn't put the bins out. Honestly, I've never taken so many long walks in my life. I really, really wish I didn't have to be stuck in the middle of it all, particularly as I'm struggling to get over Jo. Every day I resist the urge to ring her or text her, and every day my own misery about being out of work is compounded by the terrible atmosphere at home. I'd rather be anywhere but here. But at the moment I have no choice. I'm thirty-eight, single, broke and living with my mum and dad. It doesn't get more pathetic than that.

'Maybe you're right,' Mum says, pausing to stare at the vegetable aisle as if the carrots will give her the answer she's looking for. 'I'm just frightened that if he goes, he'll never come back, and then what would I do?'

She looks so worried and vulnerable when she says this that I forget my earlier irritation. She's so capable and organised most of the time, it's hard to remember that she's sixty-nine. I'm finding it tough enough picking myself up after Jo. How difficult must it be for to start again after all this time? She's been married for more of her life than she hasn't.

'Then you pull yourself together and make a life without him,' I say. 'Believe me, it's the only thing you can do.'

Good advice, Lou, I think as we make our way to the checkout. Shame that right now you're not managing to do the same.

Daniel

'Sit up straight for Mr King.'

Daniel sighed as he regarded the student before him. Jason Leigh was one of his brightest pupils, who had done spectacularly well at GSCE, but was failing badly at A Level, so his mum had demanded an interview with the Head to see what could be done about it.

Not a lot without Jason deciding it was time to pull his finger out, was Daniel's honest response, but he suspected that was not what Mrs Leigh wanted to hear. As far as he could see, she was part of the problem – the worst kind of helicopter parent, constantly on Jason's case.

Daniel felt some sneaking kind of sympathy for Jason, who clearly had had enough of the education system and had done appallingly in his mocks. Miraculously, despite having taken very little interest in the application process, he actually had two offers from universities. Daniel suspected that although Jason was more than capable of getting the required grades, he wouldn't actually bother to try.

'So how did you feel the mocks went, Jason?' he asked, trying to ignore Mrs Leigh, who clearly had the bit between her teeth.

There was a mumbled 'Dunno,' and Jason slumped into his chair even more, followed by a 'Jason, don't be rude!' from his mother.

Daniel waved her concerns away. He didn't think Jason was intending to be rude, he was just a seventeen-year-old who couldn't see the point in any of this.

'Come on, Jason,' said Daniel, 'this isn't about me or your mum. This is your future we're talking about. None of us can do your exams for you.'

Jason shrugged again. 'I just don't see the problem. It's not as if speaking French and Spanish is going to get me a decent job.'

'But Jason,' said his mother, 'you love Spanish and French.'

'No, Mum,' Jason said, looking tired, '*you* love that I'm *good* at Spanish and French.'

He slumped some more, so Daniel tried another tactic.

'OK, Jason, so what would you rather be doing? You can always go back and take different subjects next year if you like.'

A shrug. And nothing.

'Come on, Jason, there must be something you're interested in.'

'Gaming,' said Jason. 'I'd like to work on computer games.'

'That's not a career,' said Mrs Leigh in frustration. 'I don't think you'll get a degree in computer games.'

'You'd be surprised,' said Daniel. He leaned forward, turned back to Jason. 'So why didn't you take computer sciences instead?'

'Mum said I should do languages.' Jason sneaked a stroppy look at his mum.

'Those bloody computer games!' said Mrs Leigh. 'You spend far too much time on them.'

'But I like them,' said Jason, 'and I'm good at them. I don't need to go to uni to get a job in the gaming industry.'

'But you could be the first person in the family to go to university!' wailed his mum. 'Honestly, Mr King, I'm sure your children don't behave like this.'

'I think all children behave like this, sometimes,' said Daniel, thinking of Sam locking himself in the garage to play his drums for hours, spending as little time on his studies as Jason appeared to on his. Sam's mocks hadn't gone too well either. And Beth's fury about it had evoked a shrug and a, 'They're only mocks,' response. To Daniel's dismay it had led to a massive row, and Beth and Sam hadn't talked for a couple of days. Daniel was worried about Sam's future too, but sometimes he thought Beth came down too hard on him and made it worse.

'So that's where you see your career, Jason?' said Daniel.

'Definitely,' said Jason, brightening up. He began to talk knowledgeably and at length about the games that interested him and the world of computers till Daniel's head was dizzy.

'I could earn shedloads of money and not end up in debt,' he finished. 'Why should I even bother with uni?'

'Jason!' His mother was apoplectic, Daniel could see a vein bulging on her forehead. 'But what security will you have? You have to go to uni, you *have to*.'

Daniel began to feel a little sorry for her, he knew just how hard it was being a parent at times. Particularly of a recalcitrant teen. He could imagine him and Beth having a similar conversation with Sam's head teacher.

'You might not *need* a degree to work in the gaming industry, Jason,' he said, 'but you're a clever lad, and having qualifications never hurt anyone. You've only got a few months left with us, why not at least try to achieve what you're capable of? There are kids in this school who would kill to have your opportunities. You shouldn't waste them.'

'I suppose.'

'Mr King's right, Jason,' said his mother more gently. 'It's worth a try, isn't it?'

Jason nodded imperceptibly, staring down at the table.

'So what do you think?' said Daniel. 'Is it worth pushing yourself the extra mile for the next few months? It can't hurt, can it?'

'I guess not,' said Jason.

'So you'll give it a go?' Daniel said encouragingly.

Jason shrugged.

'It's up to you,' said Daniel, 'but, if you are going to take this seriously, you will need to attend the catch-up sessions your teachers are running. They give up their valuable time to help, Jason. I have to say, I think the least you could do is give it a try.'

Jason had the grace to look a little shamefaced at this.

'Listen to Mr King,' said Mrs Leigh, softening her tone a little. 'I never had the chances you did. Don't throw them away.'

'And it's not obligatory to go to uni this year,' said Daniel. 'You could take a year out, re-evaluate what you want to do. Why not go and see Mr Price in careers? He might have some suggestions for you.'

To his relief, this seemed to go down well, so by the time their conversation had drawn to a close, both Jason and his mum were smiling. Who knew, Jason might even surprise them all.

Daniel ushered them out and sat back down at his desk with a sigh. Jason Leigh was so very like Sam, who also thought school was pointless and was currently displaying no ambition whatsoever. Daniel hadn't a clue how to get through to him. Whatever he said fell on deaf ears. Daniel was reluctant to be as overbearing as his own father had been, and had seen so many pushy parents over the years that he'd always taken a rather hands-off approach with his own children. Maybe, as Beth kept telling him, that had been a mistake.

'Physician, heal thyself,' he said, and got back to work, wondering how he was ever going to cross the chasm that existed between him and his son.

Chapter Three

Lou

It occurs to me as I get home with Mum and start unpacking the shopping that I should take my own advice. In the month since Jo ditched me and I got made redundant, I have been utterly miserable. I'm missing Jo badly, and resisting the urge to call her as I know that it won't do any good. I have no money, and have been feeling so emotionally battered I can't even think about work.

I can't do anything about my relationship status, but getting a new job would go some way to restoring my low self-esteem. I've been feeling so unhappy, I haven't bothered up till now. So when we get in, the first thing I do is sign up for some job agencies, and start looking for credit control opportunities. I wasn't too long in my last job so my CV is up to date, and I know they'll give me a good reference. It wasn't as though they were unhappy with my work. It was just bad timing that I came into the company when things were starting to go badly. An unfortunate example of last in, first out.

I stare out of the window at the grey January day. It's such a bleak month, especially when you're unhappy. All that hope and expectation of Christmas gone, and nothing to look forward to. Maybe I should go away somewhere, get some winter sun, just to cheer myself up. In fact, maybe I should make Mum go with me. I can't remember the last time she and Dad went away properly. It would give us both a chance to clear our heads. I have a little money saved up, and besides, what else are credit cards for?

I've just clicked on a website offering winter breaks when my phone buzzes. *Jo*. Oh fuck, I'm not ready for this. She's sent me a couple of texts since the New Year, but I've ignored them. I'm not strong enough to cope with her yet.

How are you doing? Worried about you xxx

Really? *Really*? Why would she even care? She was the one who broke my heart. I'm so angry with her for saying this that I break my no contact rule and before I can stop myself I'm furiously typing out a reply.

You could have fooled me, I text back.

Don't be like that, Lou Lou, is the response. *Can't we be friends?*

Of course we can't. I'm far too raw. What is she thinking? I want to text something angry back, but I know from bitter experience (oh, I have so much bitter experience!) that it won't help, so I content myself with: *Sorry, not ready for that yet. Maybe one day.*

The phone beeps again. *It seems such a shame. Didn't we have some good times?*

Yes, we did, I think, and then some not so good times. I had hoped that she was the real deal, that finally I'd found someone to share my life with, but for her I was clearly a little interlude. I can't say any of that though, without sounding appallingly needy, and I won't give her the satisfaction.

Sorry, Jo, that's the way it is. Please don't text me.

Not unless you want me back, I'd like to add, but I know that's not going to happen.

I switch my phone off, and return to the website. A week in Tenerife looks like the best thing ever. Life's too short to be miserable. I click on the link before I can change my mind, and quickly book our flights. Mum will probably think I'm interfering, but I reckon we both deserve the break.

Beth

The meeting is excruciating. It's so weird having Jack sitting here, and for some reason I'm finding it hard to look him in the eye. From the outset it's clear that Vanessa hates my drawings, and she makes her feelings very plain. There is no attempt at finesse, or trying to soften the blow. My initial warmth turns to hostility and by the time the meeting is halfway through, I am boiling with rage.

'I just didn't picture the Littlest Angel like this,' she says. 'I think she needs to be cuter.'

She does have a point. My angel looks sharper than I intended, and slightly demented. Cute she definitely is not.

'I admit she's not quite right yet,' I say, 'but I don't want to draw Disney angels, I'm afraid.'

'I think that's exactly what you should be going for,' says Vanessa. 'Cute and sweet is what sells at Christmas, particularly in the US.'

She also hates the spread which has the angel talking to one of the statues on top of St Peter's.

'Hmm, I don't quite see why she would be going to Rome?' she says. 'It just doesn't work for me.'

'It just doesn't work for me,' is one of a number of Vanessa's pet sayings that I am beginning to hate.

'But why would she be going to Paris or London?' I say.

'They sell better to Americans,' was the swift response. So that's all right then.

Jack has been quiet up to this point, but he intervenes now.

'Maybe the story isn't quite right yet,' he says. 'Perhaps that's where Beth is having the problem. I know I've just come into this, but I am struggling with the concept a bit. Beth, is there a reason why the angel is going round the cities of the world? I may be missing something, but it doesn't make much sense to me. Sorry, I hope you don't think I'm being too critical.'

He smiles over at me with the crooked grin I remember so well, and my heart lurches a little, and I'm back in time again, back to the first night he grinned at me like that. I pull myself together and shoot him a grateful look.

'That's not how it was planned originally,' I explain. 'My story was actually simpler than that, but I couldn't seem to get it out right, so Vanessa suggested this direction.'

I don't say what's really in my head, namely that Vanessa's idea has made things worse, but I'm pleased when Jack says, 'Is it worth looking at it again?'

Vanessa looks deeply irritated. 'We're under a lot of time pressure here, Jack, I think we should work this current idea up till it's right.'

'Fair enough,' says Jack, and winks at me in a conspiratorial fashion. I feel slightly light-headed. I blush and look away, grateful for his intervention, but unable to process the confusion I'm feeling. I'm still reeling from the shock of seeing him again. During our three years at art school we were very close – except he never quite reciprocated my feelings in the way I wanted him to. For Jack, I was only ever his occasional hook-up, but I was blindly in love, and like a fool I always thought it would lead to more. In his own way, he was quite honest about it. He used to tell me he was a free spirit who didn't want to be tied down. I was so infatuated that I bought into it for far too long – until the day I caught him sleeping with my then best friend, Kerry. Then it was as if the scales had fallen from my eyes, and despite Jack's protestations that I was always going to be the one he came back to I finally came to my senses. After that, we drifted apart, and I met Daniel the following year at teaching college. He was so different from Jack; kind, caring, funny; it was so easy to fall in love with him. I was head over heels before I knew it, and pregnant quicker than expected. All of a sudden I was a mum at home looking after two small children, all thoughts of Jack Stevens forgotten. Well, mostly forgotten. I have had the odd wayward daydream about what would happen if I ever saw Jack again. But I never seriously expected it to *happen*.

I've never even told Daniel much about him. I felt like such a fool for falling for Jack's lines, and in the early days of our relationship, I didn't want Daniel to know about my stupidity. As time went on, it became irrelevant. Jack Stevens had disappeared from my life, and I hadn't properly thought about him in years. Seeing him in the flesh again is such a shock. I'd forgotten about those brilliant blue eyes . . .

The meeting ends inconclusively, with me promising to go away and rework both the text and drawings. As we pack up our things, Jack suggests coffee, and before I can think too much I say yes. I'm curious to know what he's been up to, and he reminds me of a part of my life that I'd almost forgotten about, when I was young and free and wanted to change the world with my art.

'Well, well, Lizzie Holroyd,' he says as we squeeze into a busy Caffè Nero near the office. 'I can't tell you how great it is to see you again.'

He flashes that gorgeous smile at me and I feel a bit dizzy. This is insane. What is going on in my head?

'It's good to see you too,' I say, because aside from the dizziness, it is. 'It's Beth now, by the way.' I put Lizzie behind me with Jack, and Daniel has only ever known me as Beth.

Jack raises his eyebrows. 'So, *Beth*, how's life as a successful picture-book artist?' he says. 'I always knew you'd do well.'

'Flatterer,' I say, but secretly I'm pleased. Emotions aside, Jack was one of the most talented people in our year. His good opinion always mattered to me back then, and I'm surprised at how much it matters to me now. 'To be honest I'm not really enjoying it much at the moment. This damned book is killing me,' I say. 'I've never had such difficulty working a story out.'

'You'll get there,' he says. 'You're disgustingly talented, you know. You always were.'

'Really?' I can feel myself blushing.

'Oh God, yeah,' says Jack. 'You had One Most Likely to Make It written all over you. I can't tell you how great it is to meet you again, and see how well you've done.'

He seems so genuine and warm, it's hard to remember the Jack who broke my heart, and all I can think of is the Jack who I fell in love with way back then. I feel as though I've entered another life, and for a minute it's as if the intervening years have slipped away. I didn't used to have responsibilities – instead I had ambitions, ideas and *fun*. Who was that girl I used to be? So full of life and love and hope? Where has she gone? I miss her.

'Thanks,' I say. My heart is doing a silly fluttering thing. Which is *ridiculous*.

Jack's worn well. He looks fit and healthy, and at nearly forty is still devastatingly handsome.

'So how's life with you?' I say. 'Any kids?'

'One,' he says, 'a daughter, aged five.'

He shows me pictures. She's cute as a button.

'I'm not with her mum though. My fault.' He looks rueful.

'Ah, right,' I say. The leopard clearly hasn't changed his spots. 'Sorry to hear that.'

'I don't have a great track record with women,' he says. 'Mainly because I have a bad habit of letting the good ones slip through my fingers . . .'

He pauses and looks at me, in a way that feels significant. Shit, he can't mean . . .? My heart is racing at the thought.

'. . . So I'm not great with commitment.'

He doesn't mean me, I admonish myself. He's just being nice.

'Unlike you, I see,' he says, clocking my rings.

'Yes, happily married to Daniel for eighteen years,' I say, looking down at my ring finger with a flash of guilt. 'Two kids, a boy and a girl.'

I find myself telling him about them enthusiastically, as if by doing so I can put a barrier between me and my fluttering heart.

Because sitting here with Jack is nice – too nice. It feels dangerous. I should go.

'I'm really glad you're happy,' says Jack, and his pleasure seems genuine.

'Thanks,' I say. 'I am.'

Which I am really, I know I am, but there's a part of me now, here with Jack, that's wondering how life could have been. Whether that girl I was wouldn't have got lost under a welter of responsibilities if Jack had stayed in my life. I think of us sitting together in the college bar, talking about life over beer and packets of crisps.

'I was an idiot back then,' he says, and I realise he's trying to apologise.

'It's a long time ago,' I say, 'all forgotten.'

'There's no fool like a young fool,' he says, and smiles at me. 'Your Daniel is a lucky man.'

He shoots me a look. It's regret, I think, mixed with something else. Desire? I am temporarily poleaxed. I have to get a grip.

'I'm the lucky one,' I say firmly. 'I have a great life, wonderful children, and a gorgeous husband. I couldn't want for anything more.'

I am deliberately hiding behind the wall of my perfect domesticity, and trying to turn away from the dangerous feelings Jack is evoking.

I think he senses it, because he comes over all business-like and says, 'If you need to chat over the storyline and pictures some more, please do get in touch.'

'That would be lovely,' I say and give him a hug. The hug I receive in return is warm and heartfelt. It is with some regret that I pull myself away. 'It's been great to see you again.'

'And you,' he says.

I watch him head back to the office, turning the card he's given me over and over. I won't take him up on his offer, I decide. It was lovely to catch up. But despite Jack Stevens' devastating blue eyes and charming manner, the past should stay where it belongs. In the past.

Daniel

Daniel got in late from work to find Beth cooking and the kids, as usual, in their rooms. Sometimes it felt as if they'd already left home and it was just him and Beth in the house. For all the notice the kids took of them, they might as well be invisible. Still, it was always good to come home, to Beth, to their shared life. He was lucky to have such a family, lucky to have a four-bedroomed detached house, lucky to have a garden. He could never have imagined this happening to him when he was growing up, in the small flat he and his mum had shared in south London.

'Good day?' Beth asked, giving him a welcoming hug. He pulled her to him, breathed her in. She was every bit as gorgeous to him now as she had been that first day he'd met her at teacher training, when she'd walked into the lecture hall and smiled at him. He'd taken one look at the pretty arty girl with the long curling hair, and known that he was smitten. All these years later and he still was.

'Busy,' said Daniel. 'How did the meeting go?'

'It was dire,' said Beth. 'That girl. Ugh. I'm more confused than ever. I feel this bloody book is going to be the death of me.'

'I'm sure it's not as bad as all that,' said Daniel. Beth always fretted when she was in the middle of a book, but she pulled it off every time. It was a constant source of astonishment to him as to how she did it. He was so proud of her.

'It really is,' said Beth. 'Oh, and you'll never guess who the new art director is.'

'Who?'

'Do you remember me telling you about a guy called Jack Stevens?'

'The guy from college?' Daniel had faint memories of Beth mentioning a friend from art school called Jack years ago. Apparently he had always encouraged her when they were students, which had given her the confidence to do what she was doing now. For some reason they'd drifted apart after college; she was always a bit vague as to why.

'The very same,' said Beth. 'Small world, huh?'

'Isn't it?' Daniel said. 'How was he?'

'Just the same,' said Beth. She seemed a bit preoccupied. 'At least I know he's on my side.'

'Well that's something,' said Daniel. He sighed. 'I'd love to stay and chat, but I've got paperwork to catch up on. How long till supper?'

'You have half an hour,' said Beth.

Daniel went upstairs and poked his head round Megan's door.

She was sitting in her bed, wrapped up in a blanket, transfixed to a screen.

'Good day?' he asked.

'It was OK,' said Megan, barely looking up.

'I hope that's homework you're doing,' said Daniel.

Megan blushed. 'Not exactly. I'm just watching something on YouTube.'

'Well, look at that after you've done your homework,' said Daniel. 'You know, you've got—'

'I've got GSCEs next year and need to knuckle down,' said Megan rolling her eyes. 'I *know*, Dad, and I am working.'

'Good,' said Daniel, smiling. Megan always had an answer for everything, but at least she still talked to him.

He paused outside Sam's room, thinking about Jason Leigh. Maybe Sam needed a similar kick up the arse.

Sam was also hunched over a computer, sitting at his desk with his back to Daniel.

'How's it going?' said Daniel, trying to effect casual. He never quite knew what kind of response he would get from his son.

'OK,' said Sam.

'What about your extra lessons? How were they today?' Sam had done spectacularly badly in his mocks and been pulled in for extra help in economics and physics.

'Didn't go,' said Sam.

'Sam!' Daniel was exasperated. 'We've talked about this. If you don't start working soon, it will be too late.'

Sam shrugged.

'It's my life, Dad. And I'm nearly eighteen, so just butt out.'

Daniel could feel a knot of tension building inside of him. Sam was frequently disrespectful, but Daniel didn't like to come down too hard for fear of sounding like his own dad, Reggie. Daniel had spent a lot of his early childhood being subjected to vicious tongue-lashings when his dad had come home drunk, and had always sworn he would be a different kind of father. He could still remember the occasion when he'd failed badly in a spelling text and Reggie had shouted at him for being stupid. Daniel had tried so hard not to be negative to his own children, and it was incredibly frustrating to feel it all being kicked back in his face.

'You might be nearly eighteen, but you're still living under my roof,' he said, trying to control his voice.

'And?' Sam swivelled around so that he was facing Daniel.

'You could at least respect me and your mum,' said Daniel, feeling his frustration brimming over into anger at his son's disinterested expression.

Sam said nothing and turned back to his screen. Daniel took a deep breath. He had a sudden image of being six years old and hiding under his bed because Reggie had erupted when Daniel had broken a cup. However angry Daniel was with Sam, he wouldn't let it control him. He refused to.

So instead, he went into his study to fire up his computer,

silently fuming. What had gone wrong with his relationship with Sam? He'd always tried to be open and honest with both his children, but over the last year Sam had closed down on him.

He opened his emails with a sigh, and then saw a name in his inbox that made him freeze.

Reggie King. *Dad*?

It had been a couple of years since Reggie had last been in contact, which suited Daniel just fine. His stomach turned in knots. Life was always much easier if he didn't think about Reggie. He read the email with a growing sense of dread.

Hi son, Long time no see, read the email. *I'm going to be back in the UK in February. Maybe we could hook up for a drink? Reggie*

Daniel stared at the message, his thoughts racing. *Maybe we could hook up* after five years of very sporadic communication? Just like that? What the hell did he want?

Chapter Four

Lou

I drive up to Beth's house, feeling the smidgeon of envy I can never quite repress when I turn into the drive of her four-bedroomed mock-Georgian home. Beth has a lovely house, a caring husband, gorgeous children. I know she's worked hard for them, and deserves all those things, but sometimes it's hard to get away from the fact that she has everything I ever wanted. Barring perhaps the husband. A wife on the other hand . . .

It feels as though life has always come easily to Beth and never to me. I flunked out at school, didn't make it to uni. When we were kids she was always the A-grade student, the pretty one, the one with the boyfriends. I was left in her shadow. She never flaunts it in my face, but being next to my high-achieving big sister always makes me feel a failure; I hate it. And I hate myself for letting it get to me.

'Lou, come in.' Beth gives me a hug, and instantly I feel like a bitch. She is always unfailingly kind; it's not her fault my life is such a disaster zone.

She's still in her dressing gown and PJs, her hair done in a messy bun, with curls straggling down her shoulders. She manages to look fabulous though. Beth is one of those annoying people who could look good wearing a paper bag. She seems a bit distracted and has smudges of paint on her hands. My heart sinks. If Beth's in full creative mode, bang goes my chance of having a sensible chat.

'Sorry, am I disturbing you?' I say. 'Maybe I should call back another time.'

'No, no, it's great to see you,' says Beth. 'It's not going well, to be honest. I could do with a break.'

She absentmindedly rubs paint in her face and sighs.

'What's the problem?' I say, following her into the kitchen. I can see the conservatory which leads off from the kitchen is littered with bits of paper, paint and discarded drawings. 'Aren't you using your studio?'

Daniel built her a studio in the garden for her work. Of course he did.

'The cold,' says Beth. 'My fingers are going numb in there. Sometimes a change of scenery helps.'

'But not at the moment?'

'Nothing helps at the moment.' Beth looks rueful. 'To what do I owe the pleasure? Mum and Dad, I assume? Sorry, I should have come before.'

I've actually been surprised that Beth hasn't been over more. She's often complained to me that Mum expects her to be at her beck and call. Now that there's a real crisis, and I happen to be around, she seems to have left everything to me.

Beth and I have had endless conversations about the parental situation since Christmas. Daniel's even taken Dad out for a drink – to no avail. Dad wouldn't say anything other than that he's in love. Like some heartsick teenager. I've tried to understand Dad's point of view, even though I'm still angry, but I just don't get it. I asked him what's so great about Lilian. He says he met her at the art classes

Beth encouraged him to take – I think she might feel a bit guilty about that – and they struck up a friendship.

'Lilian's so different from your mum,' he said, 'kind of arty, and a free spirit. I didn't realise how stultified I was till she blew into my life like a breath of fresh air. I know it's hard for you to accept.'

And I don't accept it. I won't accept it. The whole notion of my dad having an affair is preposterous. Honestly, men can be pathetic at times. Which is part of the reason why I prefer women. Although . . . I haven't exactly had a great track record there, either.

'What's the latest, then?' asks Beth as we settle down with coffee.

'Mum's finally asked Dad to move out,' I tell her.

'You're kidding me?' says Beth, looking genuinely shocked. 'I keep thinking they'll sort it out somehow. They can't be splitting up at their age. It's absurd.'

'I know. But they can't go on as they are. You've seen how vile they can be to one another. It's horrible living with it.'

'Is there any way to persuade Dad to change his mind?' Beth is clutching at straws. I totally understand why, although if she'd been living there these past weeks she would see that Dad needs to move out. It's not fair on Mum.

'I honestly don't think so,' I say. 'I think even Ged's tried.'

Ged has been conspicuous by his absence since all this kicked off. I put the fact that he has actually rung Dad down to a kick in the butt from Rachel. God knows what sort of family she thinks she's landed up in.

'How's Mum?' Beth looks guilty. 'I keep meaning to come over and see how she is, but it's been busy, and you know how it is . . .'

I do know. I am annoyed with Beth for not seeing more of Mum, but in a way I can't blame her. I'm stuck with Mum and Dad. If I had the chance I'd probably do what Ged's done and run a mile. Maybe it's time I did step up to the plate

So I content myself with, 'I'm sure Mum would love to see you,' and tell her that I've decided to take Mum away.

'It will do us both good.'

'That's a brilliant idea,' says Beth, 'but can you afford it? We can chip in if necessary.'

'I was going to pay for it, but when I saw the prices I changed my mind and told Dad he has to at least pay Mum's share. I figure he owes her.'

'He certainly does,' says Beth. 'I'm still in denial about all of this. I can't believe none of us saw the signs.'

'Me neither.'

'I guess you never know what's happening in other people's marriages,' says Beth.

'I guess not.'

'Dad and this Lilian woman . . .'

There's silence for a minute, and then Beth makes a funny noise. I look at her. She's starting to laugh, putting a hand to her mouth.

'I know it's wrong of me, but really, at his age, what can he be thinking?'

'I don't think thought has much to do with it,' I say, and Beth shrieks with disgust.

'I don't even want to go there,' she says, giggling helplessly now. 'We shouldn't laugh, but really, the thought of him and someone who isn't Mum, it's crazy.'

It's enough to tip me over the edge. We both end up laughing till the tears are running down our faces. After all the anger, it feels like a nice kind of release.

'I genuinely thought this would all blow over,' says Beth when she's recovered. 'I guess I was wrong. Sorry, I've been so stressed out over this book, I haven't given them the time I should.'

'No worries,' I say. 'You've got a lot on your plate, and at least I'm not working at the moment.'

'Thanks, Lou,' says Beth, 'I am grateful.'

'It's fine,' I say, plastering a smile on my face. I can feel myself sobering up. Good old Lou, the spinster daughter, with so little in her life she can carry the can. 'Glad to help.'

Daniel

Daniel emerged from a stressful meeting of the Senior Management team with a horrible headache. They'd been discussing the shortfall in this year's budget, and there had been several dissenting voices around the table when Daniel and the bursar had spoken about tightening their belts. Jim Ferguson had been particularly vociferous about Daniel's suggestion to scale back on the introduction of a new computer system, which had been his particular baby. The trouble was there was a lot of wastage, but the bottom line was the school didn't have enough money to implement some of the programmes Daniel had wanted to put in place to improve things. He was going to have to wait another year. He somehow didn't think the Ofsted inspectors were going to be impressed by that, whenever they showed up. He hoped he wasn't heading for trouble.

Daniel headed for his office, made a coffee, and started going over yet more paperwork. There was always so much to do. He rarely left school before six thirty, and was only grateful he had a short journey home now. It was so much easier than when he'd been working in London, when he was rarely home before 8 p.m. At least he got to see his family for some of the evening, though invariably he found himself locked away in his study for a couple of hours each night.

Not that Beth seemed to notice at the moment. She was so caught up with the combination of her new book and worries about her parents, sometimes she barely acknowledged him when he came in. He was used to her vagueness when the muse was upon her, but this was a whole new level. Most days he would find her in her shed staring grumpily at bits of paper, having completely forgotten about cooking tea. She seemed to be fed up with everything she'd produced so far, which was making her snappy. Daniel felt like he was walking on eggshells, and last night they'd had a row and both gone grumpily to bed. It was exhausting.

Daniel still hadn't got round to mentioning the fact that Reggie had been in touch. Partly because he was tempted to ignore it, and partly because he knew Beth would think Daniel should meet him. It had been the aim of her married life to effect a reunion between her husband and father-in-law, whom she'd only met once, a very long time ago. On that occasion, Reggie had been charm itself, and Beth had been surprised by Daniel's uncharacteristic rudeness to him. They had rowed about it at the time, because Beth couldn't understand why Daniel could never allow his dad back into his life.

Perhaps he should have told Beth more about his childhood, but it was all too grim. Over the years Beth had tried to get him to talk about it several times, but Daniel preferred to shut out his past. He had felt so damaged by what had happened to him growing up; it made him feel somehow ashamed. And he hated the bitterness and anger he still felt towards Reggie. Daniel had always been afraid that anger would poison the life he had built for himself, so he had decided early on that he would put those feelings away and never think about it. Most of the time that strategy worked.

Beth was so close to her own family, he couldn't explain to her what a rotten dad Reggie had been. Although Daniel had a few vague early memories of happy family days out, most of his memories of Reggie were of him being drunk and aggressive. Aged eight, Daniel regularly used to go to bed with a book and stuff a pillow over his ears to drown out the sound of his dad shouting. He had watched his mum being worn down by it, until in the end, she finally threw Reggie out in an argument that Daniel could still remember to this day. After that, although Reggie still saw him occasionally, Daniel had felt his mum was his family. Both his parents were from Jamaica, but neither had stayed in touch with their own families, who hadn't approved of the match. 'How right they were,' Mum had said once, sighing. 'But at least I have you.'

Daniel adored his mum, but he'd always missed having a wider family. It was one of the reasons he'd thrown himself so whole-heartedly into Beth's family; they represented everything he didn't have. Being with Beth had given him a joy that he hadn't known life could offer. They'd met at teacher training college. After a stint in the city, which he'd hated, Daniel had decided, with his mother's blessing, to become a teacher. He'd met Beth and fallen head over heels in love. It was a time in his life when everything should have been going right for him. Then out of the blue, his mum had developed an aggressive cancer and died just before their wedding day. To stave off his grief, Daniel had made it a point to keep looking forward, never back. Reggie brought him back to a dark place he never wanted to return to. It was as simple as that. Even if Beth wouldn't see it like that.

Her experience of family was so different from his own, he sometimes felt she couldn't understand the deep vein of toxicity which had run through his childhood. It was easier to shut the past down, look forward, and make her family his own instead. And now her parents were splitting up, and it made him feel totally disorientated. No wonder Beth was so miserable. He must try to make it up to her somehow.

He opened the email from Reggie once more, stared at it for a few seconds and then decided to get this over and done with. He'd tell Beth about it later, when Reggie was safely back in the States.

Hi Reggie, Good to hear from you. Up to my eyes in Ofsteds and general stress. Maybe next time you're over? Daniel.

His hands hovered over the keyboard for a second before pressing send. He had too much on his plate at the moment, without having to deal with his father. Life was stressful enough already. Daniel hit the button.

Beth

The email arrived this morning, and I must have read and reread it a dozen times already, trying to see if there was a hidden agenda. Jack Stevens was always a bit slippery. Gorgeous, charismatic, but very, very slippery, as I found out to my cost. But seeing him again has reminded me of the person I used to be around him: someone with possibilities. The years of parenting and being a wife have taken some of that away from me. Thanks to getting pregnant with Sam, my career ended up on hold, and I slipped into the world of picture books by accident. Daniel had known someone from college who worked in publishing and got me my first gig. He'd always been hugely supportive of my efforts, while not having a clue about the creative process involved. It had suited me to create stories for children when mine were small, and the work fitted in with being a mum. But when I was at college I'd had other ideas. I was going to be an avant garde artist and win the Turner prize. Or develop my sculpture work, which I'd loved. Or be an inspiring teacher for a new generation of artists. Daniel never understood that side of me, so I never discussed it with him. Whereas Jack . . .

Jack had always instinctively got where I was coming from when I spoke about my art. He had great ideas for how to get the best out of my work. We used to sit up till the early hours discussing our plans for the future. At the time I'd fantasised about us getting together properly, having a proper relationship, not the half-hearted moments which seemed to promise so much but ended up going nowhere.

Jack Stevens. I can remember him in my first year at art school. He was a self-confident strutting peacock, one among many, but there was something about him that made him stand out from the rest. Jack was going through a massive Bowie phase at the time, and oh, he was beautiful. He had a thin, angular face, with the most amazing cheek-bones and blue eyes which sucked you in, making you believe he could see into your soul. He knew it of course, and was quickly surrounded by a coterie of fans, both male and female. He was always ambiguous about his preferences, playing with gender before it was even a thing, but for some reason he admitted to me when we still barely knew each other and he was very very drunk that he was a through and through hetero.

I tried to ignore him at first, thinking someone as dazzling as Jack wouldn't be interested in me, but to my surprise he kept seeking me out. Then, one night in a club, we got chatting and we both felt an instant connection. I knew I hadn't imagined it, and the day after that Jack asked me for coffee. I had a feeling I was heading for trouble, but he made me feel special.

'The others are nothing,' he'd say, 'you're my muse.'

It was immensely flattering, and being young and naive I believed him. I was intoxicated by the idea of being Jack's inspiration. His room was full of sketches of me – and he even persuaded me to model for him. Even though there was evidence of other women, I chose to ignore it, because he always said that I was the only person who meant something to him, and I suppose I really wanted to believe it. Till the moment I finally realised he was bullshitting me all along . . .

I look around my lovely bright kitchen, where yet again I've caused chaos with work (memo to self, really must tidy up before Daniel gets in tonight; it's driving him mad), and know Jack would never have given me a home like the one I have. My life with Daniel is ordered, calm, stable, secure. All the things Jack is not. We'd have probably ended up living on a houseboat somewhere. Or in a squat. And I can't ever imagine having had children with him. I suspect if I had, I'd have done all the work. Unlike Daniel, Jack is not great father material. At least he wasn't back then. Maybe he is now, although somehow I doubt it. But it had been so easy to fall for Daniel after Jack; good, solid, reliable, gorgeous Daniel. I know he'll never let me down.

I stare at my wedding ring. Solid. Reliable. *Dull . . .?* I know I'm being unfair, but I can feel my nineteen-year-old self rebelling, her voice echoing in my head. *Is that what you settled for, Lizzie?* But no, that free-spirited girl is buried deep, deep in the heart that Jack Stevens broke.

And what she could never have known is the years of happiness I've had with Daniel. I know Jack could never have given me that.

I look at the email again.

Hi Lizzie,
Great to see you the other week, after such a long time.
Glad things are going so well for you. If you ever want
to meet up and chat about the book, I'm really happy
to help.
Love Jack

I'm not sure how to respond. Or whether I should respond. But then I think, what the hell? I'm reading far too much into this. He's just being friendly. This is business, nothing more.

That sounds great Jack, I email back. *Maybe we can fix some time to chat soon.*

An email pings back immediately.

How does coffee sound? If you're free you could come up to London next week?

Maybe in a couple of weeks? I suggest. I don't want to seem too keen, but honestly, I'm so stuck with the book, I'm sure it can't hurt to meet up with him. It's just two old friends getting together. One thing Jack is great at is working around creative problems. It can only be good news if it helps sort out my writing block, can't it? There's no harm in it . . . Or so I keep telling myself.

Chapter Five

Lou

'Passport, Mum,' I say as we approach the check-in desk. Honestly, it's like dealing with a small child. I've had to organise everything for this trip. I wonder how on earth she ever managed to take us anywhere when we were little. Every small decision seems to render her utterly helpless.

'I'm sure it's in here somewhere.' Mum looks flustered and starts delving into her bag, which seems to be mainly full of tissues. She takes everything out, apologising profusely to the man behind us. I'm cringing, but the man gives us a sympathetic smile.

'Oh dear,' Mum says. 'I can't seem to find it.'

'Are you sure?' I say. I know she had it before we left home.

'I'm sure,' says Mum. Her purse has now joined the heap on the floor, plus a hairbrush, some lipstick, and her make-up bag.

'Mum, you need to put all of that in your suitcase,' I say. 'You're not allowed to take liquids on board. I told you that earlier.'

I've told her three times actually, but like a lot of the things I've said it's been ignored. Back in the Dark Ages when Mum last got on a plane, the liquid rule didn't apply. She and Dad have been content to go caravanning in the New Forest for the last ten years, or when they're feeling daring, across to France.

'Did you, dear,' she says. 'I don't remember.'

We squat down on the floor, rifling through her possessions, and then I make her open up her suitcase. I motion to the man behind us to go ahead, but he kindly says he can wait.

Eventually Mum says, 'Oh I know where I've put it!' She rummages through her suitcase once again, only to reveal her passport hidden in a pair of knickers. 'For safekeeping.'

Our queue friend smiles at me and I want to die. At least Mum seems oblivious to the chaos she's causing. Aside from the man behind me, the other passengers are looking a bit mutinous.

Finally we're done and we can actually go to the check-in desk. Thank God I did it online. At least now we have all the right documentation, so it doesn't take too long. I hold on to Mum's passport and boarding pass till we're safely through security, where she causes the alarms to go off as she's absent-mindedly put her watch in her pocket. It then transpires there is some perfume at the bottom of her bag, which she's most put out to have confiscated.

'But it's my Rive Gauche,' she wails. 'Your father bought it for me in Paris. He always liked the smell.'

Why on earth has she brought that? As a reminder of everything she's lost?

'Mum!' I am so frustrated with her. 'Dad isn't here, remember? Why don't you get some other perfume?'

'I like the Rive Gauche,' she says stubbornly, and I can see she won't be budged.

'Fine, we'll get some in Duty Free,' I tell her. Any more of this and I might end up strangling her before we take off.

I feel mean for being so irritated. Mum is more agitated than normal, as she and Dad decided it would be good if he finally moved out while we're away. Beth and Daniel have taken charge of the move, for which I am immensely grateful. I know how hard this must be for Mum. It's just she's acting so helpless it's driving me mad. I have a feeling it's going to be a very long week.

But actually, once we get to Gatwick Village, she perks up a bit. She's enjoying the shops and purchases not one but two bottles of Rive Gauche on her and Dad's joint credit card. He clearly hasn't cancelled it yet. I know he's feeling guilty because he hasn't worried at all about how much money we're spending, and didn't quibble when I booked us into a four-star hotel.

By the time we're queuing up to get on the plane, Mum is like an overexcited puppy.

'It's so long since I've been on a plane,' she keeps saying, 'your dad hates flying. Thanks so much for organising this, Lou.'

She's not so excited to discover there's not going to be a film.

'I'm sure there was a film last time I went on a plane,' she says. I roll my eyes. Low-budget airlines are outside her experience. She's also absolutely horrified by the cost of everything.

'You mean we have to pay for our food?' she says, scandalised. 'I liked those little aeroplane meals. They were always free.'

'You must be the only one who liked those,' I say. 'Let's just have a snack and a glass of wine.'

Our friend from the queue turns out to be sitting next to us, and introduces himself as James Horton. He's a widower and visiting his daughter and grandchildren in Tenerife. He's perfectly nice and friendly, but I'd have expected Mum to ignore him once she'd made a few polite observations. But they get on like a house on fire, much to my relief. It turns out James doesn't live too far from Wottonleigh, so he and Mum find plenty to talk about. I sit back and read my Kindle. Shame old James isn't staying in our hotel. It looks like he's doing a good job of keeping Mum entertained. Still, at least I can relax for *this* bit of the trip . . .

Daniel

'Is that the lot?' Sam, Beth, and Daniel had piled up the back of their Volvo with Fred's possessions. Megan was out with friends, and Sam had been reluctantly coerced into helping. Fred didn't appear to have taken much with him. Daniel sensed his father-in-law felt so guilty about everything that he didn't want to appear demanding. He was slightly furtive and couldn't quite look anyone in the eye.

Daniel still couldn't quite credit what had happened. He and Beth had discussed it endlessly over the past few weeks, especially the fact that neither of them had seen it coming. What on earth possessed a man of Fred's age to give everything up for someone new? It all seemed so odd. And it made Daniel feel weirdly rudderless – he'd always assumed his parents-in-law would be together till their dying breaths. Theirs had seemed an unremarkable marriage, but a solid one, and now it felt as if one of life's great certainties had been torn away.

Fred didn't seem to be able to explain it himself. Daniel,

at Beth's instigation, had taken his father-in-law out for a few quiet drinks, to try to discuss the issue.

'There's no point asking Ged,' Beth had said, 'he'll either just pat Dad on the shoulder and say way to go, or get cross with him. Either way he won't be constructive.'

But Daniel didn't think his intervention had been any more useful. Fred had just sat staring into a glass saying, 'I didn't plan for this to happen. I know I've hurt Mary, and the children, but when I met Lilian, I fell in love, and I realised what I've been missing. I know nobody really understands.'

'Well I don't actually,' said Daniel, thinking to himself – love? Surely he must mean lust?

'It's like this, Daniel,' said Fred, 'I'm going to be seventy-two this year, old boy. I may not have much time left. I'd like to be happy for what remains of my days.'

'And this Lilian makes you happy?' said Daniel.

'Yes, she does,' said Fred simply. 'She just walked into my life and took my breath away. I haven't felt like that for a very long time.'

'But I thought you and Mary were always so right together.'

'Mary and I, well, we've wanted different things for a long time now,' said Fred with a sigh. 'You know what she's like. Everything has to be just so. I feel constricted in my own home. Lilian is a free spirit, and she's reminded me that I am too. You know, I was like Beth once. I loved art, and would have gone to art college, but it just wasn't the done thing for someone like me. So I got married and got a job in insurance instead. With Mary I've always felt there was something missing. I know it sounds corny, but I feel like Lilian completes me.'

And that was all he would say on the subject. It made

80

Daniel both sad and slightly anxious. He'd always rather assumed that he and Beth were as solid as her parents were, that after all this time nothing could rock the boat of their marriage, but if Mary and Fred could split up, who was to say that he and Beth weren't as secure as he'd thought? Ever since he'd got together with Beth he'd been haunted by the thought that he wasn't good enough for her – insecurities no doubt stemming from his childhood. Despite his mum always insisting that wasn't the case, Reggie leaving when he was so young had always made Daniel feel inadequate, as if it were somehow his fault. Beth told him he was daft for thinking it, but he had a deeply rooted fear that one day she might decide to do the same. And with Mary and Fred splitting up that fear had multiplied. Presumably they'd both thought their marriage was permanent too. Could it happen to him and Beth?

Daniel shook his head, trying to dislodge his thoughts. They were fine, just pressurised by the normal things that affected everyone: children, work, money worries. It was unsettling to discover that age was evidently no barrier to infidelity, that was all.

He and Sam got in the Volvo, while Beth and Fred took his ancient Toyota. He was keeping the car as Mary didn't drive. Which was all fine and dandy while Lou was still living there, but Daniel could foresee a time when it might be difficult. Oh well, they'd have to cross that bridge when they came to it.

'Is Grandpa really going through with this?' Sam said as Daniel turned out of the drive and headed down the road for the crummy flat Fred had rented for the next few months. To everyone's great relief he hadn't moved straight in with Lilian. That would have been beyond awkward.

'It would seem so,' said Daniel.

'I didn't think old people did it any more,' said Sam. 'I mean, can he even get it up?'

'I have absolutely no idea,' said Daniel, 'and it's certainly not a question I'm ever going to ask. And for God's sake don't ever say that to your mother!'

Sam grinned.

'Of course I won't. But you have to admit, it is funny. My grandpa, the player.'

'I don't think your gran finds it all that funny,' said Daniel.

'No,' said Sam, 'but still. Those are some genes I've inherited. Awesome.'

Even Daniel had to laugh. It was quite ridiculous, and for the first time in months his son was actually talking to him.

'Don't you dare tell Mum I laughed,' said Daniel as they pulled up outside the new flat.

'Wouldn't dream of it,' said Sam, and shot Daniel a conspiratorial wink.

'You'd better not,' said Daniel, 'your mum would kill me.'

'My lips are sealed.'

'Good,' said Daniel, and they grinned at one another.

It felt like the first time in forever that he'd actually bonded with his son. Daniel only wished it could have been in better circumstances.

Beth

The drive to Dad's new flat is excruciating. Seeing him pack up all his stuff and knowing that Mum is going to come back to an empty house has made me hopping mad. I've always got on better with Dad than Mum. We share the same arty creativity. To think I thought it would do him good to take up painting as a hobby – ironic how that turned out. I'm furious with him for what he's done to Mum. How could he? He's told Daniel he's in love, at his age! It's ridiculous. He's in lust, which is a totally different thing.

Dad tries to make polite conversation, but I ignore him. I'm worried if I say anything I might let rip and never stop, and I don't want to do that. Maybe Dad realises it, as he stops trying to chat, and we drive the rest of the way in silence.

We get to the flat first and Dad opens the door self-consciously.

'Welcome to my new home,' he says. It's horrible. The kitchen is tiny and dirty. The bathroom ditto. There's a small lounge/dining room painted in browns and tans and a depressing-looking bedroom with a lumpy double bed. It's easily as bad as anywhere I lived as a student, and there's something infinitely sad about my dad moving into some-where like this at his age. For a moment, I want to give him a big hug and say I'm sorry, but then I remember that he brought this on himself and I feel angry all over again.

Dad clears his throat.

'Look, Beth, I know I've not behaved very well, but I'm still your dad . . .'

'Don't,' I say, 'please don't.' I'm not ready for a father–daughter heart-to-heart. I don't want to hear him trying to justify himself, or saying sorry again for his behaviour. I'm still too angry. I want to punish him for what he's done to Mum, to us.

I'm spared from further conversation by Daniel and Sam rolling up with the rest of Dad's stuff, and the next half an hour is taken up with lugging boxes and unpacking. The whole thing is very unsettling and none of us speak very much. I dig out a spare kettle we had at home, and make some tea. I know Dad won't have thought to go shopping, so I've brought him some provisions. Though God knows how he'll manage. He can barely cook.

My phone buzzes. Jack. Oh. I get a little zing of pleasure, and squash it immediately. We've taken to sending the occasional text, but he's the last person I want to hear from right now.

'Who's that?' asks Daniel.

'Nobody,' I say, 'just a work thing.'

For some reason I haven't been able to tell Daniel that I'm communicating with Jack. I don't even know why. It's not as if we're doing anything wrong, but then again, if I'm not doing anything wrong, why do I feel guilty? Part of me is really looking forward to seeing Jack again, but I can't seem to find the words to mention it to Daniel. It's like I have a precious secret that I don't want to share with him. I take a sharp pause of breath. What am I playing at? For a moment I wonder whether this is how it started for Dad and Lilian – with lying and secrecy?

This is ridiculous. I am so not my dad. Yes, I have an inappropriate crush on a man I was once in love with, but it doesn't mean I am going to act upon it, and by not telling Daniel I am just emphasising how unimportant the whole thing is. And it's not like Jack has a clue how I feel about him. It's all safely locked up here in my head. Right where it's going to stay.

We don't stay long at Dad's. I give him a stiff hug and promise to call in the week, but I'm glad to be out of there. Despite the fact that Dad is the one doing the leaving, his new flat smells of sadness and failure. If I stay there too long I might start feeling sorry for him, and I don't think he deserves me to.

When we get in, I order us Chinese. Megan is back from

wherever she's been – as usual I have had a monosyllabic response to my questioning about her whereabouts – but when we we sit down to eat and watch a film together, she seems to relax and is much chattier. It's the first time in ages we've all been in on a Saturday night, and it's really cosy. I cuddle up to Daniel and count my blessings. I am with my family, where I belong. My phone goes again. Another text from Jack. Daniel strokes my hair, and I squeeze his hand. Time to knock this silly fantasy on the head. I switch off my phone and don't reply.

Chapter Six

Beth

My resolve lasts till halfway through the week. I've finally finished my next round of drawings for *The Littlest Angel*, and I know they're still not right. My angel does look a bit more cutesy, but I still can't seem to stop her pulling faces. Instead of taking her to the Vatican, I've sent her to St Mark's, where she's communing with the seagulls who tell her to take a boat heading eastward. I have no clue as to why, or any idea where she's headed after that. I eventually decide that the pyramids might be a good place for her to visit – Egypt seems about the right ballpark anyway. So I send her there, and introduce her to a rather bored camel. To be honest, I'm quite pleased with my camel, who looks suitably sardonic.

I get a phone call from Vanessa almost the moment I've sent the pictures.

'Oh dear, Beth, I don't think this is quite what I'm looking for,' she says. 'I'm not sure how a camel fits into the story.'

I'd have thought a camel fitted into the nativity better than a seagull, but what do I know?

'I was thinking the camel might lead the angel to the wise men,' I say.

'Oh right, I see,' says Vanessa in tones which suggests she doesn't. 'The thing is, Beth, it's just not quite working for me.'

I might have known she'd say that; and it makes me want to punch things.

There's a pause and then she says, 'Well, let's run it by marketing and rights to see how they feel.'

Oh God. My heart sinks. If the rights department don't think they can sell this, then I'm so done for. What if they decide to drop me? I know how hard the picture-book market is at the moment; I might never find a new home.

'I'll look at it again,' I say, trying to stop my thoughts from spiralling. 'I'll see if I can come up with another angle.'

It's the last thing I feel like doing, but I'm so anxious that I want to placate her.

'That's great, Beth, would you?' gushes Vanessa. 'I'm just really worried that it might affect sales. I think a camel isn't quite cute enough. Could she meet a lamb instead?'

Oh great, we're back to cute, although at least a lamb is appropriate. I sometimes think Vanessa and I are inhabiting parallel universes.

'I'll think about it,' I say, 'and get something to you in the next week.'

'Brilliant,' says Vanessa, 'I'll look forward to it.'

The call ends, and I go back to the illustrations, but nothing is working. I can't seem to draw cute sheep either. They either look demented or pissed off. Nothing to do with the way I'm feeling, I'm sure. By the time Daniel gets home, I'm in the depths of despair.

'What's up?' he says, kissing me on the top of the head, and making me feel instantly better.

'What if I can't do this any more?' I say. 'It's all I know how to do.'

'Don't be daft,' he says. 'You'll work it out. You always do.'

I want more from him than that, but Daniel has an unshakeable faith in me, and can't see that the odd reassurance is not quite enough at the moment. For once I wish he understood the creative part of me, and could give me some real and helpful input. But he doesn't. He's immensely proud of everything I've achieved, I know he is, but he's perplexed by the way I live in my head so much, and my constant worry that one day the muse will desert me. It's lovely when someone thinks everything you're doing is wonderful, but sometimes constructive criticism is vital. And I know Jack can give that to me, but can't work out to find a way of telling Daniel we've got tentative plans to meet. Then Daniel gives me the opening I've been hoping for.

'Have you talked to your mate Jack about it?' he says. 'Mightn't he be prepared to help?'

'I guess so,' I say, looking up at him. 'You wouldn't mind?'

'Mind? Why should I mind?' Daniel looks confused and I feel guilty, till I remember that he has no access to my innermost thoughts, and I've never ever told him how much Jack once meant to me. Perhaps I *should* tell him. But now, after all this time, it's going to look suspicious. When I met Daniel I wanted to put Jack in the past; I can't suddenly bring all that up now. It's understandable that seeing Jack again has revived the memory of those feelings, but nothing is going to happen there, so there's no need for me to feel guilty. I am, as usual, making mountains out of molehills, and Jack *could* help me. He always was incisive about my work.

So the next day I text him.

Book crisis! Help! I say. *Can we meet?*

Sure, is the response. *How are you fixed next Monday?*

I read the text over and over again, and realise that actually, it contains nothing more than professional friendliness. I have been getting myself in a state for nothing. Absurdly I feel a bit disappointed for having got it so wrong. Then I shake myself. Fantasising about Jack is ridiculous, and I do need his help. For the first time in months my book problems don't seem insurmountable, and that has to be a good thing.

Lou

Our Tenerife holiday is turning out to be quite fun. Now that we're here and in a different routine, Mum has perked up quite a lot. It's sunny enough to have breakfast on our balcony in the mornings, and we've been out on a couple of trips round the island. I even hired a car and drove us up to Mount Teide, which was a fairly harrowing experience, as it was very foggy and Mum yelped whenever we went round a corner. She squealed every time she saw a gap in the clouds and realised how high up we were.

James, our friend from the airport, is staying not too far away and has joined us for a coffee once or twice in town. Mum seems to have taken rather a shine to him, and he to her. And I'm glad. She seems a lot less sad than she did, and I swear she's even flirting a little with James. So when she suggests a shopping trip with him, I'm happy to let her go on her own. I'm more than content to spend an afternoon by myself by the pool. Even if unwanted thoughts of Jo have a tendency to intrude. Being away from home is giving me more time to think about her. Last time I was on holiday, we'd gone to Greece together. It had been such a lovely time, and now here I am alone. I shake my head with a determined effort. I am not going to ruin this holiday by being miserable. I'm not.

I'm sitting by the pool, reading my book, enjoying the late winter sunshine. It's been great to get away from home, and I'm even getting a tan. I look up and see a woman on the other side of the pool staring at me. She smiles and I smile back, and after a few seconds she comes over and introduces herself as Maria. She's a very pretty Spanish woman, with long curly dark hair, beautiful brown eyes, and a ready smile. I judge she's a few years younger than me. I take to her immediately; something about her is very appealing.

'You are alone?' she asks.

'No, here with my mum,' I say. God that sounds sad. A middle-aged singleton holidaying with her soon-to-be-divorced mum. Oh well, this woman is probably straight anyway.

'Do you fancy some sangria?' Maria asks, and so we go to sit by the pool bar and soon find ourselves chatting about all sorts. She's single too, and works as an estate agent here. Apparently the company she works for is recruiting.

'Sounds great,' I say. 'I'm out of work at the moment.'

'You should stay here,' says my new friend, 'get yourself a job. I have a great job looking after all the holiday lets. It's fun. You'd enjoy it.'

'I'd love to, but Mum . . .'

I fill her in on the situation, and she is uber-sympathetic.

'Your poor mama,' she says, 'your papa is a very naughty man.' Her accent is lovely.

'I know,' I say. 'He's never done anything like this before. It's been really weird and hard. He's hurt Mum so badly, I'm finding it so difficult to forgive him.'

'Huh, men!' she says with a toss of her long hair, and it's at that moment that I *know*. My stomach gives a little flip. Maybe I do have a chance here after all.

I'm not normally one to take the initiative, but the sun and the sangria are making me feel a bit reckless. Mum probably won't twig anything if I go off for drinks with my new 'friend.' I never disabused her of the notion that 'Joe' was male, after all.

'How are you fixed tonight?' I say with a confidence I don't normally feel. 'I was thinking of going out for a drink.'

Maria smiles at me in a way that makes me feel slightly faint, and says, 'I've not got any plans. A drink would be lovely.'

When Mum and James get back, she's delighted I have something to do. It turns out James has invited her to dinner.

'Way to go, Mum,' I say. I'm pleased that someone has made her smile, even though it will probably come to nothing, and even though I really want her to get back with Dad. She needs the ego boost.

'It's only dinner,' she says and I laugh. 'That's how it starts.'

For the first time since Christmas, I feel alive and positive. I spend ages choosing an outfit to meet Maria in, and take more care of my make-up than I have in months. By the time I've finished, I'm actually pleased with the way I look. And a little bit nervous. It's not exactly a date, but I think I like Maria, and I want her to like me. I have a moment of panic, wondering if I should go, then I shake myself out of it. I'm jumping the gun as usual. Nothing's going to happen with Maria, but an evening out with her can only do me good. I can't wait to get cracking.

Daniel got home to find that Reggie had been in touch again. This time he'd phoned the house and spoken to Beth. After a rough day at work, it was the last thing he wanted to hear. And the last thing he wanted to do right now was argue with Beth about it.

'Why didn't you tell me your dad was in the country?' said Beth. 'He's very keen to meet up.'

'I knew you'd nag me about it,' said Daniel.

'Too right, I will,' said Beth. 'He is your dad.'

'Yeah well,' said Daniel, 'that still doesn't give him any right to see me.'

Beth softened. 'Look, given what an idiot my own dad is being right now, I can understand that you don't want to see yours, but . . .'

'Good. So you get it then,' said Daniel, more sharply then he'd intended. 'I hope you didn't make any promises.'

'I didn't,' said Beth. 'I told him to ring back later.'

'You didn't,' groaned Daniel. He knew he was being unreasonable, but Beth's well-intentioned intervention had got completely under his skin. She'd never get why he wanted Reggie out of his life. 'I don't want to see him. Or speak to him.'

'I know you don't,' said Beth, in a clear effort to placate him. 'but what about the kids? Don't they have a right to know their grandad?'

'He tried that line on you, did he?' said Daniel bitterly. It was a tactic his dad had employed several times on him in the past.

'Well,' said Beth, 'He does have a point.'

'What if I said he gave up that right when he left me and Mum to struggle on alone?' said Daniel angrily. 'Now your dad has shown he's got feet of clay, I thought you might understand better.'

As soon as he'd said it, Daniel wished he hadn't as Beth looked like she'd been punched in the stomach.

'That's different,' she protested. 'And unfair.'

'Is it?' said Daniel. He took a deep breath and tried to calm down. 'Look Beth, you've never got this, but my dad isn't like yours. He's not some cuddly lovely guy who's going to come over and have a happy family reunion. It's never going to happen.'

'You always say that,' said Beth, clearly unwilling to let it go. Why did she have to be so persistent? 'But why not?'

'Leave it, Beth, please,' said Daniel, feeling suddenly tired. He hated talking about this, hated thinking about the past. 'Reggie was a terrible father, he poisoned my childhood. I don't want him anywhere near my family. I don't want to see him and that's that.'

'What if I do?' said Sam, who'd come in and overheard the conversation. 'I'd like to know more about your side of the family. Megan and I both would. We'd love to find out more about him. We know all about Mum's family and nothing about yours.'

'I'm sorry you feel like that Sam, but it's not happening,' said Daniel.

'I just don't understand why,' Sam persisted.

'That man is a nightmare, and he made your grand-mother very unhappy. I want as little to do with him as possible.'

'That was a long time ago.' Sam said in frustration. 'What if he's changed?

'Not long enough for me,' said Daniel, angry now. 'I can't ever forgive him for what he did to us.'

'He's my grandad though,' said Sam, 'and I have a right to see him.'

'Fine,' said Daniel, throwing up his hands. 'You get in contact with him then. You can all meet him, but I don't want him in this house, not ever. Do you understand?'

He got up and left the room, slamming the door behind him. He was angrier then he'd been in a long time, and bitterly cross that Reggie seemed to be causing trouble even without them seeing him. He supposed it was only natural that the kids were curious, but Daniel had fought his whole life to keep them away from his father. Sam was nearly eighteen, and Daniel couldn't stop it from happening any more. He closed his eyes, trying to keep calm. They did have a right to meet their grandad, but none of them knew what they were dealing with.

Chapter Seven

Lou

I creep into the apartment at 3 a.m., feeling like a guilty schoolgirl. Maria and I have had a brilliant night scoping out the gay clubs in Los Americanos. I have flirted and danced and drunk, and haven't had so much fun in ages. We went to a hilarious drag show in a bar called Chaplins, before going off to have a boogie. By the end of the evening we've exchanged numbers and Facebook details, and promised to keep in touch. I've told Maria all about Jo, so nothing actually happened tonight, but there's the delicious thought that something *might*, in the future. If nothing else, I've gained a friend. It's been great going out with Maria, she's made me feel young and light-hearted again. But I hadn't *quite* imagined I would be staggering in at this time. I almost laugh at myself; I'm thirty-eight, I can come in any time I like. But I haven't come home late to my mum since I was in my twenties, and I feel the same nervous pang as I did back then as I tiptoe around.

To my surprise there's a light on in the bathroom. Damn, Mum must still be up. There goes my plan just to sneak into bed quietly. Then I hear a man's voice. Bloody hell, has Mum brought James back?

I tentatively knock on the door and witness a scene I never expected to see. Mum is sitting on the floor with her head down the toilet, throwing up, and James is sitting beside her, ineffectually patting her back.

'What the—?' Oh God, I should never have left her, she's got food poisoning and it's all my fault.

'Ahem, I'm so sorry about this,' James looks shamefaced. 'I'm afraid it seems as if your mother may have imbibed too much wine at the restaurant. She kept saying she wanted more.'

Mum, drinking? I feel like I've entered a parallel universe. Mum only really has a drink at Christmas. And even then never too much.

'Are you OK, Mum?'

Mum raises bleary, tear-stained eyes at me and says, 'I'm a sixty-nine-year-old woman whose husband has just left her. My whole life has been for nothing. Of course I'm not OK.'

And then she starts to sob – huge, rackety, bone-shaking sobs. Poor James looks mortified, as if he can't wait to get away, and who can blame him? He was probably expecting a nice relaxing evening. He didn't sign up for this.

'Thanks so much for looking after her,' I say. 'It's all right, I'll take over now.'

'Your mother is a lovely woman,' James says as I see him out. 'If you don't mind me saying so, I think your father must be a fool.'

'I don't,' I say, 'because you're right.'

It's just as well Dad isn't here now. I'd give him a right talking-to.

I go back to the bathroom to find Mum sitting on the bathroom floor, washing her face with a flannel. It's terrible to see her in this state.

I don't often normally hug Mum, as she's not the cuddly

type, but she looks so woebegone, I find myself enveloping her in my arms.

'I'm such an idiot,' she says. 'Look at me, a drunken old fool, sobbing over a man.'

'You're not the first,' I say, and hold her tight. She feels bony and awkward. God she's lost a lot of weight. 'And it's not your fault. Dad's being a prick.'

'I won't have you talk about him that way,' says Mum. 'It must be my fault. I can't have been a good enough wife.'

'Mum,' I say gently, 'I know they say it takes two to tango, but Dad's the bad guy here.'

This produces a fresh round of sobs, and I hold her tightly once more, stroking her hair. I have a sudden memory of being six years old, and Mum holding me when I'd been sick. She was always there for us when we were little, and in her own way she's always been there for us as adults. I'm just not sure I've always noticed.

'But what a waste my life has been,' wails Mum. 'Forty-two years of marriage and nothing to show for it.'

'Nonsense, you've got us. You've been a brilliant mum. Of course it hasn't been a waste.'

'You think?' Mum looks at me bleary-eyed. Suddenly she seems older, more vulnerable. It's as if our roles have reversed, and I'm the grown-up. I hate seeing Mum like this; it's a weird feeling to be the one in charge for a change, but a surprisingly good one.

'Oh Mum,' I say, holding her close. I wish this had never happened to her. I wish Dad would realise he's made a big mistake, and everything would go back to normal again. 'You're the best. And we're going to go home and remind Dad of just what he's throwing away.'

Beth

I'm horribly nervous on the day I go to London to meet Jack. I wonder if Daniel has noticed that I'm different on the odd occasion when I've mentioned his name. I hope not. I know there's nothing there. I know nothing can happen. But meeting Jack again has been a catalyst, to remind me of the way life could be. I love and adore my family, of course I do, but sometimes bearing the weight of them all just feels too much. Daniel is a great father, but he has a demanding job, so even now, when the kids are older, it's still me organising their activities, picking them up from parties, remembering to book them on courses. I sometimes feel everyone else's lives are more important than my own. I definitely come at the bottom of the heap. When I text Jack or think about him, I forget all that. I feel like I've walked through a door into another world, where I'm not just a mum and a wife any more. I'm Beth, and I'm free.

I'm really early for our meeting, so I order a coffee in the Costa where we've arranged to meet. I sip it slowly, trying not to look too much like someone eager to meet a date. Despite my best intentions I feel a bit excited.

I get out my sketch pad and the manuscript so far, and read over it, frowning, trying to get my professional head on. The story just makes no sense. I wish I could get Vanessa to see that with all its faults, my original idea was better.

'You look like you've got the world on your shoulders.'

Suddenly he's here, and my heart skips a beat. I'm drowning at the sight of him. Oh God, what am I doing here? *It's business, Beth*, I scold myself. *Stop thinking about anything else.* But . . . I can't breathe, and I feel nausea rising in my gullet. I used to feel this way back then too. *Stop it, stop it*, I admonish myself. *Get a grip.*

'I'm just looking at what I've done and thinking that none of this is working,' I say, hoping my voice isn't as shaky as I feel. 'I don't know what to do. Vanessa seems to hate all my ideas.'

'I'm sure it isn't as bad as you think. Let me get myself a coffee, and then we'll go over it together. Do you want another?'

I nod mutely, barely able to speak now I'm actually in his presence. Luckily Jack doesn't seem to notice how untogether I am. I get myself back into shape while he brings over the drinks.

'It's so good to see you again, Lizzie,' he says. 'You're looking very well. Marriage must suit you.'

'It does,' I say. 'And actually, I really don't use Lizzie any more.'

'Old habits die hard,' he says lightly. 'You'll always be Lizzie to me.' He smiles. Oh, such a smile. I had forgotten how easy it was to get lost in that smile. I am quiet for a minute, till Jack brings me back to the subject at hand and asks to see my work.

He is silent as he looks through it, and I think, oh God, he hates it. I'm surprised to find how much I mind what he thinks of it. Jack always used to be dead honest about what he thought. I need to hear his opinion, even if I don't like what I hear.

'Well, you haven't lost your touch.' Jack eventually sits back and smiles. 'Lizzie – Beth – these are wonderful.'

'They are? I feel like I've lost the plot totally this time.'

'Granted, the storyline needs work,' says Jack, 'but your little angel, wow, she has so much character.'

'Vanessa hates her.'

'I think you'll find Vanessa is struggling to keep up at the moment. Karen is a hard act to follow and you're pretty intimidating.'

'Me? Intimidating?' I am stunned. My family would laugh at the idea.

'Well, you always have been a bit,' says Jack. 'You were always the one at college who knew where you were going, what you were doing – you were so certain about your vision.'

'I was?' I laugh. 'All I can remember about college is feeling I was winging it. Anyway, I think you're wrong. Vanessa can't possibly be intimidated by me. I'm an old has-been – she's the future. If anything, I'm the one who should feel intimidated. She's got me so confused about this bloody book. I had such a simple idea and she's over-complicated it.'

'Well, why don't you go back to the original idea?' says Jack. 'I know the story side of it isn't my area of expertise, but I'd always go for simple over complex.'

'But they've tried to sell Vanessa's version already,' I say. 'I'm not sure I can go back to the beginning right now.'

'I think you should get back to the heart of the matter,' says Jack. 'Forget everyone else's input, including mine, and tell your story in your way. I know you can do it.'

'Do you?'

'I do,' says Jack. Briefly, he lays his hand on mine. I feel an absurd tingle, and let it linger there a little longer than I strictly should. There's something thrillingly illicit about this, but I have it under control. Nothing wrong with some innocent flirting, so long as that's all it is.

'You've made me feel so much better,' I say. 'You haven't lost your touch.'

Part of Jack's appeal had always been how good he made me feel about myself. Particularly in the early days when I knew him, before I realised how faithless he could be.

'Then I'm glad,' says Jack in a way that makes my heart sing.

I change the subject, trying to get things back on a more even footing.

'How's the job going?' I ask, clearing my throat. 'I really hadn't had you down as someone who'd work in children's publishing.'

'I haven't always,' says Jack. 'It was when my daughter, Tash, came along. I loved the books she was reading, and was fed up in my previous job working in commercial fiction. Then an opening came up for a new head of design for Smart Books. They wanted someone with a different kind of experience, which was lucky for me. I haven't regretted it.'

'That's lovely,' I say. ' Do you get to see Tash much?' I am assuming since he isn't with her mum, Jack doesn't have custody of his daughter. Jack looks momentarily sad, and I get the slightest of glimpses into his more serious side.

'Not as much as I'd like,' he sighs. 'Her mum moved down to Kent to be nearer her family. But I do try. She means everything to me. She can be a bit of a prima donna, mind, but I think the world of her.'

'You wait till she's a teenager,' I say. 'Prima donna describes my daughter to a T.'

Jack laughs.

For the next hour or so we go through all my spreads, and throw ideas back and forth. It's really helpful and inspiring, and for the first time in months, I think I might have a chance of cracking this project. I'm enjoying Jack's company so much, I completely lose track of time, till I look at my watch and discover it is much later than I'd thought. I really should leave, although part of me wants to stay all day.

'Thanks so much for giving up your time for me,' I say. 'It's really good of you.'

'My pleasure, Beth,' he says. 'I'll always have time for you, you know that.'

The way he says it make my knees knock together slightly under the table. Oh God, what if I'm not imagining things, what then?

Daniel

'How was London?' Beth had clearly only just come in, judging by the chaos in the hall where she'd left her bags, and from the half-hearted way she was rooting through the kitchen cupboards looking for something to cook. She seemed a bit distracted.

'Fine,' said Beth. 'Jack was very helpful.'

'Well, that's good,' said Daniel. 'Do you think you can turn things around for Vanessa?'

'I have no idea,' said Beth. 'Apparently she finds me intimidating.'

Daniel laughed and kissed the top of his wife's head. 'You, really?'

'That's what I said.'

'Who's intimidating?' asked Megan as she walked into the kitchen. 'And when's tea?'

'Your mum, and not sure,' said Daniel.

Megan grabbed a pork pie from the fridge and started laughing. 'Mum is the least intimidating person I know.'

'Is it really so hard to think of me as scary?' asked Beth with a rueful grin.

'Yes,' said Megan and giggled some more.

'Afraid so,' said Daniel. 'But it's OK – I love you just the way you are.'

The doorbell rang.

'I wonder who that can be?' said Beth. 'We're not expecting anyone, are we?'

'Nope,' said Daniel. 'I was rather hoping for a quiet night.'

Unusually Sam came hurtling down the stairs shouting, 'I'll get it.'

Daniel and Beth looked at each other in surprise. Maybe Sam had a secret girlfriend they didn't know about. There was a slight pause and some mumbling before Sam ushered someone into the kitchen.

Daniel stood still from the shock, not quite able to take in what he saw.

'Reggie?' he said incredulously. 'What are you doing here?'

No. Beth couldn't have gone behind his back and asked Reggie over. Could she? Daniel turned furiously to his wife. 'Was this your idea?'

'No, it wasn't,' protested Beth.

'It's OK,' said Reggie, looking embarrassed. 'This clearly isn't a good moment.'

'Don't, please,' said Beth with a strained smile at her father-in-law. 'It's lovely to see you again.'

She glared at Daniel who glared right back.

'Well if you didn't invite him, who did?'

'I did,' said Sam, stepping forwards. 'I thought it would be good if you and Grandad could meet.'

'Sam!' Beth was clearly shocked. 'You shouldn't have done that without consulting us.'

'Why not?' Sam looked mutinous. 'Just because you don't want to see Reggie, I do.'

Reggie was looking extremely awkward. 'I'm sorry, I didn't mean to cause a row.'

'It's OK,' said Beth, which made Daniel feel even crosser. 'But Sam, you shouldn't have done that.'

'I don't see what the big problem is,' Sam said.

'The big problem is that you went behind my back,' said Daniel. 'I'm going out, and when I get back I want that man out of my house.'

With that, he got up and walked out, leaving his family open-mouthed behind him.

Chapter Eight

Beth

I am flabbergasted, first by the fact that Sam clearly hasn't thought this through at all, and second because Daniel has walked out of the house. He's not one for dramatic gestures – if anything they're usually my department. What on earth is going on? Meanwhile I have his dad to deal with, standing in my kitchen looking as awkward as I feel.

'I'm really sorry,' I say, 'It is great to see you, but I think Sam might have made a mistake here. I don't mean to be rude, but it would probably be better if you left.'

'Dad is a total loser,' says Sam. 'He's behaving like a kid.'

'That's enough, Sam,' I say. 'This is our house, you should have told us.'

'You're right, I should go,' says Reggie. 'I'm clearly not wanted here.'

'I don't want you to go,' says Sam stubbornly.

'Sam, it's not your choice,' I say. 'For now, I think your grandad should leave. But there's no reason why you shouldn't visit him, OK?'

'OK,' says Sam grumpily.

'I am so sorry about this,' I say as I escort my father-in-law from the house. 'It's not like Daniel to be so rude.'

'Well, he probably feels he has good reason. I wasn't the best dad in the world.'

'What did happen between you both?' I am curious, Daniel never talks about his dad, only his mum, whom he adored. I've always wondered, but if I ever ask him he clams up about it. I did ask him once if his dad hit him, but Daniel said it wasn't like that and then volunteered only that it was such an unhappy part of his life that he doesn't want to dwell on it. I can see how much it upsets him to think about the past, so I have learnt over the years not to pursue it, but I sometimes wonder if it would do him more good to talk. And right now I don't have a clue what he's thinking. I wish I did.

'It was a long time ago, and I was in a bad place,' sighs Reggie. 'Too much booze, I'm afraid. I wasn't there for Daniel, and I regret it. I don't blame him for hating me, but there's a lot of water under the bridge now. I'd really like to put things right though.'

'I can try to help,' I say, 'but Daniel can be very stubborn.'

'Yeah, well, so can his old man,' says Reggie, smiling wryly.

'Your grandson too,' I sigh. 'Must be a King thing.'

'He seems like a good lad.'

'He has his moments,' I say. I don't want to go into how much of a crap parent I feel most of the time around Sam.

'Well, Beth, it was nice to see you,' says Reggie. 'Maybe we can meet again before too long.'

'Maybe,' I say as I close the door.

But I recall the look on Daniel's face as he stared at his dad. Somehow, I don't think we'll be seeing Reggie again any time soon.

Daniel got into the car and drove and drove. He had no idea where he was until he found himself drawing into Evelyn Avenue in Tooting, miles from where he now lived, and pulling up outside the flat where he'd grown up. They had lived on the top floor of a crumbling old Victorian house, with sash windows, which had been hot in summer and freezing in winter. He sat staring at the building, now spruced up for a new generation. So much anger in that flat. So many memories of his dad yelling, his mum crying, and him hiding from it all wishing he could be somewhere else. He wondered if that anger was part of the fabric of the place; whether all that misery and decay had seeped into the walls and stayed there.

All his life he'd been running from this. Running from the anger he'd grown up with, the damage he'd seen his parents inflict on one another. Daniel prided himself on his even temper – it was partly what made him good at his job. He'd barely ever raised his voice at home or at school, and fought very hard against anger if it came his way. And yet now, faced with what Sam had done, he found himself incandescent with rage. He wanted to hit someone – *something* – very hard. How could Sam have gone behind his back? Daniel had made it perfectly clear he didn't want anything to do with his dad and Sam had gone and invited him anyway. Their brief moment of unity on the day they'd helped Fred move had faded away. It was as though whatever Daniel did, Sam would do the opposite to get a rise out of him. And boy was it working.

Daniel banged his hands on the steering wheel in frustration. What was he even doing here? He ought to get home. This was no way to behave.

A text came through from Beth. *He's gone. Please come home.*

Daniel took deep breaths. He was not going to let this get the better of him. He *was not*.

On my way.

By the time he got back, Daniel had managed to calm down.

He accepted the glass of wine Beth offered and sat down to eat the meal she'd left in the microwave.

'Where are the kids?' he said.

'In bed.'

'Good,' said Daniel. He wasn't up to a row with Sam about what he'd done. 'I can't believe Sam did that. How did he even get hold of Reggie's number?'

'He didn't,' said Beth, 'Reggie rang when we were out. Sam didn't see anything wrong with inviting him over. He didn't mean to cause trouble.'

'Didn't he?' said Daniel flatly. 'That's not how it feels from where I'm standing.' He felt tired and strung out. He just wished Reggie would go back to America and leave them alone.

'Daniel,' began Beth. 'I know you never want to talk about this, but I'm worried about you. Wouldn't it be better if you tried to make amends with Reggie?'

'No,' Daniel said shortly. 'He made my childhood hell, and I don't see why he should just swan back into my life now. He doesn't have the right.'

'But maybe he had his reasons,' argued Beth. 'I got the impression he wants to make it up to you.'

Daniel laughed sardonically.

'Make it up to me how?' he said. 'How can he make up for the times he came home drunk and hurled abuse at Mum? Or the times I spent cowering under the bedclothes pretending to be asleep in case he turned on me? I think it's a bit late to make it up to me.'

'Oh,' Beth looked shocked. It was the most open he'd ever been with her about Reggie. 'I don't know what to say. I'm so sorry, I hadn't realised it was so bad.'

Daniel sighed. This wasn't Beth's problem, it was his. 'I know. It's my fault for not telling you. That's why I hate talking about it. I decided long ago Reggie had done enough damage to me, and I wasn't going to let it affect the rest of my life. And I've succeeded. Beth, I'm proud of the fact that I'm nothing like him. I don't want him anywhere near me, or my family. He's poison.'

'Oh Daniel,' said Beth, coming over to him and giving him a hug. 'If that's really how you feel . . .'

'It is,' said Daniel. He held her tight, blinking back tears from his eyes. His family was so precious to him. It was his greatest fear that something would happen to change that. He couldn't let Reggie in, however much he might have changed. It was a relief that Beth finally seemed to understand.

'We'll say no more about it, then,' said Beth, kissing him.

As Daniel kissed her back, it felt as if a burden had been taken from his shoulders. His own family was what counted. No one else.

Lou

The taxi deposits us outside the front door at 9 p.m. Mum and I are both shattered and a bit bad-tempered after a rather drawn-out flight home and a long wait at the airport. I think Mum's a bit anxious about going back to a house which doesn't contain Dad, and she's very quiet. We didn't see James on the flight back; I think Mum is relieved. She hasn't referred to what happened at all, and has been avoiding James. She spent the rest of the holiday being very self-restrained. Shame. I rather liked wild Mum. It also meant that I didn't get out much again either. Although I did manage a farewell drink with Maria, in which we promised to keep in touch. Probably just as well we didn't see each other again. I've got enough of a track record for boomeranging from one unsuitable relationship to the next, and though it was fun flirting with Maria, I didn't really want a sleazy 3 a.m. encounter that wouldn't amount to anything and would only have made me feel worse about myself.

'Oh lovely, Beth's been in,' says Mum as she goes into the kitchen and discovers a bunch of flowers on the table, and a ready meal in the fridge.

'Actually, I don't think it is Beth,' I say in surprise. There's a note from Ged, saying *Welcome Home, Mum*. Hmm. Ged is not known for such thoughtful gestures. I detect the hand of the new woman. Well, good for her. It's about time Ged started taking more responsibility, even if he has to be pushed into it. Perhaps now that he's going to be a dad he finally gets it.

Mum is obviously touched beyond belief and starts rhapsodising about how wonderful Ged is, going on and on until I want to scream at her. He's done *one* little thing, and probably not off his own bat. I never hear Mum singing mine or Beth's praises. It's always been like that. She doesn't even know she does it, but Ged definitely gets an easier ride from her than we do.

She's on the phone to him immediately, inviting him and Rachel to come round, while I start to sort out some food and unpack. The house seems strange without Dad in it. *Wrong*. I keep expecting to trip over his slippers in

110

the hall, or find him pottering about in the garden. This is going to take some getting used to.

'We'll get Beth and Daniel over too, make a family day of it,' Mum is saying. Oh God, she's talking about her birthday. It's her seventieth and Beth and I have been agonising about what to do for her. And now she wants a family celebration? We haven't been together as a family since Christmas Day. It's going to be so weird doing this without Dad.

'Yes, and I shall invite your father too,' she continues. 'Time to put this unpleasantness behind us, and go back to being a proper family.'

I blink in surprise. Unpleasantness? She's talking as if they've had a little tiff. I didn't quite have this in mind when I told her to show Dad what he was missing.

'Mum,' I say as gently as I can when she gets off the phone, 'I'm not sure it's such a good idea getting Dad to come over for your birthday. It's not going to fix anything.'

'That's where you're wrong,' says Mum with a fierce determination. 'We've been together for over forty years. I am *not* going to give him up without a fight. We're a family, and families should stick together.'

Ouch.

This is a really, really bad idea.

Chapter Nine

Lou

I'm sitting in Beth and Daniel's kitchen regaling them with tales of our holiday. Megan is sitting there too, open-mouthed.

'Nana got drunk?' she says. 'I can't believe it.'

'Neither could I,' I say. 'I thought it might do her some good, but now she's fixated on this seventieth birthday thing and somehow getting your grandpa back. I can't imagine how that will work out.'

'Me neither,' says Beth, looking sad. 'When we dropped him off, he seemed pretty sure he wasn't coming home. He's still on about being in love.'

'Oh God,' I say, 'it's worse than having a teenager.'

Megan gets the giggles.

'Do you think Grandpa and that woman actually do it?'

'Megan!' says Beth, 'I don't want to think about it.'

Daniel laughs.

'It's not funny,' says Beth crossly, even though we've laughed about it too. Is it my imagination or does she seem a bit tetchy with Daniel?

'I know,' says Daniel. 'It's just . . . your dad. I can't get my head around it.'

112

'None of us can,' I say.

'So is Ged going to turn up for this famous party?' says Beth.

Apart from the flowers, Ged still hadn't been round. He doesn't 'do' awkward situations or emotions, and Mum's house is bang full of both.

'I might give Rachel a ring,' I say. 'I'm pretty sure she was behind the flowers, and it does look like she could be our future sister-in-law.'

Ged's girlfriends are usually of the fleeting kind, so Beth and I have given up trying to befriend them. But he actually seems devoted to Rachel, and of course she's pregnant, which makes her family as far as I am concerned.

'What about your dad?' says Daniel. 'Does he know anything about the party? Maybe someone should talk to him.'

Beth sighs. 'I'll go and see him,' she says, 'I've been avoiding it for too long.'

Poor Beth. She's always been Dad's blue-eyed girl. I think she's taken his fall from grace a lot harder than the rest of us. She's certainly not in any mood to forgive him just yet.

'I can't see him agreeing to come to the party,' she says, 'but I can try.'

Beth

'Hi Dad.' I give him a brief hug as I walk through the door. He looks tired, and thin. I bet he's not eating properly. The flat is even more dismal than I remember, and he hasn't done anything to make it better. The sink is full of dirty cups, and the lounge has papers and magazines and empty takeaway dishes scattered all over it.

'So, solo living going well?' I ask, glancing at the chaos.

I am both horrified and sad that he seems to be living in such squalor.

Dad grimaces.

'I have to say I hadn't *quite* appreciated how much your mum does around the house.'

How have I never noticed before what a Neanderthal my dad is? I suppose I put it down to a generational thing and blamed Mum for running around after him. For the first time I wonder if I've been fair. What if Mum felt she had to do that to keep him? For all I know Dad's strayed before. His behaviour seems uncharacteristic, but what if it isn't? Mum has had jobs in the past, but never what you might call a career. She always said we were her career. And then we left, and she made Dad her focus. What does that leave her with now? They always had a very traditional marriage: Dad was in charge of the garden, DIY and the bills, Mum the domestic stuff and the cooking, but I thought it suited them. Suddenly I see that Dad really took it all for granted.

I sigh with exasperation.

'Dad! It's not hard. You need to clean up as you go.'

'I'll get used to it,' he says. 'I suppose I'll have to get used to a lot of different things now.'

I look at him sharply. Does he think he's made a mistake?

'She misses you, you know.'

Dad looks a bit shamefaced.

'Well, I miss her too,' he says, 'but that doesn't change anything. Lilian and I want to be together.'

Where is she now? I feel like asking. It's Saturday night, but Dad is here on his own. Maybe he's having second thoughts. And maybe pigs will fly. I know I'm kidding myself, but he's clearly feeling guilty, so I press home my advantage.

'You know it's Mum's birthday coming up.'

Dad looks distinctly panicky.

'Her *seventieth* birthday. Which she never imagined spending on her own.'

Dad's look of panic disintegrates into guilt.

'Yes,' he mutters. 'She did mention something about a party.'

'She wants you to come. Would you?'

Dad fiddles unnecessarily with the kettle.

'Would I be welcome? I know what I've done has been very hard on you. Please believe me, Beth. I don't want to upset your mum, but Lilian's the best thing that's happened to me in years. I wish no one had to get hurt, but sadly that doesn't seem possible.'

He looks so forlorn, and even though I'm still cross, I can't help but want to give him a hug.

'You're still our dad,' I say. 'It won't be the same without you. Please come.'

Dad looks pleased I've said this.

'OK,' he says, 'I'd like to come. But it doesn't change anything You have to understand, it's over between me and your mum. It has been for a while.'

'I know,' I say.

I'm not sure Mum will see it like that, but still . . .

Daniel

'Where are you off to?' Sam was heading for the door looking shifty. Since the debacle with Reggie, he had been even more uncommunicative than ever. Daniel had no idea what he was doing any more. He came and went as he pleased, despite Beth shouting at him. Their constant screaming matches were giving Daniel a headache and achieving nothing as far as he could see. He'd tried to keep out of it for fear of making things worse, but he was fed up with Sam taking Beth for granted.

'What's it to you?' Sam's belligerence came over Daniel in waves.

'Despite your near-adult status, you do live under my roof,' said Daniel. 'And it's polite to let other people know what you're up to.'

'I'm going out,' said Sam.

'Where?'

'Out.'

'When will you be back?'

'Later.'

'How much later?'

'Don't know,' said Sam. 'I'm taking the car.'

'No, you're not,' said Daniel, 'I might need it.'

He didn't need it, and knew he was being petty, but Sam's assumption had him riled.

'OK, can I take the car, please?'

'Why do you need it?'

'Because I'm going out.'

'Perhaps if you told me where you're going I might say yes.'

'Oh for fuck's sake, Dad, I'm nearly eighteen. I don't have to tell you everything I do.'

Suddenly Daniel felt very tired. He didn't want to argue with Sam, and he didn't want a situation where Sam decided to take the car without asking.

'Fine, then,' said Daniel. 'Take the sodding car. But don't be back late.'

Sam muttered his thanks, grabbed the car keys and was gone, leaving Daniel feeling an utter failure.

Megan appeared ten minutes later.

'Can I have some money?'

116

'What for?'

'I'm going out with the girls to Nando's,' said Megan.

'What about dinner?'

'It's OK, I told Mum,' said Megan airily.

'Fine,' said Daniel, giving her twenty quid and feeling like he'd been stitched up.

'When will you be back, and how are you getting home?'

'Text you later,' said Megan. 'And Ali's mum's bringing us back.'

'OK, keep in touch,' said Daniel.

He watched his daughter disappear in a whirl of make-up and perfume and went and sat down in front of the TV with a heavy heart. His children were growing up and away from him. As difficult as it had been when they were small, he missed the simplicity of those days.

Once, he and Beth would have relished a Saturday night without their offspring, but now he felt as if they were slipping through his fingers, running away from them both into a future that didn't include them. And instead of enjoying some downtime with her, Beth was still at her dad's and he was suddenly all alone. It made him feel bereft. He decided to ring Josh, see if he fancied a pint. He was his best friend from his college days, and they hadn't seen each other in a while.

Daniel picked up his phone and glanced at his Facebook feed.

The first status that came up was a picture of Sam, posted just a few seconds ago . . . He was with Reggie.

Meeting my grandad at last, Sam had written. *Awesome*.

Daniel sat back in horror. He couldn't believe what he was seeing. Sam had lied to him again. Or, if not lied outright, he certainly hadn't been straight with him. There it was in black and white, Sam with his arm round Reggie's shoulder. The shock of the betrayal was like a punch in the gut. Sam looked happy, and relaxed in a way he never was with Daniel.

Daniel sat back on his chair, feeling sick as he stared at his son's happy face. It felt as though he was losing his son to Reggie. And there was nothing at all he could do.

The Littlest Angel

The Littlest Angel flew and flew, as fast as her wings could take her. She was such a very long way from home.

Eventually she arrived on the tower of a large cathedral. She stopped to pause for breath. She was still following the star, but it was so far away.

'Bonjour! Who are you?' A rat poked its head up from the rafters.

'I'm an angel and I've got lost,' said the Littlest Angel. 'I'm trying to get home to find the new baby and announce his birth.'

'You 'av to keep going zat way,' said her new friend. 'Good luck!'

Vanessa Marlow: I'm not sure we want to include actual French. This is for small children.

Vanessa Marlow: Also isn't this a bit stereotypical??
Beth King: Um, it was a joke?

Vanessa Marlow: Not quite sure this is right yet. Do we need to have a rat? Wouldn't a mouse be cuter?
Beth King: OK, Vanessa. I'll let you have a mouse.

Part Two

A Long Way Home

April–June

The Littlest Angel

The Littlest Angel set off with renewed purpose. She flew and flew, and kept flying east until she came to the land of the pyramids that the pigeon at St Mark's had told her about.

There, she met a <u>grumpy-looking</u> camel.

'Hello,' she said. 'I'm the Littlest Angel, and I'm looking for the new baby.'

'You need to go that way,' said the camel. 'The star will take you.'

'Oh, thank you,' said the littlest angel, and she set off on her way.

<u>Vanessa Marlow:</u> Does the camel have to be grumpy?

<u>Beth King:</u> What's wrong with a grumpy camel? I quite like my grumpy camel.

<u>Vanessa Marlow:</u> Can't it be cute?

<u>Beth King:</u> Does it have to be?

<u>Vanessa Marlow:</u> Yes.

Chapter Ten

Daniel

'Are you ready, guys?' Daniel was waiting by the front door, wondering not for the first time why it took his family so long to get out of the house.

Beth was fussing over last-minute alterations to the cake; Megan was redoing her hair for the umpteenth time, and Sam was nowhere to be seen. He'd moaned so much about having to go, Beth had threatened to cut off his allowance, resulting in a huge row. She had a tendency to go in all guns blazing, which Daniel always found difficult, particularly at the moment. He'd spent the last two weeks stewing on the fact that Sam had seen Reggie behind his back, and not managed to find the words to articulate how he was feeling. When Sam had been rude to Beth, Daniel had nearly snapped, but just managed to restrain himself. Shouting never solved anything in Daniel's book. Although in this case, after he'd calmed down a bit, Sam had actually apologised to Beth and agreed to show up, which was better than they could have hoped for.

Daniel was in two minds about the party. What had started off with a few family members seemed to have escalated into something much bigger. He couldn't help thinking it might have been better for Mary to keep it low-key, and wondering if inviting Fred was a good idea after all.

'But she should be able to celebrate her milestone birthday,' Beth had argued, 'and Dad owes her, he has to come. Besides, Mum wants to show Rachel she's not getting involved in a totally dysfunctional family.'

'Inviting your dad to the party isn't going to change anything though, is it?' Daniel said. 'I shouldn't think Rachel will be unaware of what's going on.'

'Maybe not,' said Beth. 'But you know what Mum's like. She's adamant that she wants Dad there.'

'I hope it doesn't end in tears,' said Daniel, and then left it. In the last few weeks it felt as though he and Beth seemed to have been quite snippy with one another. It was partly her preoccupation with the new book, which still wasn't going well, and partly the situation with Reggie. Although Beth had been supportive about Daniel's stance with Reggie, she still felt it wasn't fair to stop Sam and Megan from meeting him.

'Fine if you don't want to see him,' she'd said, 'but I really don't see why it's such a problem for the kids. They should have the chance to find out about their family history.'

Daniel hadn't yet told Beth about the picture he'd seen on Sam's Facebook page, but he was worried that if he probed too deeply, he might find that she knew all about it anyway. Despite their often fiery relationship, Sam did tend to tell Beth stuff. Daniel knew he'd put a barrier up since Reggie had turned up on the scene, and he didn't know how to pull it down. It was making them both irritable, and Beth was snapping at him over little things, like not pulling his weight around the house, and not supporting her when

Megan stayed out later than she was meant to. They didn't quite have full-blown rows, instead retreating into silence if the conversation got too tetchy. It worried Daniel that they weren't talking to each other enough, but then there were days when he'd come home and everything felt normal again, and he decided he was being paranoid. Every marriage went through its ups and downs, this was just one of those times when theirs was a bit patchy.

Beth eventually appeared with the cake and a bunch of balloons, followed by Megan, who tripped out in the shortest of short skirts – 'Not appropriate, young lady,' said Beth, sending her back to change – and finally Sam came growling down the stairs, looking like he'd just got out of bed, moaning about his lot.

'Can you just do this one thing for your grandma?' said Beth in exasperation, and Sam at least had the grace to look a little embarrassed.

Finally, a full half an hour after Daniel had wanted to leave, they were off, and Daniel breathed a sigh of relief. He hated being late for things.

'Dad's not here yet.' Lou greeted them at the door, looking anxious already. 'Mum's doing her nut. He *is* coming, isn't he?'

Beth shrugged her shoulders. 'He said he was. Unless the evil witch known as Lilian has got to him, and persuaded him not to.'

'He has to come,' said Lou. 'It will be so awful for Mum if he doesn't.'

Daniel was in two minds about this, but thought better than to say anything. Instead he went to greet his mother-in-law.

'You look lovely,' he said, giving her a kiss. She did, she was wearing a simple velvet dress and a pearl necklace, her short grey hair cut in a smart bob. She'd lost weight since Fred had left, and it made her look very elegant. Fred was a fool to let her go.

'Now have you got a drink, Mary?' Daniel added, and made sure his mother-in-law sat herself down while he and the kids organised the balloons and decorations, and Beth and Lou disappeared into the kitchen.

The doorbell rang, and Ged and Rachel arrived, followed swiftly by a whole host of friends and relations. It seemed like Mary had invited everyone she knew. Daniel could only pray that it wasn't a total disaster.

Beth

The party is in full swing, but there's still no sign of Dad. Lou, Ged and I have a rapid conference in the kitchen.

'Should I call him again?' says Lou.

'No point,' I say. 'He seems to have switched off his phone. I can't believe he's not coming. He *promised*.'

I had been thawing to Dad a bit since I last saw him. Despite him living in a chaos of his own making, I couldn't bear to think about him in that horrible flat, but now I'm furious all over again.

'Maybe he changed his mind,' Ged says. 'Perhaps he's decided it's not such a good idea.'

'I'm inclined to agree with him,' says Lou, 'but Mum was adamant she wanted him here.'

'Well if you ask me, she's better off without the old sod,' says Ged. 'He's treated her appallingly.'

'Yes, well, you ought to know all about that,' I say sweetly. 'It's never stopped the poor fools who've chased after you.'

'I'm a reformed man these days,' says Ged loftily.

'Ha, that'll be the day,' I snort.

'Oh ye of little faith,' said Ged, pretending to be hurt. 'I'd never met the right person before.'

'Aw, Ged's met the right person at last,' teased Lou. 'The women of the world can relax.'

He play-thumped her and said, 'Maybe I should go round to see Dad and have a chat, man to man.'

'Bad idea,' I say. 'You'll either end up rowing or drunk, or both.'

Ged and Dad have never exactly seen eye to eye. The last time they got into a discussion about the appalling state of Ged's finances it had got so heated I thought they might actually have a fight.

At that point the doorbell rings and I rush to open it.

Dad is standing on the doorstep, holding a rather squashed bunch of flowers and looking extremely awkward.

'Any room for a little one?' he says.

Lou

We all breathe a sigh of relief when Dad arrives. Whatever happens next, at least he came. Mum is magnificent. She air-kisses him briefly.

'Hello, darling, so pleased you could come,' she says. 'You look like you haven't slept for a week.'

'Happy Birthday, Mary,' he says awkwardly, thrusting the flowers into her hands.

'How sweet of you,' she says. 'You needn't have bothered. I'll just go and put these in a vase. The children will look after you.' She disappears off into the kitchen and then deliberately goes off to charm her guests. I watch her talking and laughing, being funny and entertaining. No one who didn't know her would have any idea that this was the woman who a few short weeks ago could barely make it out of the house.

129

I can see the effort it's costing her though. Look at me, she's saying to Dad, do you *really* want to give this up?

Dad ends up in the kitchen, chatting with Ged and Daniel. I think all three of them are eager to stay out of the limelight.

'Don't hide out here too long, boys,' I say. 'Someone will notice.'

'We'll be in in a bit,' says Daniel. 'I was just talking about Beth's birthday. I'm thinking of holding a surprise fortieth in July. What do you think?'

'Oh that's a great idea, Daniel,' I say. 'We'll talk about it another time. Now please do remember to socialise.'

I go back into the lounge to find Rachel, who is sitting on her own, looking a bit lost.

'Ged hasn't abandoned you already has he?' I say. 'Particularly when you're so close to your due date. He should be at your side at all times. I've a good mind to tell him.'

She laughs.

'I'm fine,' she says. 'It's not as if I'm going to pop right this minute. Ged's finding this all a bit awkward, and I think he wants to escape with the men.'

'Yup,' I say. I like Rachel, she seems to have the measure of Ged.

'Don't let him push you around,' I warn her, 'I love my little brother, but—'

'—he can be a prize jerk?' says Rachel. 'Tell me about it. You know, I actually had to leave him for a bit to make sure he'd do the right thing by the baby. But I think he's ready to settle down now.'

'Really? What happened?'

'I found out I was pregnant in Bali, and he had a bit of a panic about it,' says Rachel.

'I bet he did,' I say. I can just imagine how freaked out my devil-may-care brother must have been to find out he actually had some responsibilities.

'So I said if he didn't want to be with me and do this properly, I was going to go back home to Oz and would never see him again.'

'Blimey,' I say. None of Ged's other girlfriends would have either the nerve or the nous to call him out like that. 'Then what happened?'

'I got as far as the airport, and he rushed up to find me at check-in, threw his arms around me, and said he couldn't stand the thought of life without me, and would I like to come to England and meet his family.'

I burst out laughing.

'That's priceless. Go Rachel, the girl who tamed Ged.'

Rachel grins. 'We do love each other, you know.'

'I think you're very good for him,' I say. 'I take it it was your influence with the flowers for Mum? I don't think Ged would think of that one on his own.'

'Ged is far too naughty to your mum,' says Rachel. 'I certainly won't let our son get away with that kind of behaviour.'

'Oh, you're having a boy? How lovely,' I say. Typical Ged, not bothering to let anyone know.

'We are indeed,' says Rachel, 'and I'm going to make damned sure he doesn't learn any bad habits from his dad.'

I laugh. I'm liking Rachel more and more. Ged has finally met his match.

There is a clinking of glasses and suddenly I realise Mum is about to make a speech. She hadn't said she was going to. Oh lord, what is she planning to say?

Rachel and I look at each other nervously. I hope Mum hasn't been drinking again. I'm not sure I can cope with that.

'Thank you, everyone, for coming to my party,' Mum says. 'This wasn't quite the way I planned to spend my seventieth birthday, but it just goes to show you're never too old for a change of circumstances, even if they're forced on you. Here's to a dissolute old age!'

She raises her glass and everyone toasts her. I'm not sure if most people even know what's happening. I look over to see Dad standing in the doorway. He looks lost and forlorn, as if he's a kid left out of the sweetshop.

Oh, well played, Mum, well played.

Chapter Eleven

Lou

'Hi, Louisa.' Dad sounds uncharacteristically nervous on the other end of the phone. 'Er, is your mum in?'

I try not to laugh. He sounds like all Beth's boyfriends from school used to when they rang up to speak to her. It's odd hearing him sound so uncomfortable.

It's been two weeks since Mum's party and Dad has rung every day. I can't work out what's going on. Is he still seeing Lilian? Does he want to come back? If so, he's not being very obvious about it. Mum is being very naughty and is either not answering the phone or managing to be out when he calls. I'm quite impressed. I had no idea she had it in her. She's been out nearly every night. She's started going to Zumba classes, volunteers at the local charity shop, and has even been on a date with James. Well, she says it wasn't a date, but she spent a very long time choosing what to wear. I don't think she's being quite fair to James. He clearly likes her, and I don't think she should be using him in her campaign to get Dad back.

I told her off about it, but she shrugged and said, 'James

is a friend. He understands I'm not ready to have a relationship with him.'

'You're playing with fire,' I warned, but she's ignored me, and keeps making excuses not to speak to Dad.

The one and only time they did speak, she made a big point about how she was going out for dinner with a friend. I hope she knows what she's doing. I know she's playing hard to get, but I'd hate to see James caught in the middle. Strangely, it does seem to be working. Dad is certainly trying to re-establish contact, while Mum is doing a grand job of being elusive.

'Mum's not in, Dad.'

'Do you know when she'll be back?' The million-dollar question. I am frequently in bed by the time Mum gets back home these days.

'No idea,' I tell him. 'She's a bit of a law unto herself at the moment.'

'Oh,' Dad sounds so downcast, I feel quite sorry for him. So on impulse I say, 'Why don't you come over for Sunday lunch? I'll cook if Mum's out.'

'That would be good,' says Dad. 'And you can tell your Mum . . .'

'Yes?' I prompt.

'Oh . . . nothing,' says Dad and puts the phone down.

'Who was that?' Mum has just come in from Zumba. It suits her. She looks glowing and healthy.

'Dad. He wants to see you.'

'Does he indeed?' Mum looks triumphant.

'I've invited him for lunch on Sunday,' I say. 'It's OK, you can go out if you want.'

'No, I'll be here,' says Mum, with a smug smile. 'I think lunch is an *excellent* idea.'

Daniel was in bed catching up on some paperwork. He was dog-tired and wanted an early night. He'd left Beth downstairs pottering; she'd said she was quite happy as Sam was out and she wanted to make sure he was home before she went to bed. Sam hadn't said where he was going, but Daniel had a good idea.

Daniel heard the door slam, and then Sam and Beth talking in the lounge before eventually there were footsteps on the stairs and he heard Sam shout 'Night!' It wasn't much, but at least it was some communication.

Beth came into their bedroom shortly afterwards. She looked preoccupied.

'Sam have a good night?' said Daniel.

'Yes,' said Beth. She looked as though she wanted to say something else, but disappeared off to the bathroom.

'Did he say where he went?' Daniel asked when she came back in.

Beth paused, 'You're not going to like this . . .' she said.

'He's been seeing Reggie, hasn't he?' Daniel said flatly. He could tell straight away that she knew. How long had she been keeping it secret from him? He could feel the familiar rage welling up inside.

'How did you know?'

'Last time he put it on bloody Facebook,' Daniel said.

'Is it really such a bad thing?' said Beth gently, but Daniel wasn't to be pacified.

'I don't want our son going near that man,' said Daniel. 'I've told you why I want nothing to do with him.'

'I know, and I do understand that, Daniel,' said Beth, 'but he's not Sam's dad; he can't hurt Sam the way he did you. Sam has us.'

Daniel sighed. 'I suppose so, Beth,' he said. 'It's just so hard, knowing what he was like. It worries me, Sam getting to know him.'

'But he doesn't seem to be like that now,' said Beth. 'Maybe he's changed.'

'Maybe he has,' said Daniel, 'but I can't forget.'

'Do you think you could learn to forgive?'

Daniel might have known she'd say that. Beth always wanted to put things right with people.

'Oh forget it,' said Daniel. 'If Sam wants to see Reggie I can't stop him, but I don't have to like it.'

'Daniel, don't be like that.' Beth reached over to take his hand, but Daniel shook her away. He knew he was being unfair, but he turned his back on her.

'I'm going to sleep,' he said, and turned off his light.

Sighing, Beth got into bed with him and turned her own light off, while Daniel lay in bed festering. Despite his exhaustion, he couldn't sleep, his thoughts turning back to the things he'd tried so hard to forget.

He just couldn't talk about it. All those years before Dad left, feeling sure it was his fault that Reggie was angry all the time, even though Mum said it wasn't. And that fateful trip to the States, in the year before he met Beth, when he'd turned up at his dad's new pad to find him shacked up with another woman, being a dad to her children in a way that he'd never been to Daniel. Although that relationship was long over, and Reggie never mentioned her again, Daniel had never been able to explain the crushing sense of rejection he'd been left with to anyone. He'd decided on that day that he would have nothing more to do with his dad, wouldn't run the risk of being hurt again.

From then on, Daniel had had intermittent contact with Reggie, and he wanted to keep it that way. He couldn't stand the fact that Reggie had turned up and was trying to muscle his way into the family Daniel had spent the last eighteen years building for himself.

What really hurt was that Sam wanted to spend so much time with Reggie. Having been the kind of dad he'd always wanted for himself, in the last few years Daniel had felt Sam pull away from him. He didn't seem to want the things that Beth and Daniel wanted for him, preferring to focus on his music rather than academic success. By luck more than hard work he'd managed to scrape through his GSCEs, but he was doing a worrying lack of work for his A Levels. Daniel could see the appeal of a long-lost musician grandad, who probably seemed a lot more fun than his boring parents. It didn't seem fair that Sam could barely give Daniel the time of day, and yet have time for the man who had been such a shitty father himself.

Over the years, Beth had tried several times to probe Daniel about Reggie, but he had always pushed her away. Up until now she'd accepted it, but he knew he'd hurt her tonight by refusing to open up. So not only was Reggie successfully driving a wedge between him and his son, he'd managed to cause Daniel problems with his wife too. And at the moment, for the life of him, Daniel didn't see what he could do about it.

Beth

'You seem really preoccupied.' I'm in London meeting Jack the week after the Easter weekend. It's a lovely spring day, and I've left the kids at home. Sam is supposed to be revising, Megan is seeing friends and Daniel has gone into work to oversee some revision workshops. I get on the train, feeling like I'm shedding my normal life. I feel simultaneously guilty and excited. I have rung Jack a few times to sound him out on a couple of ideas, and though he has been nothing but professional, I can't help indulging myself in a fantasy life where I don't have to think about family pressures, and the only thing I need to concentrate on is how to sort this wretched book out.

With Jack's help, I finally feel like I'm making some headway. I relish our conversations. I haven't felt this creatively inspired in years.

I sigh. 'It's Daniel,' I admit eventually. 'I'm worried about him.'

I feel guilty talking to Jack about Daniel. It seems like a betrayal of sorts, but it's such a relief to get my worries off my chest. Daniel seems to be closing down on me, and I can't seem to reach him at the moment. I hate it. I explain about Reggie turning up, and before I know it I'm also pouring out the story of Mum and Dad's split, and how much I worry about the kids.

'It's as though everything I thought was certain in my life has become rocky,' I say. 'It's all falling apart.'

'Nothing in life is ever certain,' says Jack, 'and I'm sure it's not as bad as you think.'

He smiles that lovely smile, and I feel warm all over.

'Maybe not,' I say. 'But in a funny way, I wish I could go back a few years. It all seemed so much simpler when the children were small.'

Back then, life had been hard, but Daniel had been starting out in his teaching career, we had our first family home, and while looking after small children was exhausting, I somehow felt we were in it together. Now? I'm not so sure. I had never imagined parenting teenagers would be harder than having little ones, but in some ways it really is.

And more than anything, I wish I could go back to before

Christmas when Mum and Dad were still together, rubbing along the way they always had. Although Lou seems to think that Dad is angling to come back, nothing is ever going to be the same again. It makes me feel unsettled about my own relationship. Time was I'd have thought Daniel and I were rock solid and nothing could split us apart, but right now I feel we're cracking round the edges. And here I am sitting talking to another man about it. A man I find very attractive.

Moments like this with Jack are making me fantasise about another kind of life, another kind of reality. What would have happened if all those years ago, Jack and I had got together? What would happen if I acted on my feelings for him now? As we sit closer and closer together, I know that I am being tempted in a way I never have been before. Dare I even go there?

Jack is talking again. He reaches over and grabs my hand. I let him, kidding myself he's just being supportive, but knowing I like the solidity of it grasping my own.

'It will be OK, Beth. You and Daniel seem to have a strong marriage. It's bound to be unsettling at the moment. But you're lucky. You have something I never had.'

I'm lucky, I think. He's right, I'm lucky. And then I stare into those beautiful blue eyes and think, *Fuck, what am I doing?* This is playing with fire. I quickly withdraw my hand. Is it my imagination or does Jack give it a slight squeeze before I do?

'I think I'd better go,' I say. 'I really ought to get back for the kids.'

I don't. Sam will be probably be out by now, and Megan will be sitting in the lounge on Snapchat if she's in. Neither of them care whether I'm there or not most of the time; I feel like I'm just part of the furniture. But I can't stay with Jack, otherwise I might do something I regret. I check my phone. A missed call from home. That's it, I really need to go.

'If you ever need to chat,' says Jack, 'you know where I am.'

'Yes of course,' I say. He stares at me for a moment longer, as though daring me to look away. I peck him on the cheek and flee the café. I feel like I've betrayed Daniel, and I don't exactly know why.

Chapter Twelve

Beth

'Daniel,' I say rather breathlessly as I get on the train home, 'I've had three missed calls. Is everything OK?' I look at my watch. The afternoon has slipped away from me; I'm going to be back much later than I'd intended.

'Where have you been?' Daniel sounds stressed and angry. 'Megan's gone AWOL.'

'What do you mean, Megan's gone AWOL?'

'We had a row about her doing her homework,' says Daniel. 'I sent her up to her room, and now she's not there. She's not answering her phone either.'

Shit, shit, shit. My heart is beating erratically; I can feel the panic beginning in my chest. Megan has been volatile over the last few months, the slightest attempt at discipline setting her off, but she's never disappeared on us before. She's generally good at letting us know where she is. Megan would choose to vanish when I'm in London and miles away. The majority of the time I am at home, working in the shed; why does this have to happen today? Even though it's not my fault, I can't help but feel guilty.

'Look, don't panic,' I say even though I can feel myself starting to. 'I'll ring round the mums I know and see if

141

anyone knows anything.' This is easier said than done. Megan keeps me as far away from her friends' mums as possible. Just in case I find her out, I suspect, like the time I thought she was at a sleepover with one friend and it turned out they'd bunked over to another's and gone to a club for under-sixteens. I do have a couple of her mates' mobile numbers on my phone though, so I message them and ask them if they know where she is. Eventually I get a message back from her friend Chloe. *Sacha says she's in the park.* Relief courses through me, only to be followed by a horrible thought.

Which one? I text back urgently. Please don't let it be Prince's Park – it's the local teenage hangout where all the bad things happen. Drink, drugs and sex, from what Sam has told me. And, of course, when Chloe texts me back, it turns out that's where she's gone. How has Megan ended up there? She knows I disapprove. We've had chats about it, and she always says she wouldn't be so stupid. Like an idiot I've believed her.

I ring Daniel. 'Found her,' I say, 'she's in Prince's Park. My train should be in in about fifteen minutes. If you pick me up from the station we can go straight there.'

Daniel groans. He knows far more than I do about the local teen subculture.

'What the fuck is she up to?'

'Whatever teenagers normally do in the park?' I say. 'Let's just find her, shall we? We'll worry about what to do then.'

By the time the train pulls into the station, I am jittery beyond belief. I just pray that Megan is safe.

Daniel barely speaks to me when I get in the car.

'Why were you so late?' he asks. 'I've been going out of my mind with worry. Why the hell didn't you answer your phone?'

'Sorry, I turned it off in our meeting and forgot to turn it back on again. Then lunch went on a bit longer than planned.'

'You stink of booze.' Daniel looks at me disapprovingly.

'I had one glass of Prosecco,' I protest. I'm too anxious to row though, and I can see why he's cross. I should have been back sooner.

We pull into the parking bays by the park and head down a wooded path to the playground, where a bunch of teenagers are swinging desultorily on the swings. My heart sinks. They're all smoking and there's a vodka bottle in evidence, plus the distinctive smell of pot. Oh great.

There's no sign of Megan, but I recognise one of the girls in the group. They all seem a lot older than Megan, which isn't reassuring.

'Do any of you know Megan King?' I ask. There's a collective shrug, apart from the one girl I recognise.

'I think she went home.'

'When?'

'About ten minutes ago.'

Damn, we've just missed her. At least I know that ten minutes ago she was safe, but I'm dreading what kind of state she might be in now.

'She went that way.' The girl points us to a path leading to another park entrance, which goes to the other side of town. Megan is heading in completely the wrong direction.

'Was she alone?'

More shrugs, and then someone says, 'I think Jake was with her.'

Jake? Who's Jake? As far as I was aware, Megan barely knows any boys.

'Why don't I walk down the path and you bring the car round to the other entrance?' I suggest, heart pounding.

'Good idea,' says Daniel. He heads off one way, and I the other. I am almost sick with anxiety and guilt. What if something has happened to Megan? I'll never forgive myself.

It doesn't take long to find her. I'm halfway down the path when I come across her crouched on the ground, throwing up over a flowerbed while a boy I don't know is patting her awkwardly on the back. The mysterious Jake, I presume.

'Oh Meg,' I say. I am so angry with her but also relieved that she's safe.

She looks up at me, and says, 'I am so fucked,' before throwing up over Jake's feet.

Daniel

'I've got her.' Beth's voice on his mobile was a welcome relief. Daniel had spent the last few hours torturing himself with thoughts of what could have happened to Megan, unable to get hold of Beth. Thank God they'd found her. 'I warn you though, it's not pretty,' Beth carries on. 'She's very drunk.'

Bloody, bloody hell. He heard about this sort of thing all the time in the staffroom at school. But it was the first time to his knowledge that Megan had been drunk. Daniel shook his head. Who knows what she might have been getting up to when she'd gone on sleepovers with her mates? She never told them anything. Megan was his little girl, he couldn't bear the thought of her behaving like this, even though he knew other kids did. You trusted your own children, but you never knew what they got up to behind your backs. He'd had enough conversations with distraught parents unable to comprehend what their children had been doing to know that. He and Beth were going to have to sit down and have a serious chat with Megan. But not right now.

As Beth and Megan appeared through the park gates, he could see Megan could barely stand, and she was covered in vomit.

'Bugger,' he said.

'Bugger indeed,' said Beth. 'I'll make her clean the car tomorrow as a punishment.'

Daniel's anger quickly evaporated into relief. At least she was safe.

'I'm so sorry,' Megan kept saying. 'I didn't mean to do it.'

'Have you ever been drunk like this before?' Daniel couldn't help going into head teacher mode as he put another arm around Megan and helped Beth lead her to the car. They needed to know how much of a problem this was.

'No!' Megan's indignation was a little forced.

'I'll take that as a yes then,' said Beth. 'You, young lady, are grounded.'

'Yes of course,' said Megan, who seemed unable to do anything but apologise through a bout of violent hiccups.

Despite his anxiety, Daniel had to repress the desire to laugh. Megan was such an earnest and remorseful drunk. He was reminded of the way she used to apologise profusely as a small child when she'd got into trouble. His little girl was still in there somewhere.

They eventually got Megan home and Beth had to clean her up before putting her to bed with towels and a bucket in case she threw up again.

'Well that was fun,' said Beth, when she eventually came downstairs.

'I knew there was something going on,' said Daniel. 'She's been so secretive lately.'

'Well, why didn't you say?'

'Because you're always so hard on her,' said Daniel.

'And you're too soft,' said Beth, exasperated. 'And look where that's got us.'

They glared at one another angrily, and Daniel was about to say something else, when he thought about his daughter lying upstairs.

'Oh forget it,' he said. 'Let's not row about whose fault it is; at least she's safe.'

'Thank God,' said Beth. 'When I think about what might have been . . .'

'Don't,' said Daniel. 'Everything turned out OK. We just have to hope she doesn't do it again.'

Lou

Sunday morning and Mum is up bright and early. It's a lovely day and the sun is shining through the kitchen window. Mum's picked some daffodils from the garden, and they're giving an air of spring cheer. The whole house is spotless by the time I come down. I've been Skyping Maria; we've been talking a lot lately, and as usual after I've been chatting with her, I've come away feeling more cheerful about life. She has a knack of making me feel better about myself.

I had planned to do the cooking today, but Mum has got the roast on already. She's dressed up to the nines and looks very glamorous in a slim-fitting red dress. She's wearing a necklace and earring set Dad gave her one Christmas, and even has high heels on.

'Wow, look at you, hot mama,' I say. 'Dad will be certain to know what he's missing now.'

'That's the idea,' said Mum. 'Now be a dear and set the table for four.'

'Four?'

'Oh, didn't I mention? I've asked James.'

'Mum!' I'm scandalised. 'Do you think that's fair on James?' Dad deserves it, but James has been sweet as anything to Mum.

'It was his idea,' she says. 'Honestly Love; I know what I'm doing.'

She goes back into the kitchen, where she has Gloria Gaynor's 'I Will Survive' playing at top volume. Really, she couldn't be less subtle if she tried.

Lunch is not a success.

James arrives first and seems ill at ease. Maybe he's having second thoughts about this being a good idea. I have a tortuous conversation with him about cricket, which is clearly a passion, while Mum clatters around in the kitchen. I hope she's not on the sherry.

Dad turns up late. This time without flowers.

'Dad, this is James,' I say brightly. 'Mum and I met him on holiday.'

'I know,' growls Dad, barely extending the hand of greeting.

James goes back to talking about cricket, while Dad glowers in the corner.

'Are you a fan of the game?' James asks, trying to engage him.

'Not my cup of tea,' says Dad.

'Shame,' says James.

'Racing's more my thing,' Dad eventually ventures. I've been shooting him filthy looks and I think he's finally picked up on the fact that he's being pretty rude.

It turns out James is fond of racing too, so by the time Mum has appeared from the kitchen, looking a little pink

(I think she has been on the sherry), they're chatting away like old friends. Oh dear, I don't think that was part of Mum's plan.

'Can I do anything to help, Mum?' I ask.

I'm finding the whole thing excruciating. Dad had slipped out at the end of Mum's party without making a scene, but it's clear from his behaviour since that she's got under his skin. There are the phone calls for a start, and the sheepish way he asks about her. I wonder if he's getting cold feet about being with Lilian. Maybe he wants to come back? He seems very nervous today, and is drinking a lot faster than usual. He and James seem to appear to be on the point of swapping rude jokes – definitely time for me not to be here.

Mum just smiles sweetly when I offer to help, and says, 'It's all under control, darling.'

Another half an hour elapses before lunch is served, and everything is awkwardly polite until she turns to Dad and asks, 'So how have you been? And how is dear Lilian?'

'Er,' Dad clearly doesn't know what to say. 'I'm – she's OK.'

'Good,' says Mum. 'I'm happy for you.'

I nearly choke on my food. Despite the new and improved version of herself, I know that's not what Mum actually thinks.

James looks embarrassed and starts to talk about the weather, which has just turned warm after weeks and weeks of rain. Dad gratefully drops into a chat about global warming and the flooding up north.

By the time pudding is served, I'm beginning to think that maybe we can get away without a scene, but I haven't bargained on Mum, who suddenly pops up with, 'So, when should we talk about the divorce?'

I am so going to hide the sherry from her next time.

This time it's James who nearly chokes on his coffee. I don't blame him; he probably hadn't bargained on this.

'I think I should leave,' he says. 'These are private matters.'

'No, stay, please, James,' says Mum. 'I'd like an independent witness. I don't want to get stitched up. You're not planning to stitch me up, are you Fred?'

Dad looks horrified.

'Mary – how can you think such a thing? We've been married for forty-two years!'

'Which still wasn't enough to keep you faithful, was it?' says Mum. 'You've betrayed me once, why shouldn't you do it again?'

James gets up. I can't say I blame him. Mum is behaving appallingly.

'Look, Mary, you know I want to support you, but I really am not comfortable about the turn this conversation has taken. I'll see myself out.'

Mum looks temporarily remorseful, but she's on a roll now, and barely notices when I awkwardly walk James to the front door.

'It is a shame that our forty-two years of marriage weren't on your mind when you went off with Lilian,' she is saying when I come back in the room. 'So I rather think I'm entitled to say what I like.'

'Mary!' I can tell he's shocked by her bitterness.

'So – the divorce,' says Mum, as if he hasn't spoken at all.

Dad says nothing, and then, 'I don't think I want a divorce, Mary.'

'Neither do I,' says Mum, suddenly softening, 'but I also don't want to be married to a man who's unfaithful.'

There is a pause and to my astonishment, I see tears in Dad's eyes.

'Mary, I know I don't deserve it, after what I've done to you, but what if I said I'd made a terrible mistake? The last few weeks it's been all I can think about; how badly I've treated you, how thoughtless I've been. Do you think you might – I mean, would you consider – Mary, would you possibly have me back?'

Chapter Thirteen

Beth

'So do you think Dad's fancy woman might actually have bitten the dust?' I'm having coffee with Lou in town, and she's been updating me on Mum's outrageous behaviour on Sunday.

'It would seem so,' says Lou. 'He certainly doesn't seem to want to go through with a divorce. I must say, much as I want them to get back together, I think it's rather spineless of him to come crawling back again.'

'Will Mum have him back?'

'I'm not sure,' says Lou. 'She's not rushing anything, which is sensible, but honestly she's not behaving much better than Dad. The way she's been stringing poor James along is shocking.'

If you'd told me I'd be having this conversation about my parents six months ago, I'd have laughed in your face. This still feels so weird. I'm cautiously pleased that Dad wants to come back, but I hope he's not going to pull the wool over Mum's eyes again.

'It just goes to show, doesn't it?' I say.

'Show what?'

'That you never know what's going on in other people's

lives.' I sigh. If anyone had told me six months ago that Daniel and I would be struggling this much, I don't think I'd have believed them, either.

Lou looks at me, sudden concern in her eyes.

'Is everything OK, Beth? Has Megan settled down yet?'

I'd given her a very loose account of Megan's adventure. I'm too ashamed to tell anyone all the details. I feel like a failure as a mum at the moment, especially as Megan has clammed up and is refusing to tell me anything about what's actually going on in her life.

'Sort of,' I say. 'We're keeping a close eye on her, and she's still grounded. So hopefully it was a one-off. It's not just that though. I don't know . . .' I take a deep breath. 'Daniel and I are having a tricky time at the moment. The kids are such hard work, and he's really upset about Sam getting closer to his dad, and . . .'

'And?'

'And we just don't seem to connect any more, you know?'

I feel bad saying this. Is it true? Or am I exaggerating? I don't normally discuss Daniel with Lou. I just feel so churned up at the moment and confused about my feelings for Jack.

'I do know,' says Lou with feeling. 'I'm sure it's just a phase though. You and Daniel are made for each other. You've always been perfect together.'

'Have we?' I gaze wistfully out of the café window, toying with my spoon. Suddenly I feel the need to confide. Apart from a very brief conversation with my mate Gemma from college, who knows all about our history, I haven't told anyone about Jack or the way I feel about him. I'm not sure Lou will approve, but I have to tell someone. It's driving me nuts.

'Do you remember Jack Stevens, Lou?'

'What, that up-his-own-arse arty guy you used to see at college?'

'Yes, him. And he wasn't up himself.' Suddenly I wish, Elizabeth Bennett-like, that I hadn't been quite so down on Jack in the past.

'He totally was,' says Lou. 'You were just too besotted to notice. What about him?'

'He's the new art director at Smart Books.'

'Really? God, that must be weird,' says Lou.

'It is a bit,' I say. 'He's been helping me quite a lot with this new book though, and . . .'

Lou looks horrified, even though I haven't said anything. 'No, no, no, Beth. You cannot go there. You mustn't.'

'Nothing's happened,' I say hurriedly. 'And nothing's going to happen. It's just . . .'

'Just what?'

'He reminds me of the way things used to be. The person I used to be.'

Lou narrows her eyes and purses her lips. She is usually the least judgemental person I know, but I can tell she's judging me now.

'Beth! You're married, you have two kids. I cannot believe you're pining after some tosser who treated you badly in the past. You must be crazy.'

'I'm not pining after him, exactly,' I protest. 'It's just the way he makes me feel.'

'Have you any idea how lucky you are?' Lou looks really angry now. 'You have the perfect life, Beth – the gorgeous husband, two lovely children. Why would you even think about throwing that away?'

'Nobody's life is perfect,' I say, annoyed that she's judging me. 'You have no idea how dull domesticity can be. It's all right for you and Ged, you've had the freedom to do what you like while I get to play the dutiful daughter and wife. Is it wrong to hanker after something else occasionally? Thinking about it isn't the same as doing anything.'

'But it's dangerous,' says Lou. 'You should be careful.'

'I am being careful,' I say, 'it's just that sometimes I find things at home . . . overwhelming. I feel the real me gets lost under a layer of being Mum and Wife. There's nothing wrong with trying to find her again.'

'Grow up, Beth. You can't just chuck eighteen years out of the window because you've hit a bad patch,' says Lou bitterly. 'At least you're not single and childless.'

Wow. When she says this, I suddenly realise how jealous Lou might be of what I have. She's never really said it before. Although she's had her fair share of heartbreak, she's always been outwardly positive about being single. I had brushed any worries about her under the carpet, pushed away the nagging thoughts that maybe she isn't so happy with the way her life has turned out after all. Poor Lou, I can see why I've made her cross. I really don't want a row. I wish I hadn't mentioned Jack to her now; I just needed to confide in someone.

'You're right,' I say. 'I shouldn't have said anything. Daniel and I will get over this, in time. I'm sorry, I didn't mean to upset you.'

'Good,' she says firmly. 'Because one thing I've learnt is that if you have something precious the way you two do, you should fight as hard as you can to keep it.'

I know she's right, I know she is. But a small part of me wonders if I really have the strength for the fight.

Daniel

The Ofsted inspectors had finally come in during the second week of term, and the atmosphere in the school was very tense. Daniel had already had two female members of staff in tears, added to the fact that his head of geography, Andy Barlow, was having a not very silent row with the head of PE over the use of the shared school minibus.

'You know I booked it for the sixth form geography field trip next week,' Andy was angrily saying in the corridor outside the staffroom. 'It's been in the calendar for weeks.'

'Well the under-thirteens rugby team weren't expected to get through to the final,' said Malcolm Chalmers loudly. 'We need the minibus.'

'You two! In here!' hissed Daniel fiercely. He pulled them into an empty office next to the staffroom.

'What's this all about? I've got Ofsted inspectors roaming the corridors, and you two are having a full-on row in public.'

'Sorry,' said Andy, 'but the geography department booked the minibus all day on Thursday and I don't think we'll be back in time for the rugby match.'

'Can any of the parents help?' said Daniel. 'If the worst comes to the worst, we can ask for volunteers among the staff. I'd take some of them, except I don't want to be off premises while the inspectors are here.'

'OK,' said Malcolm. He accepted the situation with a surly nod, and Andy looked triumphant. Oh dear. There was already a healthy rivalry between Geography and PE; Daniel hoped it wasn't going to develop into an all-out feud.

'Now, out!' said Daniel. 'It's worse than dealing with the kids.'

He leant back and sighed deeply. As if he didn't have enough on his plate. The Ofsted inspection had come at such a difficult time for him. Megan was still sulkily grounded and Beth was watching her like a hawk in case of any further misdemeanours. So far she seemed to be behaving herself, but she was such a secretive kid. She barely confided in them at all, and it worried Daniel. He'd seen enough teenage girls exhibiting similar behaviour and ending up in a spiral of self-destruction; the last thing he wanted was for the same to happen to Megan.

Sam, in the meantime, grew ever more silent and appeared to be doing no revision whatsoever for his A Levels. If either he or Beth mentioned exams, he would tell them to get off his case and claim to have it all under control; a claim Daniel thought was fairly unlikely. And instead of he and Beth working together to sort this all out, they seemed to be pulling in opposite directions. With all that going on at home, he needed the extra pressure from grumpy staff like a hole in the head.

The inspectors had been polite and non-committal, but he knew of at least three lessons that hadn't gone according to plan. The thought of not getting an Outstanding result was making him feel sick. Although Daniel felt he was making inroads with the younger staff, and he knew he could rely on the support of people like Carrie Woodall, Jim Ferguson was still a thorn in his side, having spent most of this term obstructing every suggestion that Daniel made. He knew that Jim and his cronies would like nothing more than to see him fail. And if he did, he wasn't sure he could rely on the support of the governors. It was giving him a huge headache.

'Mr King?' It was his secretary, Jenny, who had popped her head round the door. 'I think the inspectors want a word.'

Daniel smiled tiredly. 'No rest for the wicked.'

On balance, he wasn't sure where he wanted to be, work or home. Neither option was appealing.

Lou

'So is Dad moving back in then?' I ask as I load the dishes after dinner. Mum has been very cagey about Dad since the infamous lunch. I think James might be out of the picture now; I caught her on the end of a rather tetchy phone conversation with him the other day. I don't think he was terribly impressed with Mum's behaviour, and I can't say I blame him. Both my parents seemed to have turned into irresponsible adolescents in the last few months. I must say it's very trying.

'Possibly.' Mum is applying lipstick and fluffing up her hair before she goes out to Zumba. I hope to God she hasn't got her eye on a man there as well. That would be all I need.

Is this what happens after so many years of marriage? You start acting like a prisoner who's been set free?

I know I've wanted them to get back together, but I do feel a bit wary on Mum's behalf. I've been talking to Maria about it a lot on Skype, and she agrees with me.

'Your lovely mum should be careful,' she says. 'When a man has cheated once . . .'

I know what she means, but this is my dad we're talking about. I can't believe that he'd come back and then hurt Mum again, but still, I can't help wondering what changed his mind. He seemed so sure in the beginning that he was never coming home.

'Are you sure, Mum?' I say. 'Dad behaved so badly. It feels like you're letting him off the hook.'

'Yes, I'm sure,' says Mum. 'Your dad and I have been married a long time. We understand each other. I think he realises he's made a massive error of judgement. I know he's put us all through the mill, but he really is trying to put things right. So cut him some slack, please, for my sake.'

'Fine,' I say, with a sigh. 'I just hope you're making the right decision.'

'I am,' says Mum firmly. 'And for your information, I'm not letting him off the hook. I'm going to make him wriggle on it for a bit longer.'

I laugh. One good thing about all this is the new Mum who won't take things lying down. True to her word, she says, 'If Dad rings, say I'm out, and I'll be back later.'

Go Mum, using the old make-yourself-unavailable trick.

'Sure,' I say. 'Have fun.'

I watch her go with a bemused smile. More and more now, I feel like I'm living in a parallel universe. Everything is so bizarre.

The phone goes.

Joy. It's probably Dad and I'll have to have another agonising conversation where I make excuses for Mum.

'Hi Dad—' I begin, but I'm cut off by a hysterical sounding voice. A voice I know very well. My heart starts pounding. What is she doing ringing me? And how did she get this number?

'Lou, it's Jo,' she says. 'I'm in a total mess. You have to help me.'

Chapter Fourteen

Lou

'What's up, Jo?' I try to stop my voice from shaking. 'And how did you get this number?'

'I looked it up,' she says, 'Oh Lou, everything's such a disaster.'

Months of silence, and now she rings me when she's in some kind of trouble. I grip the phone hard. Part of me wants to stop the conversation right now, but what if she really needs me?

'So?' I say. 'My life hasn't exactly been a bed of roses.'

'I know, and I'm sorry. No one understands me the way you do. I can see that now.'

Right. That's new. I think I have a fair idea of what's going on.

'Have you had a row with Nikki?' I ask. Nikki is my replacement, who came on the scene indecently soon after I had vacated it. It turns out I hadn't been wrong to be suspicious about Jo having an affair. I belatedly found out about Nikki a couple of months ago when a mutual friend mentioned it, thinking I knew. I didn't know. A few months ago, it would have killed me, but meeting Maria has given me more confidence, so now part of me is quite amused.

From what I've heard, Nikki is much tougher than I am, and I suspect she won't put up with Jo's bullshit like I did for so long.

'Not exactly,' says Jo. There's a pause. I wait. 'Well OK, yes we did, and no one has taken my side at all. I don't feel like I have any friends any more. I feel so let down. There's no one I can trust but you.'

Great, just great. Jo is so good at this manipulative shit. I know I'm supposed to say, poor Jo, how horrible everyone is to you, but I refuse to get sucked into this.

'You mean someone has finally called you out on your crap?' I say.

'Lou,' I can almost hear the pout, 'do you have to be so mean? I know I owe you a lot, but I'm having a really bad time here.'

She does sound genuinely upset. I can feel myself softening. I've been trying to put her out of my mind for months. I haven't seen or spoken to her for ages – but now she's actually sought me out. Pathetic as I am, I like the fact that she appears to need me.

'What do you want me to do, Jo?' I say.

'I just need a break, to get away from everything,' says Jo. 'So I was wondering . . .'

'No,' I say. I know what she's going to ask. She wants to come and stay, I bet she does. 'Don't even think about it.'

'Please, Lou, it would only be for a little while. I wouldn't ask if I weren't desperate.'

'This isn't my house, remember?' God how pathetic, if she did stay I'd have to check with my mum. Aged thirty-eight. I give myself a little shake. I wouldn't let her stay even if it was my house, the last thing I need is to have to work out how to bring my ex-girlfriend round without Mum suspecting anything.

'Lou, I know you're mad at me, but can't we at least try to salvage some kind of friendship here?' Jo asks. 'It would mean so much to me if you'd at least let me come to see you.'

I hold the phone, wavering. My heart is beating too fast; I can't help but feel excited at the thought of seeing her again.

'You can't stay here, Jo, I'm sorry,' I say eventually. 'But look, maybe we can meet up sometime. Or something.'

I don't want to make any firm plans, but I can't help but feel a bit excited about the thought of seeing Jo again. I just hope that I'm not going to regret it.

'Good old Lou Lou,' says Jo, her tone lightening. 'I knew I could rely on you.'

'I haven't promised anything yet,' I warn. But Jo doesn't listen, she just starts talking about how much she wants to see me, how lonely she is. Oh dear, what have I let myself in for?

Daniel

'Hi Dad.' Megan was the only one to acknowledge him as he came into the house, which was in a pretty untidy state. He discovered Megan 'working' in the lounge in a nest consisting of her duvet, iPod, computer and phone. How much actual work was going on was a moot point, but there were books and papers scattered everywhere so she certainly looked the part.

Beth had clearly retired to the shed to work. The kitchen was in chaos. The dishwasher hadn't been emptied since breakfast, the washing was still in the machine. That only meant one thing: Beth was in full creative mode.

Sam's blazer, school bag and shoes were abandoned

161

carelessly on the hall floor. There was no sign of Sam, but Daniel heard drumming in the garage. If Sam spent half the effort he used on the drums as he did focussing on his exams, he'd get A*s no problem. As it was . . .

He popped his head round the garage door.

'Sam?' he shouted over the noise.

Sam didn't hear him to begin with, so Daniel shouted louder.

'Sam!'

Sam stopped and looked at him defiantly.

'Aren't you supposed to be doing revision?'

'Did it at school.'

'Really?'

'Yeah. Get off my case, Dad. My first exam is maths. All I need to do is practise.'

'Well, go and practise now then,' said Daniel.

Sulkily, Sam got up and went upstairs. But at least he'd listened for once. If only Daniel could break through that hostility and actually make Sam see they were on the same side. It was killing him that he couldn't. Sighing, he slackened his tie, unbuttoned his shirt, grabbed a beer from the fridge and wandered down to the shed to see Beth.

'How's it going?' he asked.

Beth was covered in paint and staring critically at a picture she'd just painted. It depicted a little angel sitting on a hillside, talking to a small boy. Something about the picture tugged at Daniel's heartstrings. It reminded him of Sam and Megan when they were little, and he felt a pang of regret for those days. They seemed to have more joy out of life then. Right this moment, he felt drained from the weight of his responsibilities.

'That looks great,' he said.

162

'Do you think?' Beth turned a dazzling smile on him. 'I actually think I might have turned a corner.'

'You've got paint in your hair.'

'Have I?'

'And on your nose.'

'Just as well there's only you to see,' laughed Beth.

'Isn't it?' said Daniel and he kissed her.

As they kissed, the tension of the day gradually drained from him. Work might be stressful, but home was where his heart was. Any day of the week.

Beth

I sigh with relief as I get off the phone from Vanessa. She's cautiously approved the new direction I'm going in with the book, and she hasn't once said 'It's not quite working for me.' Thank God for that. One less thing to worry about.

I'm also feeling happier about Mum and Dad. According to Lou, Dad is moving back home, which is quite a turn-around but another thing less to worry about. I make a mental note that I must go round to see them. Make him see how much it means to us all that he's come home. Perhaps after our rocky start to the year, life is looking up.

Megan is being a little more communicative with me, though I have no idea who the mysterious Jake is, or whether she's seeing him. I do some surreptitious searching of her Facebook page, but she doesn't seem to talk about anything much on there. Most of the time she Snapchats her friends, and I can't access those conversations. I feel torn between wanting to respect her privacy and terror that she's going to get herself in a worse mess. But at least she's outwardly behaving herself, which means Daniel and I are less tense with one another.

Sam is still a worry. His exams are coming up and he seems to be spending more and more time with Reggie and precious little time on revision. I try to talk to him about it, but he doesn't want to know, and for once I think Daniel's approach of sitting back might be the right one. You can lead a horse to water . . . It's not as though I can physically pin him down to a desk and stand over with him with a whip. He's nearly six foot and towers above me. Short of Daniel physically restraining him (which he'd never do) we've resigned ourselves to just hoping for the best.

Reggie does seem to be a good influence, as the few times Sam does sit down to work are when he's been over there (though of course I haven't mentioned that to Daniel). Megan's taken to joining them occasionally, and she seems equally dazzled by Reggie. I know Daniel is finding it difficult to see his children and his dad getting on so well. Apart from that one moment when he confided in me, he's clammed up about Reggie again. At least now I have some small understanding as to why Daniel's relationship with Reggie is so bad, but I feel sad that he can't find a way to sort it out, and it's so hard being shut out when all I want to do is help. While ultimately I think the children should see Reggie, I can also see how galling it is for Daniel when Sam comes home bursting with enthusiasm about the music industry he so desperately wants to join.

My phone rings. It's Jack. I try not to let it, but my heart gives a faithless little leap.

'Hi Jack, how are you?' Keep it light, Beth, keep it light.

'I see the Wicked Witch has approved your new designs,' he says.

I laugh; Jack had taken to calling Vanessa the Wicked Witch after an occasion when I had ranted at him about how unreasonable she was being.

'You are a very bad man,' I say.

'But you love me.' Oh. I know it's a joke, but I quickly gloss over it.

'It's such a relief,' I say. 'Finally, the end is in sight.'

'We should go for a drink to celebrate,' says Jack, his tone casual.

'That sounds lovely,' I say, *but impossible,* I think. Right at this moment I don't think I should be gallivanting up to London. What if Megan decides to take off again? I feel bad enough that I wasn't around last time; I can't do that again. I fantasise about another world, where it's possible for my real life and my imaginary life to live side by side without any repercussions.

'It sounds great, Jack, but things are a bit hectic here at the moment,' I say. 'Maybe in a few weeks when things have calmed down.'

'I'll hold you to that,' says Jack.

It's when I put the phone down that I wonder, is that a threat? Or a promise?

Chapter Fifteen

Daniel

'Sam! Get out of bed, now!' Beth was yelling up the stairs to no avail. 'You're going to be late.'

Daniel wondered why she still bothered. Sam had pretty much been late every day of sixth form; there seemed little point trying to get him to change his habits now. Megan meanwhile had wandered downstairs in her T-shirt and shorts, wailing, 'Where's my uniform?'

'In your bedroom,' said Beth, exasperated.

'I've looked there,' said Megan.

'Well look again.'

Megan went upstairs, complaining loudly, while Beth pottered around in the kitchen eating toast. Cautiously, Beth and Daniel were beginning to hope that Megan was getting back on track. She wasn't grounded any more and there had been no repeats of the park incident. Beth kept fretting that her daughter didn't open up more, as some of her friends had daughters who told them everything. Megan hardly confided in either of them, but Daniel had concluded there wasn't a lot they could do about it.

'Want a cuppa?' Beth asked.

'No time,' said Daniel. 'I've got an early meeting.'

'Daniel!' said Beth. 'You know breakfast is the most important meal of the day.'

Daniel grinned. That had been his mum's favourite mantra. 'OK, I'll grab this then,' he said and took a bite out of Beth's toast.

'You could get your own.'

'Share and share alike,' grinned Daniel and kissed her on the cheek. 'Have a good day.'

'You too.'

'Oh, I'm going to be late back. I've got a governors' meeting.'

He wasn't looking forward to it. The Ofsted had resulted in a Good result rather than the hoped-for Outstanding, and he knew he was going to have to justify it to the governors.

'Good luck with that,' said Beth, but he had a feeling she wasn't really focussing on what she was saying as she was already heading for the stairs, shouting up at Sam again. She'd been so distracted recently, she had forgotten to ask him about the Ofsted, and he was too depressed about it to tell her.

'Bye, Dad,' said Megan, coming downstairs in the missing uniform.

'Where was it then?'

'In my room,' muttered Megan.

'Look properly next time,' said Daniel, ruffling her hair, and he left the house, quite relieved to escape the domestic muddle.

He wasn't looking forward to his day. In the wake of the worse than expected Ofsted he was going to have to get through a series of debriefings from staff as to what had gone wrong. A hellish day only to be followed by the governors' meeting when he was going to have to defend his style of management. No matter that he led a happy school. No matter that his students achieved well, often exceeding expectations. Ofsted hadn't given them the result they wanted and his neck was on the line. Daniel knew that he'd managed to make changes to improve the school, but he also knew that a Good result wasn't enough for the governors, and he was sure that Jim Ferguson for one would be delighted that things hadn't gone his way.

The day went pretty much as expected. The staff were demoralised at being told by Ofsted that their teaching wasn't up to scratch. It infuriated Daniel. He could have played the game of keeping the troublemakers at home as some schools did, making sure that the weakness of Year Eight geography teaching was hidden by sending them out on a field trip, but he hadn't. The geography teacher in question, Ellie, was newly qualified, and had the makings of a great teacher. Currently her class were running rings around her, and proceeded to do so in her Ofsted lesson too. It was such a shame because Ellie had made progress of late, and this had been a real blow to her confidence.

'Maybe I'm in the wrong job,' she said. 'Perhaps I should hand my notice in.'

'Please don't do that,' said Daniel. 'You're going to be a very good teacher. This is a horrible setback. Those Year Eights are tricky even for the more experienced staff. I'll get you some training and support, and I'm sure next year will be better.'

It frustrated him so much. None of this meant the school wasn't outstanding – in so many ways it was – just not in the narrow-minded way Ofsted looked at things. Daniel wished there was another, better way of analysing success.

After a rancorous governors' meeting in which Jim Ferguson started mouthing off about poor leadership letting the school down and the chair of governors expressed her disappointment, Daniel was relieved to get home.

Until he actually got home that was.

Beth and Megan were having an almighty row. Beth wouldn't let Megan go out on a school night, which left Megan running up the stairs in floods of tears and shaking the house to its foundations as she slammed her bedroom door shut.

Beth was so angry she barely acknowledged him. 'That girl is going to be the death of me!' she said. 'I thought she'd learnt her lesson, but no. She was all for going out with her pals to the park tonight. She erupted when I said she couldn't go.'

'Leave her for a bit,' said Daniel. 'I'm sure she will calm down.'

'*I* won't,' said Beth. 'I'm going to do some work.' She was halfway out of the room before she paused.

'Oh – how was your day?'

'Just peachy,' Daniel said to her departing back.

So much for happy family life.

Lou

It's my first week in my new temporary job. I'm working in the credit control department of an office in Wottonleigh, and despite my usual fears about whether I'm up to it or not, I'm enjoying it so far. The people are friendly, the work isn't too onerous, and it's a great relief to be out of the house. I wouldn't say I was wholly enamoured of credit control, but I'm good at it, and it feels fantastic to actually be earning money again. With any luck I can save up enough to move out of Mum and Dad's.

I haven't heard from Jo since her hysterical phone call, and part of me is relieved. I have been tempted to ring her, but Maria counselled restraint, which is probably right. I don't really want to open a can of worms and have Jo come to stay, particularly as Dad has moved back in, and there's enough tension in the air already.

Dad came home a week ago. It was an odd day. I went over to help him load his car while Mum stayed home and cooked the dinner. She did help unpack, but she was prickly to begin with, which I suppose was fair enough. After a bit of awkward silence, Dad cleared his throat and said seriously, 'Mary, I can't say sorry enough for what I've put you through. I hope you can forgive me.'

I could feel myself holding my breath. There was a long moment where they looked at each other, and then Mum seemed to fold in on herself, reaching out her arms to him and smiling.

'Oh, Fred, of course,' she said, and then Dad opened a bottle of bubbly to celebrate and we all got a bit teary, but in a good way.

So far things between them seem to be OK. Dad is trying really hard. I even found him asking Mum how the washing machine worked. Unheard of! Mum seems happier too. Though she's understandably wary, she's thrilled he's back. She's also throwing herself into preparations for the new baby's arrival. Rachel is due to pop soon, and both Mum and Dad seem to be focussing on that as a means of rebuilding their relationship. Ged actually seems to have picked up on this, so he and Rachel have been over a lot. Mum is making a massive fuss over Rachel, as her own mum is so far away. I'm trying not to feel jealous, but from initially having been cross about the new arrival, Ged's firmly back in golden-boy territory again.

'Just imagine, another grandchild,' she'd said to me glee-fully. 'Just when I'd given up hope.'

'Well I think you can give up hope on this one of your children providing you with another one,' I said snippily.

'Yes, that is a shame,' she replied, making me feel both furious and sad.

I know she doesn't really mean it, but her ambition since we left home has always been to have lots of grandkids, and up until now Ged and I have both let her down. Now I'm the only one who's failed, and that's not likely to change any time soon.

I'm tidying up my desk to get ready to go home when the receptionist rings to say I have a visitor waiting for me. Which is odd. No one knows where I work. Oh God, maybe something's happened to Mum and Dad. I go flying out to reception and run smack bang into – 'Jo?'

'I'm sorry to do this to you at work – I just didn't know who else to turn to,' says Jo as she bursts into loud and noisy tears.

Beth

I'm sitting in my studio feeling miserable. Work has been going well for the last few weeks, but today it's not. Every time I draw my angel she's looking at me accusingly. As well she might. Daniel and I seem to being increasingly scratchy with one another these days too. After Megan stormed off the other night, he managed to calm her down and coax her into the lounge with chocolate pancakes, her favourite thing in the world. He then accused me of being too hard on her, which led us to another row. We seem to be in a circular pattern at the moment: rowing, making up, living a few weeks in a sort of truce-like state, and then rowing again. I'm getting so worn down with it, but I don't know what to do.

Maybe Daniel's right and I am too anal and controlling with the kids, but it infuriates me when he doesn't support me. I just don't want either of them going down Lou's path – she dropped out of school in the sixth form and took years to find her focus, and it's taken her months to find work again after losing her job at Christmas. Is it so wrong of me to worry that the same will happen to them, particularly with Sam doing so little work for his exams?

I feel so tired of being the responsible one. All my life it's been like this. The phrase *'look after your little brother and sister'* was a constant in my childhood, and one I took with me into adolescence, frequently getting them out of scrapes which I myself wouldn't have dared to get into. The only bit of rebellion I've ever managed in my life is persuading Mum and Dad I wanted to go to art college, and then falling for the most unsuitable boy when I got there. When that went tits up, I retreated back to my normal routine. And then when I married, I had to be the perfect mum, wife and daughter. I've tried to do that, I really have. But right now I feel sick of it all. Sometimes I really, really wish my life could be different.

My angel seems to know how I feel. Now the look on her face seems to say, be careful what you wish for.

But do I really know what I wish for anyway? Do I wish that Mum was relying on me as much as she seems to be relying on Lou at the moment? Her moving back to Mum's has been a godsend; I get far fewer requests to come round at the drop of a hat than I used to, but part of me feels my place in things has been usurped. Why can't I feel pleased that Lou has managed to do what I couldn't and get Dad to move back in with Mum? I'm still in two minds about

their reunion; I hope Dad isn't trying to have the best of both worlds. But when I went to see them the night he moved back, he was being conciliatory, and promised me that he would do his best to make things work. So I have to try to believe him.

I sigh heavily. Why can't I be more sympathetic to Daniel, who's having such a rubbish time at work? Or be nicer to my kids and try to understand their point of view? I feel like I'm not being fair to anyone, and I hate it.

I know why, of course. It's because although I know Daniel loves me and cares for me, it gets lost in a welter of domestic responsibility. He probably feels the same about me. Maybe it's inevitable the longer you're married, but sometimes I want to feel special again. I want that heady feeling of being the only important person in the world. When I'm with Jack I feel different. I *am* different, freer, more creative. It's tearing me in half feeling this way, but I can't seem to help it.

I draw my angel again and this time she looks at me with disapproval. Disapproval I should share. Because despite my best intentions, despite what I said to Lou, and despite the fact I know it can only do harm, I cannot stop thinking about Jack and how life would have turned out if I'd stayed with him. Disastrous probably. But would it have been like this? I don't know, but the thought of it excites me and terrifies me at the same time. I'm scared that one day soon I'm going to give in to my feelings, and what will I do then?

Chapter Sixteen

Lou

'Let's get out of here,' I hiss, glancing around my office reception to make sure none of my colleagues are around. I am beyond embarrassed. Why on earth is Jo here? How is she here? And causing such a scene as well.

I smile awkwardly at Gina, our receptionist, and mouth an apology before escorting a snivelling Jo out of the building.

I don't know what she's expecting, but I am not going to tell her everything is OK and we're going to be best buddies again. I am *not*.

We walk for a bit in silence as I furiously work out what I should say or do.

'Don't be mad at me, Lou Lou,' she says in that wheedling tone that I've always detested.

'Why shouldn't I?' I say. 'You ditched me, remember? You don't get to turn up at my work causing a scene. That's my right. And I'd be a damned sight more dignified about it than you.' (Not *strictly* true, I stood outside her workplace more times than I care to mention in the early days after our split, but I never had the nerve to go in. I do have some pride.) 'And please don't call me Lou Lou.' Lou Lou was

her endearment for me early on in our relationship when the world seemed bright and our future happiness assured.

'I'm sorry,' says Jo, eventually. 'I shouldn't have come. I just didn't know where else to go.'

'How did you find out where I was?'

'I phoned your mum,' she says.

Oof. That will make for an interesting dinner conversation.

'Look, I know you probably don't want to, but could we go for a drink? I could really use a friend right now.'

A friend? I look at my watch, prevaricating. I haven't actually got plans this evening. I'm still angry with Jo, but part of me is pleased to be with her. After all these months, I am actually in her presence. I look at her, feeling sick when I realise that she's still as gorgeous as ever, and despite my attempts to bury my feelings for her, they're just as strong as before. I can feel myself weakening.

'One can't hurt,' she says, 'for old time's sake?'

'OK' I give in. I'm curious, with a little flare of hope that I'm trying to suppress. Could she possibly want me back? I can't allow myself to let that flare burn any brighter, I need to protect myself – but it's there nonetheless.

'So why are you here?' I say when we've found a seat in the closest bar. I order her a glass of Soave and a red wine for myself.

'You remembered,' she says, looking gratified.

'Of course I remembered. I remember everything about you, how your favourite colour is blue, how when you were thirteen you broke your arm, and that's why you decided to be a nurse. We were in love, remember?'

'Were?' says Jo.

'Unless you're here to tell me you've changed your mind, I think our relationship is firmly in the past.' I am trying

so hard to be firm, but part of me wants to give in right now. If I'm going to get back with Jo it needs to be on my terms.

There's an awkward pause, and suddenly Jo looks shifty. 'Lou,' she says, 'I am so sorry.'

'You've said. Frequently. But it doesn't change anything.'

'No, it really does. Or it could.' She leans over and grabs my hand, and treacherously my body tingles in delight. 'I'm sorry. I thought you weren't in love with me. Not the way you wouldn't let me meet your family.'

'That? That bothered you?'

My jaw nearly drops to the floor. I had no idea that Jo felt like that. I know she had suggested Christmas together but she always affected not to care about family, saying we didn't need them when we had each other.

I hadn't been quite ready to introduce Jo to Mum and Dad, but I had been working my way up to telling Beth and Daniel. Mum and Dad had had enough difficulty dealing with Beth bringing a black boyfriend home. I couldn't imagine how they'd cope with me turning up with a woman. I knew Beth wouldn't really care but I just never found the words to tell her. Besides, until Jo, none of my girlfriends had lasted very long. It was a measure of how much she meant to me that I was prepared to introduce her to at least some of my family. But every time I tried to get Jo together with them both she'd always blown me out.

'Of course it did. I thought you were ashamed of me – of us. I had to jump ship before I got too hurt. I thought you couldn't possibly love me the way I love you.'

Love, she said love. My heart sings. I take a deep breath.

'I did – I do – love you,' I say. 'It's just my parents. They're quite old-fashioned – at least, I thought they were. I wanted

to be sure before I dug up that particular minefield. I wanted to find the best way of telling them, but it never happened.'

'And are you sure now?' says Jo.

'I was,' I say. 'Now . . .'

'What if I told you the last few months of my life have been utterly miserable,' says Jo, 'and that I realise I made a terrible mistake. I know I've hurt you badly, but I want you back more than anything.'

'It's not that easy for me,' I say. 'I just . . . Jo, you broke my heart, and there's Nikki . . .'

'It's over with Nikki,' says Jo. 'I made a massive mistake. I realised very quickly that she's not a patch on you.'

'But – how can I trust you?' I say, every fibre of my being jangling with nerves. I want to believe her so much, but I'm also frightened of where it will lead me.

'Because of this,' she says, and she leans in and kisses me.

Daniel

An uneasy peace was reigning in the house. On the surface, he and Beth were getting on fine, but Daniel felt somehow that his wife had retreated from him, gone somewhere in her head that he couldn't follow. She refused to discuss the kids with him, and kept conversation to light, safe topics. Sam was spending even more time at Reggie's, although his exams had started and he ought to have been home revising. Megan was quiet and uncommunicative. Sometimes Daniel felt like a stranger in his own home. So one Friday in early June, he came home from work, went down into Beth's studio and said, 'How about a night off?'

Beth looked up, her eyes tired from staring at her work, her hair muzzy and straggling over her shoulder. Tentatively,

Daniel leant forward and pulled a stray tendril over her ear.

'What did you have in mind?' asked Beth.

'Dinner for two at Prezzi's?' he suggested.

Prezzi's was their favourite restaurant, a cheap and cheerful Italian in the centre of the village. They hadn't been there in ages. It would be nice to have dinner out together for a change.

Beth stretched her arms in the air, then grabbed his hand and kissed it. 'That sounds like an excellent idea, I could use the break.'

'How's it going?' asked Daniel.

'Much better now, thanks,' said Beth. 'Do you want to see?'

She showed him the latest spreads she'd been working on. There was a great one of the angel looking quizzically at some sheep, and another one where she was encountering the three wise men. Daniel was no great judge, but there was a liveliness to her drawing that had been missing in her earlier attempts.

'These are great, Beth,' he said, kissing her. 'I'm so proud of you.'

'Are you?' Beth's eyes looked wistful.

'Of course I am,' said Daniel, crushing her to his chest. 'Always. I'm sorry if I don't always show it.'

'What's this in aid of?' said Beth, laughing.

'Because you're my gorgeous lovely wife, and I love you and I don't tell you often enough.'

'Oh Daniel, I don't tell you enough either,' said Beth. 'I'm sorry we keep rowing.'

'Me too,' he said. 'So, dinner?'

'Dinner would be great,' she said. 'I haven't eaten much today.'

'Or drunk much either, by the looks of things,' said Daniel, pointing to a row of undrunk coffee cups lined up on the windowsill.

'I get distracted,' said Beth. 'Give me a minute to get cleaned up and sort out some tea for the kids and I'm all yours.'

'Just as long as you always are,' said Daniel.

She paused for a fraction of a second, and he suddenly had a stab of anxiety, before she kissed him on the lips, and said, 'Always.'

Daniel smiled with relief. This was going to be a great way to start the weekend.

Beth

Daniel suggesting dinner is such a lovely idea, and I'm feeling excited at the thought of a glass of wine until I realise that Megan has made last-minute plans and needs picking up late. Daniel offers to drive, but I know he's had a rough week, so I do the honourable thing and say I'll stay sober.

Sam is off out to a gig – I suspect with his grandad, although he hasn't said who he's going with. I know he's got quite close to Reggie, and it makes me sad that Daniel can't see it as a good thing. It's not doing his relationship with Sam any good at all. Sam is baffled by his attitude, and quite frankly so am I, but Daniel refuses to discuss it properly, and I'm at a loss as to what to do to make things better.

Things start to go downhill at the restaurant. We get there later than intended, and it's busy. As we haven't booked, we have to wait in the bar which is noisy and crowded and we can barely hear ourselves think. Daniel has had a couple of pints before we're shown to our table.

We don't talk much at the bar, and by the time we sit down I am racking my brains for something to say. It's so long since we've been out together alone, I seem to have lost the knack.

When we finally get served, Daniel orders wine. Great. He's going to get drunk and I'm going to be stone-cold sober. Not quite my idea of a fun evening.

'How has your week been?' I say. I'm aware that Daniel has been stressed about work, but he's not been talking about that much either. Maybe I should have shown more interest, but sometimes he's so closed down I don't know what he's thinking.

'Rubbish,' he says, and launches into a long rant about the iniquities of the education system and the idiots in charge who don't understand teachers, and how unfair the Ofsted report has been.

Oh God. The Ofsted. I've been so preoccupied I'd forgotten all about it. He hasn't mentioned it and I haven't asked. I feel terrible.

After about five minutes, he stops and says, 'Sorry, I didn't mean to go on.'

'I'm so sorry,' I say. 'I should have asked you about it. I'm glad you told me. In fact, I wish you'd talk to me more. I never know what you're thinking.'

'Don't you?' Daniel looks surprised. 'I thought I was an open book.'

'You?' I laugh. 'You're ridiculously good at keeping your thoughts to yourself.'

'Whereas I always know what you're thinking, of course,' says Daniel, laughing.

I'm pretty sure that's not true. I certainly hope so anyway . . . I really don't want him to have any idea of my inner-most thoughts at the moment.

180

'So what am I thinking right now?'

'Whether to have steak or swordfish.'

OK that's fair enough. Those are usually my choices here.

'Aside from that?'

'You're going to give me a lecture about how I'm too soft on the children.'

'Not tonight,' I say. 'Although it is true.'

'What then?' He reaches out and touches my hand.

'Daniel,' I say very carefully. 'I know that it's difficult for you, and I know I said I wouldn't bring it up again, but it's really bothering me. Sam is getting on so well with Reggie. I genuinely think he's changed. Would it really be so terrible if we saw your dad?'

Chapter Seventeen

Daniel

'Oh.' He really hadn't expected Beth to raise this issue again, not after everything he'd told her. He withdrew his hand from hers. 'Do we have to talk about this?'

Beth looked a little helpless. 'Sorry, maybe it's a stupid thing to say, it's just . . .'

'Just what?'

'This is one of the things I don't understand about you,' she said. 'I know you said you wanted to put everything with your dad behind you, but I'm wondering if it's such a good idea. Reggie's here, whether you like it or not, and he's forging a relationship with our son. That's not going to go away. So I think you should face up to the past, not run from it any more.'

'I thought you understood,' said Daniel. 'For me the past is better buried.'

'I get that,' said Beth, 'but it's a little bit hard to do that when the past turns up on your doorstep. Maybe it's time to face your demons.'

Daniel tried to laugh, but found he couldn't. He took a sip of wine, but it tasted bitter and he pushed it away.

'I don't think I can,' he said.

'Why not?' said Beth. 'I think it might help you. This whole thing clearly upsets you.'

'Which is why I don't want to think about it,' said Daniel. 'It was such a bad time in my life. I know Reggie seems friendly and relaxed now, but when he drank he was vile to Mum and me. We were both glad when he left. Mum and I put it behind us, and then Mum died. I want to remember the good bits, you know? Not the bad. It's over now, and I don't want to think about it any more. It's in the past.'

'Except it's not, because it's affecting our present,' said Beth gently. 'Sam seems to like Reggie, and it's hard for him to understand why you aren't OK with that. It's hard for me to understand, if I'm honest. Would it hurt so much to try and build some bridges?'

'Thank you for reminding me that my dad and my son have a better relationship with each other than I have with either of them,' said Daniel angrily.

'Daniel, I didn't mean that,' said Beth. 'Please, just for once, let me in.'

Daniel felt tears prickle at the back of his throat.

'I can't, Beth,' he whispered, 'I just can't.'

Beth

Our meal fizzles out after I mention Reggie. I wish I'd kept my mouth shut. Daniel pretends we haven't discussed it at all after our initial spat, and we spend the rest of the evening chatting about banalities. I wish we'd stayed at home.

Towards the end of the evening, a text arrives from Jack. *New spreads look brilliant! Great buzz about them in the office.*

I smile. That's cheering. Both that Jack thinks the book is doing well and that he's texted me on a Friday night. I wonder where he is and what he's doing. I like the fact that he must be thinking about me. Then I suppress the thought. I'm out with my husband, I shouldn't be thinking about other men. I'm a terrible person.

'Who's that?' asks Daniel, irritated that I've looked at my messages.

'Jack,' I say quickly, 'just to let me know that the spreads have gone down well.'

Daniel looks at me speculatively.

'Why is Jack texting and not your editor? Isn't it a bit late to be talking about work on a Friday?'

'Oh, he knew I was worrying about it and promised to get back to me and then forgot. He said he wanted to put my mind at rest over the weekend, and he has, which is great.'

I plaster a smile on my face, hoping it isn't too fake.

'How well did you know Jack at college?' Daniel asks suddenly.

I feel a bit sick. Is he getting suspicious? I haven't done anything wrong, but I feel guilty that I haven't been more honest with him about Jack and I at college

'Well, you know how it is at college,' I say feebly. 'We were close for a while and then we – we drifted apart.' Now is the time to come clean, tell him how it really was. Except . . . something stops me. Daniel keeps secrets from me, I know he does. Take tonight, with Reggie. Why should I tell him about something that happened so many years ago? What good can telling him now do?

'So he wasn't your secret love then?' Daniel says teasingly. I feel my heart quicken slightly.

'Jack?' I snort. 'Jack Stevens only ever loved himself.'

I am in total shock after Jo kisses me. I wasn't expecting that at all, much less her declaration of love. I want to believe her so badly. I know I still love her; one evening in her company is enough to make me realise how much I've been kidding myself for the past few months. As it turns out, I've barely moved on at all. But can I trust Jo? I can see she's trying really hard, and I am tempted to give it a go, but after another drink I decide I'm going to take a leaf out of Mum's book and not make it too easy for her. So I make my excuses and go home, and even though she's suggested meeting up again, I don't give her an answer. I tell her I'll think about it; I'm not ready for more.

And I do think about it. I don't rush it, even though she's taken to ringing and texting me every day. After a week though, I end up giving in. We meet in a busy wine bar in London. It seems suitably neutral. I don't want her coming to Mum and Dad's and I sure as hell don't want to go to hers. I am beyond nervous, not sure if I'm doing the right thing. But life is short, right? I've got a chance to get things right with the woman I love. It seems foolish not to at least give it a go.

She greets me with a kiss, and I can see that she's nervous too, which relaxes me instantly. She was always the cool, detached one in our relationship. It makes me feel stronger to think that I might have the upper hand here.

Jo is talking too much, rattling on about her day, updating me on various gossip about her friends – most of whom I haven't seen since we split. I realise with surprise that this is my fault. I allowed my usual sense of despair about another disastrous relationship to take over and assumed they'd side with Jo. When people have texted me, I've ignored them. Maybe I shouldn't have.

We're getting on so well, I agree to go to dinner.

'So,' says Jo as we sit down at a table in a discreet Italian restaurant in Soho.

'So,' I say.

'Where do we go from here?'

'Jo, I have absolutely no idea,' I say. 'You tell me at Christmas it's over. On Christmas Eve, for fuck's sake. Within weeks you're with someone else. Then you turn up months later to tell me you've made a mistake and do love me after all. What am I supposed to think?'

'I know you don't want to hear me say I'm sorry again,' says Jo.

'I don't,' I say.

'I made the biggest mistake of my life,' she says. 'I can see that now. Nothing's the same without you. I miss you so much.'

'You do?' I really want to believe that. Jo is the first person in a long while that I've had such deep feelings for. I'd been prepared to spend the rest of my life with her, and the shock of her rejection had rocked me to the core. I want nothing more than to get back together with her, but can I really take that chance? What if she rejects me again? I'm not sure I'm strong enough to stand it. 'I don't know,' I say.

And then she stops me. 'Shh, let's not talk,' she says, giving me such a look that I am completely lost. God I'm pathetic.

'Why don't we get out of here?'

And like an idiot, I follow her.

Chapter Eighteen

Lou

'So who is Jo?' I've been waiting for this. Mum has been surprisingly quiet about the mysterious woman who rang her up to ask for my work number. I might have known it wouldn't last.

'A friend,' I say. I'm not sure I'm ready to go into further detail. Not quite yet, anyway.

'Just a friend?' Mum raises an eyebrow. 'I thought your *boyfriend* was called Joe.'

'Erm,' I'm flummoxed. 'He was. This is a girlfriend. Called Jo.'

There is a pause.

'Lou, I'm not stupid, you know,' she says gently. 'I do know that lesbians exist. I just feel sad that you couldn't tell me.'

'Oh!' I'm so shocked, I don't know what to say. I've been keeping this part of my life hidden for so long, it hasn't occurred to me that Mum might actually work it out for herself.

'I'm your mum,' she said. 'I always suspected it when your relationships with boys didn't last very long. I'm not necessarily saying I understand, but I accept it. I just want you to be happy.' She pauses. 'I'm right, aren't I?'

I am totally staggered. All these years of fretting and worrying and feeling unable to share my true self with my mum, and she knew all the time.

'I wanted to tell you,' I say. 'I just didn't know how. You and Dad . . .'

'. . . grew up in different times,' says Mum, 'I get it. But we're not totally out of touch. Still, I'm glad you're telling me now.'

'Me too,' I say, a tear in my eye. It is such a relief to have someone to talk to about this. Finally, after all this time. And her reaction is so different from how I imagined it would be. To my amazement, Mum seems to be taking this completely in her stride. The sense of relief is overwhelming.

'So what's going on with this girl then?' says Mum.

'Oh Mum,' I say. 'We broke up, and now she wants me back but I don't know what to do.'

'Do you love her?'

'I did,' I say. 'I think I still do, but I'm not sure I can trust her.'

'Sometimes you need to take a chance on love,' says Mum. 'But there's no rush. You have to do what feels right for you.' She pats my hand and then changes the subject, asking me to go and tell Dad dinner's ready. As if nothing had happened at all. I am still reeling from the shock of how well she's taken it. And I know that if she's happy with it, Dad will be too. That's always been the way things are in our family.

I pop my head round the door of the study, and Dad jumps away from his laptop as if I've caught him watching porn. My heart sinks. He's not talking to *her* again is he? I hate the way I've become suspicious of my own dad. But

I can't help it. He seemed so convinced that Lilian was the woman for him at the time. What if he only came back to please us?

'What are you up to?'

'Looking for holidays. I thought I might take your mum somewhere as a late birthday present.'

I can see there's a website up on his screen advertising Spanish holidays. Maybe I'm just jumping to conclusions.

'That's great,' I say, 'I'm sure she'll love it.'

He looks so guilty, though, I can't help wondering if he is hiding something. He doesn't appear to be doing anything other than being a dutiful husband, but I feel the atmosphere around them both is still tense. I suppose that's inevitable, given the circumstances. I decide it's none of my business. I've learnt far more than I've ever wanted to about my parents' love lives in the last few months. It's up to them to sort their shit out. I have enough problems of my own.

Since the night Jo and I spent together, I haven't been able to think of anything else. Does she really mean it when she says she wants me back? She certainly seems sincere. And that kiss was a reminder of what I'm missing. I look at Mum and Dad over dinner and see how hard they're trying to make things work. Maybe Mum's right, sometimes you need to take a chance on love.

I pick up my mobile and dial Jo's number. 'Hi,' I say, without preamble. 'What are you doing on Friday night?'

Daniel

The house was positively shaking with the sound of Sam's drumming. Before too long the neighbours would be round to complain. Despite Daniel's best efforts at soundproofing, there was something about the beat of the drums that resonated through the entire house. It set his jaw on edge. Was it his imagination, or was Sam practising harder at his music since he'd met Reggie? His exams were nearly over, and Daniel and Beth had no idea how they'd gone. All Sam would say after each one was that it was 'OK', and all Daniel and Beth could do was hope for the best. The only thing that seemed to inspire Sam was Reggie.

Reggie wasn't famous by any means, but he'd always managed to make a living as a session musician. As a very small boy – before things went sour – Daniel had loved it when his dad had got out his sax and started to play, or crooned a few tunes at Mum on the mouth organ. Those were happy days, despite what came later. He did have some happy memories; those that hadn't quite been overtaken by the bad ones.

Not for the first time, Daniel wondered what had really happened between his parents. He supposed it was the usual stresses; Reggie was away a lot playing, and Mum had hinted a couple of times that he'd been easily tempted. And then there was the drinking. By the time Reggie left, Daniel had forgotten what it was like to see his dad sober. Daniel had hated to see the way his bubbly, outgoing mum became a shadow of her former self, until the moment she had made Reggie leave.

At ten years old, Mum told Daniel that he was now the man of the house, and slowly the fun-loving mum he adored returned. But still she struggled so hard to work for him, to keep food on the table and make sure he was clothed. She was determined he was going to have the opportunities she hadn't had, and thanks to that love and determination he hadn't gone off the rails as so many of his peer group had. So many people he knew had fallen into unemployment and crime. It could so easily have been him, but thanks to his Mum it wasn't. When she died, cruelly taken from him in her mid-fifties, Daniel had vowed to make the best of the opportunities she'd given him.

Daniel's mum had been gone a long time now, but he never stopped missing her or thinking about her, and wondered what she would do in his shoes. She had always been one for keeping the door open, and making amends with people. She'd always been scrupulous about not criticising Reggie to Daniel, though she had such good cause to. Maybe she'd want him to hold out an olive branch.

Daniel came to a decision. He went into the garage to watch Sam play. Though the music was deafening this close up, Sam was really good. He felt a sudden surge of pride in his son. He might not be succeeding academically, but he *was* musically talented. Daniel knew he should tell him so more, or else risk alienating his son for ever.

'Someone been giving you lessons?' he asked.

Sam looked a little wary. It pained him to see his son nervous around him, the way he had been nervous around Reggie. He'd spent all these years trying so hard for that not to happen.

'I take it you and Reggie talk music when you meet?'

'Yes,' said Sam, 'we do.'

'Look,' Daniel cleared his throat, suddenly awkward. 'I'm sorry I've been difficult about Reggie. It's just old stuff between us, it's nothing to do with you.'

'So will you see him?' Sam looked so hopeful, Daniel suddenly felt he couldn't refuse.

'Yes, I'll see him,' said Daniel, 'but I doubt we're ever going to be best buddies.' He took a deep breath. 'How would you feel if I invited him over for lunch?'

'You OK?' Daniel comes up and gives me a hug while I am sorting out the dishwasher.

'Yes, fine, why wouldn't I be?' I'm a little snappy, but I feel so tense round Daniel at the moment. He hasn't mentioned Jack again, and I haven't mentioned Reggie, but I know both subjects are there, bubbling under the surface. To make matters worse, Jack keeps texting me. I delete them as soon as I've replied, but it's making me feel guilty and I know I'm taking it out on Daniel.

'I've been talking to Sam,' he says.

'That's good,' I say; they've hardly spoken in weeks.

'And, well, how would you feel if I asked Reggie to come for lunch one Sunday?'

'I think that would be fabulous.' I am surprised, but pleased. 'What's brought this on?' I narrow my eyes, suddenly suspicious. 'You're not going to have him round so you can row with him again are you?'

'No,' says Daniel. 'It's just Sam and he seem to be getting on so well, and I can see it's hard for Sam. Megan should know her grandad too. I'm the one with the problem. I shouldn't impose it on the children. You're right, it's not fair to keep Reggie from his grandkids.'

'I'm so glad, Daniel,' I say, 'I think you're doing the right thing.'

'This doesn't mean there's going to be a big reconciliation,' he warns.

'Understood,' I say, but secretly I'm hopeful – at least it's a beginning.

As I'm giving him a hug, the phone rings. It's Mum and she's in a hell of a state.

'Is your dad there?'

'No, why?'

'He said he might pop over,' says Mum. 'Rachel's in labour, and he's got the car, so why isn't he answering the phone?'

'Woah,' I say, 'Rachel's in labour – that's wonderful.'

'It's not going according to plan,' says Mum, 'she's in surgery having an emergency caesarean. I'm with Ged at the hospital, but we can't get hold of your dad.'

'Don't worry,' I say, 'I'll find him. Keep calm.'

I ring round Dad's cronies, but no one has seen him and he's still not answering his phone. Honestly, I don't know why he has one. Eventually one of his friends offers, 'He might have gone down the Swan.' Which is odd; the Swan isn't Dad's local. Why would he be there? I grab the car keys, and dash off in a blind hurry.

I've never been in the Swan before. It's lunchtime and full of elderly couples taking advantage of a midweek lunch deal. Why on earth would Dad be in here?

I scan the room frantically, and at first see no sign of him. Where could he be?

Then I spot him, in the corner, talking earnestly to a tall, artistic-looking woman with her hair in a messy bun. They are holding hands and have eyes for no one else. Oh my God. He's with Lilian Mountjoy.

The Littlest Angel

The Littlest Angel was very tired now. She flew down and sat on top of a hill to catch her breath.

Suddenly she saw a <u>little boy</u> holding a lamb.

He was walking very slowly and looked sad.

'Are you all right?' she said.

'Yes,' said the little boy, 'but I'm trying to look for the special new baby who is born tonight, and I've lost my way.'

'I've lost my way too,' said the Littlest Angel. 'Maybe we can <u>help one another</u>.'

Vanessa Marlow: Who is this little boy?

Beth King: A shepherd. He's lost the rest of the shepherds.

Vanessa Marlow: But how can the angel help the little boy? She can hardly carry him there can she?

Beth King: I'm working on it.

Part Three

A long way from home

July–September

The Littlest Angel

The Littlest Angel was getting quite excited. The star seemed to be nearer, surely she was getting close now?

She could see a caravan heading away from the star.

She flew down to join one of the pages who was walking on the end, holding a box.

'What have you got there?' she said.

'Gold for the new king,' said the page.

'Do you mean the new baby?' asked the angel.

'I don't know,' said the page. '<u>My masters</u> are looking for a king. They said we should follow a star and that will lead us to him.'

'Oh,' said the angel. 'I think you're going the <u>wrong way</u>.'

Vanessa Marlow: I'm not sure what's the point of this?

Beth King: Trying to reference the wise men in this story?

Vanessa Marlow: Why are they going the wrong way? Confused!

Beth King: Um, have you ever read the Nativity story, Vanessa? They're going to see Herod first.

Chapter Nineteen

Beth

'Are you guys ready? We're going now.'

Sam and Megan come thundering down the stairs as Daniel reverses the car out of the drive. We're off to Sunday lunch with Mum and Dad to welcome Ged, Rachel and the new baby – Thomas – home. After a slightly harrowing few hours, Thomas was born safe and well, but Rachel had a couple of complications so had to stay in hospital for a few days. Mum has gone into full organisational mode and taken complete charge, virtually moving in with them to help while Rachel recovers from the birth. Which is probably just as well. Coward that I am, coward that Dad is, neither of us have broached the subject of where I found him the day Thomas was born, and more to the point, who he was with.

There hasn't been a moment to ask Dad what the hell he's playing at. All he would say to me at the time was, 'This isn't how it looks,' followed by 'it's complicated,' like he's in some twenty-something romcom. I wanted to scream and shout at him, but it wasn't really the time or place. So I had to pretend nothing had happened, and delivering him to the hospital to be with Mum without losing my rag was one of the hardest things I've ever done. There hasn't been the opportunity since to talk to him alone.

Daniel is of the mind to let sleeping dogs lie, and leave them to sort it out. But I can't help fretting that I should at least let Mum know that everything in the garden isn't as rosy as she thinks. She's so happy with the new baby though, I don't want to burst her bubble. I've toyed with telling Lou, but she does have a tendency to turn things into a drama, and I think our family has had enough of that recently.

When we get to Mum and Dad's, Rachel, Ged and the baby are already there. Mum is fussing over Rachel like a mother hen, and I notice she and Ged occasionally rolling their eyes at one another.

'Don't worry,' I say, when Mum's out of earshot, 'she'll get over it. She's been waiting a long time for this. May I hold him?'

'Of course,' Rachel passes me my new nephew and I cuddle him close.

'Oh, you perfect little man,' I say. I breathe in that lovely new baby smell, and have a sudden pang of longing for my own at this age. I didn't get much sleep, but at least they didn't answer back. I look back on Sam and Megan's baby-hood with huge fondness now. It was hard work, but Daniel and I were so happy, and it felt like we were going on a wonderful huge adventure together. I had no idea that all these years later, life would feel so hard. Thomas grabs my finger and stares at me with beady blue eyes. I love the way babies look at you, as if they have all the knowledge in the world and you don't.

'Oh, he is so cute,' says Megan, leaning over and taking his finger.

'Do you want a cuddle?' Rachel says and I show Megan how to hold Thomas, who gurgles softly in her arms.

'I want one,' says Megan.

'Not yet, you don't, young lady,' I say. Though Megan has been behaving herself lately, a pregnant daughter is all I need. 'And don't you be fooled. He might be gorgeous now but I'm sure he's keeping his mum up all night, eh Rachel?'

'Actually, he's keeping his dad up,' Rachel says, with a fond grin, holding Ged's hand. He looks down at her sappily. 'I've been expressing milk, and Ged's been taking the 2 a.m. shifts.'

'Where is my brother and what have you done with him?' I laugh. 'Well done, Rachel. Finally, a woman has tamed Ged.'

'Oh he knows his place now, don't you darling?'

Ged gives her another soppy look. Bloody hell. I never thought I'd see the day. From Jack the Lad to devoted dad. Rachel must be one hell of a woman.

I go into the kitchen to see Dad assiduously chopping vegetables under Mum's strict instructions. Blimey. What is happening to my family?

'Why don't you let me take over for a bit, Mum?' I say, sensing an opportunity to talk to Dad alone. 'I know you want to spend time with Thomas.'

Mum smiles, gives me some instructions and slips away. Another first. I'm never normally allowed anywhere near the kitchen.

I start fiddling with the roast, wondering how I'm going to start this conversation, when Dad clears his throat.

'I expect you want an explanation,' he says.

'It's the least I deserve.' I'm not sure I want to hear his excuses, and I'm worried if I let rip I'll end up causing a scene, which is the last thing I want to do.

Dad sighs. 'I'm trying to do the right thing here.'

'By meeting Lilian again behind Mum's back?'

'Please believe me when I say that's the hardest thing I've ever done,' says Dad. 'I realise I've made a mistake, but Lilian and I have developed strong feelings for one another. It's not as easy letting go as I thought it would be. But I owe it to your mum, and to all of you to give my marriage another go. I saw how much it hurt you all when I left. I'm trying so hard, Beth, please believe me.'

I want to believe him so badly.

'How can seeing Lilian again help?' I say. 'You've moved back in with Mum. She thinks it's over between you two.'

'It is, I promise,' says Dad. 'But . . .'

'But, what?' I demand. I feel that he's vacillating and not being quite straight with me.

'Look. I know you're on your mum's side here, which I understand. But nothing about this situation is easy, and quite frankly I'm in a bit of a mess. Lilian is an amazing woman, and I thought I wanted to be with her. But I can't be, not when it's making everyone so unhappy. The trouble is it's making her unhappy too. I don't want to let anyone down. Please can you at least believe that?'

I can, actually. Dad is essentially kind, and he hates hurting anyone. I worry, though, that by trying to do the right thing, he might be hurting people more than he intends.

'So why were you with Lilian?'

'To say goodbye, for good,' he says. 'I was only there to tell her it's over, I swear to you.'

There's a pause. He looks nervously at me. 'Have you said anything to your mum about this?'

'No,' I say.

'And will you?'

I think about what he's said. And I think about the way I haven't been totally honest with Daniel about Jack. Maybe

204

sometimes, honesty isn't the best policy. Telling people truths they don't need to know can only cause pain.

'Not if it really is over.'

'It is.'

'We'll say no more about it then,' I say, kissing Dad on the cheek, and then go back to cooking the dinner, only praying I've done the right thing.

Lou

Wow. So, from having been single and my parents having no idea about my sexual proclivities, I seem to have entered a totally different dimension, where not only have they accepted who I am, but I am back together with the woman I love. It's a bit dizzying, but in for a penny, in for a pound. When Mum invites Jo to Ged and Rachel's welcome home lunch I decide to go for it. I'd rather get it over with in one fell swoop than introduce everyone individually. Plus there's less chance of any awkward questions with so many people milling about. To avoid such questions, I've opted to meet Jo first before going to Mum and Dad's. I've stayed over at hers a couple of times now, and gradually we seem to be getting back on track. She's definitely making more effort than before. She even cooked for me one night, which she barely ever did before. It was a bit awkward actually; Maria Skyped me halfway through and I had to ignore the call. I've still been speaking to her, a little bit, telling her about Jo. She's been very supportive, but somehow I don't think Jo would like it if she knew I was discussing us with a girl in Tenerife and I don't want to do anything that might rock the boat. Jo and I haven't mentioned the future. She keeps hinting about making our arrangement more permanent, but it feels too soon, and I'm too raw from what happened before to agree.

Beth opens the door to us and to my relief gives Jo a big hug.

'Lovely to meet you at last, Jo. I knew you weren't a boy.'

I stare at Beth in surprise. 'Why didn't you say?' I demand.

'I was waiting for you to tell me,' shrugs Beth. 'I've known for ages.'

Great, I've been holding back from telling my family and they all *knew*? I am gobsmacked.

Mum and Dad's lounge feels very crowded with all the baby paraphernalia and two teenagers lying around. I swear Sam grows every time I see him.

'Hi Sam, how did the exams go?'

'Don't ask,' he groans.

I have a soft spot for Sam. Like me, he and school don't see eye to eye, and I can understand his hatred of the system in a way that Beth can't. She was always the high-achieving one.

'They're only exams,' I say. 'Life will go on if you don't pass them.'

'Thanks,' says Beth. 'That's not really on message.'

'Sorry,' I say, but wink at Sam.

'I agree,' says Jo. 'You need to pass them at least to open the next door.'

'Music to my ears,' says Beth, grinning at Jo. I'm relieved. They've found something in common. It's a start. Discovering too that Jo has trained as a midwife as well as a nurse, she and Beth are soon bonding over the joys of small babies. I'm grateful to Beth for making such an effort with her.

I'm dreading introducing Mum to Jo, but all she says is, 'It's lovely to meet one of Lou's special friends at last,' before returning to coo over the baby. *Special friend?* I wince.

Thank God for small babies. I should carry one around with me as a permanent icebreaker in awkward situations.

In fact, we have a lovely time. Mum and Dad reminisce about our babyhoods.

'So which one of us was the best baby?' says Ged. 'I bet it was me.'

'Beth was the easiest, Lou cried the most, and you slept the least,' says Mum.

'I knew I must have been the best baby,' crows Beth.

'You were all lovely,' says Mum firmly, 'in your own unique ways.'

'But I'm still your favourite,' says Ged with a grin.

'I don't have favourites,' says Mum. Yeah, right. Ged has definitely always been the favourite.

Ged and Rachel seem deliriously happy, Beth and Daniel seem more relaxed than they have of late, and the kids are besotted with their new baby cousin. All in all it's a really relaxing day. When I drive Jo back to the station, she says, 'You're so lucky, you know. I envy you your family.'

'Why?' I ask. This is curious. No one's ever said that to me before.

'Because despite your snarking at each other,' (which we do frequently, particularly Ged and I) 'I can see there's a really strong bond between you all. I envy that. I never see my siblings.'

'Family is family, isn't it?' I say. 'Maybe I'm luckier with mine than I thought.'

It's a strange idea. I have spent so much of my time feeling like the failure of the family, and slightly resenting them, I hadn't appreciated that maybe I am lucky.

'So when will I see you again?' Jo says as she gets out of the car. It's so weird the way she's suddenly turned into the needy one.

'Soon,' I say. 'I'll call you.'

'You better had,' she says, kissing me goodbye.

'It's a promise,' I say. I wave her off, and then drive off home, suddenly feeling hopeful. Maybe we can make this work.

Daniel

Seeing Beth's family happily settled once more was balm to Daniel's soul. He had always felt the lack of his own family – Mum had run away from Jamaica with Reggie against her parents' wishes, and the wound had never healed. After her father had died, she'd attempted to patch things up with her mum on a disastrous trip back home when Daniel was twelve, but it had failed miserably. Daniel's grandmother had taken great delight in pointing out how she had been right all along, and Mum had spent most of the time either fighting or crying. She had no siblings, just one cousin who had come to England before her, but Daniel rarely saw her. It had always made him extra fond of the family he'd married into. He was glad that his parents-in-law were back together, and that, according to Beth, who'd told him in a whispered aside, Fred had finally ditched the other woman. He hoped that spending time with their new grandson would help cement their reunion.

It was better for the kids too, who, despite finding the idea that their grandpa could still do that kind of thing hilarious, had definitely been a bit unsettled by it. Megan in particular had found it hard, being close to Fred. She had missed seeing him in the months when he was living away from home. It was good to see them back together, teasing one another the way they were wont to do.

All in all they'd had such a good time, it made him think

more about Reggie. The Sunday lunch Beth had arranged the week before had been OK. He and Reggie had been polite but distant to one another, and it was clear that Megan and Sam were fascinated with Reggie's tales of growing up in Jamaica. There were a couple of times, when Reggie had raved about how wonderful it was to meet his grandchildren at last, that Daniel had had to bite back a snappy comment. But watching them drink up Reggie's stories, Daniel realised with a jolt that by keeping them away from their grandad he had accidentally deprived his children of the chance to find out more about their roots, and he felt bad about that. It made him think perhaps he should try and reach out to his dad some more. Sam's eighteenth was coming up. He had eschewed a party, preferring to go clubbing with his mates, but perhaps he and Beth could kill two birds with one stone. If Daniel organised something involving Reggie, maybe Sam would unbend a little towards them.

'Maybe we should go away for Sam's birthday weekend,' he said to Beth. 'After all, we haven't got a holiday booked this year. We could use a break.'

'Do you think Sam would want to do that?' said Beth doubtfully.

'Well, I was thinking of asking Reggie,' said Daniel.

'You think it wise to spend a whole weekend with your dad?' Beth looked surprised.

'It might be a good way to reconnect with him,' said Daniel. He was feeling more positive and open to change. He'd never be close to his dad, but Reggie was the only family he had. Maybe it was time to build some bridges.

'I think that's a brilliant idea,' said Beth, and gave him a hug. 'Reggie will be pleased.'

In fact Reggie was delighted when Daniel emailed to

suggest it. It turned out he was doing a gig in Brighton in a couple of weeks' time.

'I have a place to stay,' he said, 'but it would be good to meet up.'

Sam hadn't jumped at the chance of a family weekend, but responded enthusiastically to the suggestion of going to one of his grandad's gigs. Daniel swallowed his pride and tried not to let that bother him. If they were to move forward, he had to try and shed some of his irritation about Sam's relationship with Reggie. So Daniel booked them into a Premier Inn, and hoped against hope that he was doing the right thing.

Chapter Twenty

Lou

I awake sleepily on a summer morning in Jo's flat, curled up next to her. I've been staying at hers more and more often lately. Despite my initial wariness, things are going well. Jo and I are having a lot of fun together, going on dates to the theatre, to gigs, to dinner with friends, all of whom seem thrilled we're back together. My new job is going well, and life feels good. Better than it has in a long time. Maria is the only one to advise caution. 'This Jo has broken your heart once,' she told me earlier in the week, 'be careful.' I know she's only looking out for me, but I am feeling so much happier than I have for months, I want to throw caution to the wind and enjoy the moment.

I stretch lazily and look at my watch. Yikes. Nearly 7 a.m. The only problem with being at Jo's midweek is I have to trail across London and get on a train back home to get to work. Jo starts at 8.30, but it's a five-minute drive to her surgery.

'Can you make me a cup of tea, babe?' she asks lazily.

'Sure,' I kiss her briefly, before heading for the kitchen. By the time I'm back she's in the shower. Damn, I should have hopped in first.

'Will you be long?' I shout. 'I have to leave in twenty minutes.'

'Give me a sec,' she says.

I scrabble around on the floor to find my clothes. Last night we got a bit carried away after one too many at Jo's local, and our clothing was still scattered everywhere. I've been here for two nights on the trot and I've nearly run out of clean underwear, yesterday's shirt has a wine stain on it, and the day before's is scrumpled up on the floor. Better give it a quick iron. With any luck Jo will be out of the shower by the time I'm done.

She's not. I check my watch. I've only got five minutes. I'm going to just have to go to work as I am and face the walk of shame comments. I don't know my new colleagues well, but they've picked up on my renewed relationship and I get a lot of gentle teasing.

'Jo, I've really got to go,' I say.

'Come and join me then,' says Jo, pulling open the door, looking provocative.

'Would love to. Really no time,' I say.

I brush my teeth, damp down my hair, roughly wash and shove some deodorant on.

'Will I see you tonight?' Jo follows me into her bedroom, clad only in a towel, still looking gorgeous. The temptation to stay is enormous.

'Can't,' I say. 'I've run out of clean clothes.'

'So? I have a washing machine,' says Jo.

'I'd really like a night in my own bed. You could come to me if you like.'

Mum has been remarkably relaxed about things. But then I'm marking her on my experience in my late teens, when having a boy, let alone a girl, sleep over was a definite no-no. I guess now that I'm thirty-eight she figures it's OK.

Jo wrinkles her face.

'No offence, babe,' she says, 'but I prefer my own space in the week.'

'OK, then I'll see you tomorrow.'

It's Friday tomorrow; maybe I can persuade her to come over to me for the weekend.

'We could hang out at mine, have a meal?' I suggest.

'That would be lovely,' says Jo. 'But I've already said to Tash and the others we'd meet them in the Green Man. Sorry.'

'Oh,' I say, trying not to let my disappointment show.

I grab my things, give her a quick kiss and dash to the station, aware that I am already late. On the way there, the sinking feeling starts, the feeling I used to get when we were together before. Why am I beginning to get the impression that I'm being run around in circles?

Daniel

'We're all going on a summer holiday,' Daniel warbled in the car. He was feeling cheerful, the sun was shining, and they were headed for Brighton. His favourite place. He loved everything about it, the drive down there, the pier, the sea, the Lanes. It was where he and Beth had spent a lot of time when they were courting, and as a result it would always hold a special place in his heart.

'Lame, Dad, really lame,' said Sam. 'We're only going away for a weekend.'

'Still, it's nice to have a break,' said Daniel. He felt the weight roll off his shoulders. It was ages since the four of them had done anything together, and it was great to be going away.

'If you say so,' said Sam, retreating behind his iPhone.

213

Megan, meanwhile, was sitting next to her brother, iPod at full blast, seemingly determined to cut out all contact with the real world.

Time was when any journey would have been punctuated with cries of, 'Are we nearly there yet?' and 'I feel sick!' Daniel wasn't sure the retreat into technology was much of an improvement.

'Nice to see you looking so cheerful,' said Beth, squeezing his hand.

'I am,' said Daniel, 'I'm looking forward to this weekend.'

Their journey to Brighton was relatively speedy, and they found themselves drawing up at the hotel an hour later. After the usual nightmare of trying to find somewhere to park, they'd settled on an underground car park half a mile away and had to drag their luggage through the streets.

Consequently, when Daniel suggested going for a walk, his offspring regarded him with horror. 'No,' they said in unison, preferring to be locked into Snapchat or watching rubbish on TV. Oh well, that meant he and Beth got some time together.

They took themselves off for a walk along the beach. The sun was shining, the sea calm, though there was a light summer breeze blowing, and gulls swooped overhead. Daniel felt absurdly happy as he and Beth crunched their way along the beach, holding hands. They stopped for an ice cream, and then walked to the end of the pier.

'Fancy a game on the fruit machines?'

'Oh go on then,' said Beth.

Newly married and with a very small Sam in tow, he and Beth had often come for days out in Brighton, and part of the ritual had always been a go on the fruit machines. Those had been happy days, alive with possibility. And *easy*. Well, in some ways anyway, Daniel decided. Back then, Daniel had been Sam's hero. He could never have imagined then that his devoted small boy would turn into such an uncommunicative young adult.

They settled down with chips on a bench and sat watching the seagulls, and the families playing on the beach.

'This is great,' said Beth. 'Though I do feel a bit guilty about not buying the kids chips.'

'Don't,' said Daniel. 'I left Sam some money. They're perfectly capable of grabbing some food if they want to.'

'True,' said Beth, feeding her last chip to a stray seagull. 'Shall we have a wander down the Lanes before we head back?'

'Great idea.' The Lanes had always been a favourite of theirs too. So they wandered through them, mooching about in joke shops, and antique markets, reminiscing about the first time they'd ever done this, way back when they first met all that time ago.

By the time they got back, it was gone six.

'Drink before we go up?'

'I'll just see what the kids are up to,' said Beth.

'No need, they're here.'

Despite himself, Daniel felt a cold clutch of pain as he saw his children standing with Reggie, laughing at something he'd said. He hadn't anticipated that Reggie would come straight to see them at the hotel, and felt slightly resentful that Reggie was impinging on their family time. Reggie gave Megan a big hug, and then ruffled Sam's hair. They both looked so thrilled, it was all Daniel could do to control the sudden stab of jealousy. He fought to overcome it, and he and Beth went to the bar to join them.

'Great to see you, Reggie,' he said, holding out his hand. He couldn't bring himself to hug the man, but he could at least be polite.

Beth was more forthcoming and gave her father-in-law a big hug and a kiss, which made Daniel feel jealous all over again. This was ridiculous; he needed to get a grip.

So he ordered a round of drinks and made a strenuous effort to be friendly, and tried to suppress the dark flame of envy which was threatening to overcome him. It was only a weekend. He had to make the effort, for Sam and Megan's sake, if not for his own.

Beth

Honestly, I could kill Sam sometimes. He could have warned us that his grandad was already here. I can see by the look on Daniel's face that he's struggling to deal with it. But to his credit, he pulls himself together, plasters on what Megan calls his 'fake teacher smile', and goes to meet Reggie, hand outstretched.

'Great to see you, Reggie,' he says. As if he's meeting an old acquaintance. It seems infinitely sad to me that Daniel, who has so much love to give, is incapable of showing his dad any.

'And you,' says Reggie. He shakes Daniel's hand stiffly, and I detect a slight hurt behind his eyes. I go over and give him a kiss and a hug to make up for it. Daniel might have a problem with his dad, but Reggie's never done me any harm, and I like him.

'So what's the gig tomorrow?' I say.

'Some jazz, some blues, some rock,' says Reggie.

Sam chimes in enthusiastically. 'Grandad's band is awesome. They have a great lead singer, and Grandad's brilliant on sax.'

'So I've heard,' I say. Daniel has talked about that aspect of his dad. It put him off ever learning a musical instrument himself. He says he's not musical – though I'd disagree, he has a strong rich baritone – and that that gene has skipped a generation and come out in Sam. But I wonder if he deliberately put music out of his life as a means of distancing himself from his dad.

Daniel comes back from the bar with drinks, and we chat politely about the kids, the weather, and nothing at all important. It's excruciating, but at least no one is arguing.

'Shall we eat in the hotel, or out?' I ask.

'Hotel—' begins Daniel, but Reggie stops him.

'I insist on taking you out,' says Reggie. 'My treat. How about Giovanni's?'

Giovanni's is a swanky restaurant we've always fancied going to but could never afford.

Daniel is opening his mouth to protest, but I shush him.

'That would be lovely, Reggie,' I say. 'Thank you.'

'I don't want to be beholden to that man for anything,' grouches Daniel when we're back in our room getting ready to go out.

'You're not,' I say in exasperation. 'He just wants to treat his family. Play nice.'

'OK,' grumbles Daniel.

'Come on,' I say. 'You were the one who suggested this. It's just a weekend. If you promise to behave you might just get your reward.'

I kiss him seductively and he grins.

'I'll hold you to that,' he says.

Chapter Twenty-One

Daniel

Daniel awoke to see Beth smiling down at him.

'You're a sight for sore eyes,' he said, enfolding her in an embrace. He hadn't slept well the previous night, and it was reassuring to wake up to Beth, the one strong constant in his life.

'You too,' said Beth, and they giggled as they rolled over together. At times like this it was as though the years had been stripped back and they were young lovers again. It was so easy to get caught up in the day to day of work, and worrying about the kids; it was good to remember what really mattered.

'This was a good idea, wasn't it?' Daniel felt suddenly anxious. The previous night had gone as well as could have been expected. Daniel had swallowed his jealousy and found that by treating Reggie as a casual acquaintance he was able to maintain a detached but polite air, which meant conversation, while not exactly flowing freely, had been manageable. It cost Daniel a huge pang to see how well the kids got on with Reggie, and he was doing his best not to let it get to him. It was his problem, not theirs. It was hard though. But still, at least they hadn't had a row. Sam had gone for a drink with Reggie afterwards, and sent Beth a drunk text about 1 a.m. saying, *Awesome night.*

Daniel thought back to when he was Sam's age. He'd have killed for Reggie to take him out for a drink, but his dad had been long gone by then. Daniel had always hoped to be able to take his son out for pints, but there was no point asking Sam – he wouldn't want to go.

He mustn't get cross. This was Sam's weekend, not his.

'OK, what's up?' said Beth. She was frowning at him, as though trying to work out what he was thinking.

'Nothing,' said Daniel.

'Yeah, right. You have that look on your face.'

'What look?'

'The look that says you're trying not to get angry.'

Daniel rolled over.

'I'm being stupid,' he said.

'Try me,' said Beth gently, reaching over to stroke his arm. God, he was lucky to have her. He wished he could get to the root of the misery inside him and explain it to her, but he'd kept it repressed for so long that he didn't really know how to begin.

'It's just Sam and Reggie . . .'

'It's OK to feel jealous,' said Beth. 'I do a bit too. Sam barely speaks to us, then five minutes with his new grandad and they're best buddies. And Megan's equally besotted. I know it's hard, but you've got to remember that it's all new to Sam at the moment. It doesn't mean he doesn't love us. Love you.'

'I know,' said Daniel, 'I just find it hard to accept.'

'You have to,' said Beth, 'for Sam's sake. Otherwise we'll lose him.'

'When did you get so wise?' said Daniel.

'I've always been wise,' said Beth. 'You just haven't noticed.' She kissed him. 'So, are we going to take advantage of this very nice hotel or what?'

Lou

It's Saturday, and I've finally managed to persuade Jo to come over and stay the night. I know it's not ideal to be at my parents' house but if we're going to be a proper couple again, I need to stand firm on a few things and I don't want to be the one who does all the running. I'm really pleased when she says she'll come over early. It means a whole day together, so I can show her the sights of Abinger Lea, such as they are. I really want to share the place I grew up in with her properly.

Mum is delighted.

'It will be nice to meet your young woman again,' she says.

My young woman? I do love Mum's euphemisms.

'She's my girlfriend, Mum,' I say. 'You are allowed to say it.'

'Whatever she is, I shall look forward to getting to know her. It was so busy the last time she came.'

Busy? It had been manic to say the least, for which I had been profoundly grateful. Now that I am surer of myself, I do want Mum and Dad to get to know Jo. If we have a future together, I want her to get on with my family. I want them to love her as much as I do.

The day doesn't start well. Jo rings at lunchtime to say she's been delayed. She's been asked at the last minute to do a Saturday surgery, so I suppose it's fair enough. I try to ignore the nagging doubts which tell me she'd deliberately chosen a Saturday to come over so she could opt out of it if she needed to.

I've told Mum not to make a special fuss, but she's ignored me and is preparing a massive lunch. Dad is out somewhere and rang to say he'd be late too, so Mum is pretty fractious when Jo arrives, all perfume, floaty scarves and apologies.

'Mrs Holroyd, I am so sorry,' she says. 'I had so much paperwork to catch up on. Lou never said you were going to cook lunch.'

'I didn't actually know,' I say. 'I think Mum went a bit rogue.'

'Never mind,' says Mum, softening, 'you're here now, and please, do call me Mary.'

Jo's being perfectly charming, but I can tell that Mum is not too impressed by her slightly sniffy comments to me about Jo's timekeeping. Mind you, some of that is clearly aimed at Dad, who has sneaked in late. He mumbles something about being in the library, but he looks a little shifty, and I am suddenly suspicious. I hope Dad isn't mucking her about again. Mum doesn't seem to notice anything though. I wonder if I'm imagining things. I hate not trusting Dad, but it's just such a huge hurdle to overcome.

It's a relief though when Dad gets on with Jo like a house on fire. He seems surprisingly unfazed by the latest turn of events; he merely gave me a hug when I told him, and said 'Who am I to judge? So long as you're happy.' He spends most of lunch asking Jo a myriad of questions about his imaginary health problems. There's nothing wrong with him, but he's always been a bit of a hypochondriac, and Jo is doing a great job of placating him. One out of two happy parents isn't bad.

We have a relaxed afternoon, and I manage to drag Jo out for a walk along the canal. It's my favourite place in Abinger Lea. It's lovely in summer, full of families and dog walkers crossing paths over into the woods that run alongside the water. Although it's busy, it's easy to take any of the paths in the wood and get off the beaten track.

'This is gorgeous,' exclaims Jo in delight, as we emerge from the shadows of the trees into a sunlight meadow, where cornflowers, buttercups and cowslips sway in the gentle breeze. Somewhere in the trees, a woodlark is calling, and the field is alive with the sound of bees. I feel so happy. Finally I am getting to that place that I've always longed to be ever since I was young: in a stable, happy relationship with someone my parents approve of.

It's as we go back to the house that Jo drops her bombshell.

'I'm really sorry, hon, but I won't be staying after all.'

'What? Why not?'

'I've double-booked by mistake. Tash and Becky got tickets for a gig months ago – when we weren't together. I've paid for the ticket, and couldn't get rid of it at such short notice.'

'Oh,' I say, a dull weight settling on my chest. Why does she always do this to me?

'You don't mind, do you?' she says. 'I am so sorry. I thought it was next week. I'll make it up to you, I promise.'

Sorry. How easily that word trips off her tongue. I'm really annoyed with her, but we've had such a lovely day. I don't want to spoil the rest of it, so I let it go.

Jo breezes back into the house, thanks Mum for a lovely lunch, gives Dad some more health advice, and then she's gone, leaving me feeling bereft. We have plans to meet tomorrow evening, but I had been so looking forward to tonight. I swallow my disappointment and try to hide from Mum and Dad how upset I am.

But Mum can see right through me.

'I hope you don't think I'm interfering, love,' she says, 'but sometimes I can't help feeling that Jo isn't altogether fair to you.'

'It's fine,' I say. It isn't.

'If you say so, darling,' says Mum. 'But don't let it be a one-way street. There are two of you in the relationship.'

'Just like you and Dad then,' I say a bit snippily, and then feel guilty. That's the way their marriage has always been. No wonder I'm rubbish at relationships.

'Like we were,' says Mum firmly. 'I had to learn the hard way. Please don't let it happen to you.'

Beth

We get to the gig early, which is in a local olde worlde pub. It's heaving at the bar, and Reggie and the band are setting up in one corner. He wanders over and insists on buying us all a drink.

We chat about this and that, carefully controlled conversations, as it's been all weekend. Daniel is tight as a wire though, clasping my hand tightly throughout.

After a bit, Reggie wanders back to the band and Sam goes over to help him. They chatter together happily. Sam looks like he's in seventh heaven. Maybe I've been pushing him in the wrong direction. When he chose his A Levels, he seemed to want to take the scientific route, but sixth form has quite frankly been a disaster. I can see that music is a passion for him in the way that art is for me. I just wanted him to get some A Levels too. Perhaps I've been too strict with him.

The gig starts and we all relax a bit. The band are great, and seem to be able to turn their hand to anything, thrashing out some good old blues and some more modern stuff. Turns out Reggie doesn't just play sax, he can play bass and sing too. He does a great rendition of 'Pinball Wizard', donning some big Elton specs to the hilarity of the audience. It's a great night, and even Daniel can't resist tapping his feet.

When the band take their break, Sam is pumped.

'This is really good, isn't it, Dad?' he says.

'Brilliant,' says Daniel, and for once it doesn't look like he's forced the words out of his mouth.

'I had no idea Grandad was so cool,' says Megan in awe. She's been Snapchatting all her friends in the interval, taking selfies with the band.

'What with him being so old and all that?' I tease.

'He doesn't seem old,' says Megan, 'not the way Grandpa and Nana do.'

Which is true. Maybe that's what a life without responsibilities does for you.

We are all having a great time, and I think Daniel is finally starting to relax.

It's at the start of the next set that it all goes horribly wrong.

Reggie comes up to the microphone and says: 'I recently had the good fortune to meet up with this fine young man, whose eighteenth birthday it is today. Sam King, come up and join your old grandad on bass.'

What? Daniel and I look at each other; we weren't expecting this. Sam clearly was as he leaps straight up to the stage, looking like he's just won the lottery.

Reggie hands him the guitar, and Sam says shyly, 'This is for my dad and my grandad, who are awesome in different

224

ways.' And he promptly launches into a rendition of 'Father and Son' by Cat Stevens.

Oh, how lovely. Maybe Daniel will see that both Sam and Reggie are trying to reach out to him. Perhaps it will help. I lean over to say so, but then I look at Daniel's face. He looks as if he has just been kicked in the guts. Something has gone badly wrong.

'Daniel, what's the matter?'

'They could have chosen any song,' he mutters. 'Any bloody song. Why did they have to choose that one?'

'Daniel, you're not making sense.'

'Sorry, Beth, I can't – this is too much. I have to go.'

He puts his pint down, and pushes his way out of the bar. I can see the hurt on Sam's face on the stage as he watches him go. But it's too late, Daniel has disappeared. I run after him, and find him standing across the road by the promenade, staring out to sea.

'What's wrong, Daniel?' I say. 'Sam was trying to do a nice thing there.'

'I know,' says Daniel. 'It's just that song. Reggie used to sing it to me when I was little. It felt like he'd just punched me in the guts.'

'Oh, Daniel,' I say. 'Sam didn't know that.'

'But Reggie should have,' says Daniel.

I give him a hug.

'Come on, let's go back in. Sam will be wondering what's going on.'

Reluctantly Daniel agrees, but as we head back to the pub we bump into Sam, who is flying out in a fury.

'You just can't do it, can you?' He is raging.

'Do what?' says Daniel.

'Be proud of me for once!' shouts Sam. 'I'm so fed up with it. At least Reggie gets who I am.'

'Sam, it's not like that,' protests Daniel.

'Isn't it?' says Sam. 'I'm out of here. Don't wait up.'

And with that he's gone, into the night, leaving Daniel and I feeling utterly bereft.

Chapter Twenty-Two

Lou

The weeks are rolling on and Jo and I have settled back into a routine. Mostly good. We spend the majority of our time at hers, and the occasional weekend at Mum and Dad's. I'm away so much, it's a while before I notice to my dismay that they seem to be leading increasingly separate lives. Dad often seems to be on his own in the house on the evenings I am there. Mum is still enthusiastically going to Zumba twice a week, and refuses to miss it. She's also spending a lot of time with Rachel and Thomas during the week, leaving Dad on his own, a point he brings up frequently.

'Your mum's at your brother's again,' he'll say huffily.

'Well why don't you join her then?' I usually retort in exasperation. I'm beginning to get really cross with him, and anxious about Mum and Dad's relationship. It doesn't seem like the great reunion I thought it was going to be. If anything, they seem to talk to each other even less than they did. I hope I'm worrying about nothing.

I notice that Dad has changed his tune round the house too. He doesn't seem to be trying nearly as hard as he did when he first moved back in. He barely helps in the kitchen and the house is often a tip when I come back from work.

Mum clearly isn't chasing after him any more – good for her – but it's just a tad irritating as I now find that I am instead.

Just as I seem to be constantly clearing up after Jo in her flat. I'm starting to think that she's a bit on the spoilt side. She may not get on with her parents, but they've paid for her to have this lovely two-bedroomed flat in Stoke Newington. Her dad had a new kitchen and bathroom put in for her when she moved in, and she takes it completely for granted. She never looks after it properly, and it's a constant mess. When I'm there it always seems to be my turn to cook. She has a stressful job, I get that, but domestically, she is incredibly lazy. Her room is always littered with dirty clothes. And she's shockingly wasteful. She'd rather go out and buy a new shirt than put some washing on. Her level of debt is terrifying, but I guess she knows the Bank of Mum and Dad will pay up if she needs them to. I put up with it; after all, it's her flat not mine. But when I'm there at the weekends, sometimes I can't stand the chaos and find myself tidying up. I must have mug written all over my face.

'Oh leave it, babe,' she'll say, lazily flicking through a mag. 'It'll keep.'

But the point is it won't keep, it will just get worse. Maybe I'm really anal, like Jo keeps telling me, but I do like to be in a clean-ish and tidy environment.

'I don't know how you can live like this,' I say one day, after I've exhausted myself scraping six weeks' grime off the bath.

She shrugs her shoulders. 'I'm not expecting you to,' she says. 'I didn't ask you to clean up. You don't have to be a martyr, Lou, it's not a very attractive quality.'

'But you'll expect me to do it all if we live together,' I point out. She keeps asking me to move in, and so far I am prevaricating. I'm not entirely sure why.

'Is that what you want?' says Jo. 'You know I'd love it if you did.'

Is it what I want? I don't know. I've been talking it over with Maria a lot. Even though I feel a bit guilty that I'm gossiping about Jo. But there's no one else I can talk to about this, and Maria, who's been through similar, has such sensible advice.

'I would take it easy,' she advises. 'If it's meant to be, all these problems will iron themselves out.'

I think Maria is right, and while part of me wants this, I'm in no hurry, not the way I was. If I move in with Jo, I'll be wholly dependent on her – it's her flat after all. And I know I'll end up skivvying for her the way Mum has done for Dad for all these years. It's imprinted in my DNA. I love Jo. I really do. But I'm beginning to think I might have made a mistake. In January, I thought I'd do anything to get her back. Now? I'm not so sure.

Daniel

It was a sunny afternoon in early August, and Daniel had been busy in the garden all day while Beth had been working really hard on new ideas in the studio. Daniel loved his garden. Having grown up first in a flat, and then in a house with a tiny courtyard, he relished the space he and Beth had. His mum had been very green-fingered, and always transformed their little yard into a wonderful floral display in the summer months. She'd even managed to grow tomatoes and herbs. It had left him with a love of gardening and it was a way he felt close to her. So today, he had mowed the lawn, weeded the vegetable patch, and picked beans, tomatoes and spuds. He found it both satisfying and soothing.

When he finished, he met Beth coming out of the shed, ready to down tools for the day. It had just gone three, and the sun was still blazing away. It seemed silly not to make the most of it.

'Shall we have a barbie?' asked Daniel.

'Great idea,' said Beth. 'Though I think it will just be the two of us. The kids are both out.'

Sam was working in a local bar for the summer. Since his birthday, he had been even less communicative than ever. They barely saw him, and he was spending more and more time away from home. Daniel had tried to explain his reaction to what had happened at the gig, but Sam didn't want to hear it. Beth kept saying they should give him time and space, but Daniel was increasingly worried that Sam was moving further away from them.

Megan had been at the cinema with friends and had popped home but was planning to go out again to Nando's. At least Daniel hoped that's what she was going to do. So far as he and Beth knew Megan hadn't been drinking again, but they couldn't be sure, and they both fretted about it.

'Let's invite Josh, Helen and the kids over then,' said Daniel, kissing her on the cheek.

Josh and Helen responded with enthusiasm, and they arrived bringing beer, burgers and two very excitable small children. Josh had had kids a bit later than Daniel, and it was nice to see the younger ones. It was so hot, Daniel got the hose out and for the first hour the kids ran around screaming with Megan who organised a water fight before she went out again. Sam had already disappeared, for which Daniel was vaguely relieved. The tension between them was unbearable at the moment, and he didn't know how to sort it out. He felt he'd locked himself into a situation where he couldn't get down from his incredibly high horse.

'Come on, food's up!' said Daniel as Beth and Helen dried the children off. They used to have fun like this when Megan and Sam were little. It made him sad that those days were over.

It was a lovely evening, and all too soon, Helen and Josh were getting up to go, the downside of little ones being that they flaked out rather early.

'Time we got these two into bed,' said Helen. 'Thanks for a lovely evening.'

'We must catch up again soon,' said Josh as he shook Daniel's hand at the door.

'Don't forget Beth's surprise birthday party,' whispered Daniel. He and Lou had been planning it for weeks. With her help, he'd managed to get hold of most of Beth's friends, and had lost count of the number of whispered phone calls he'd had, or surreptitious chats in the kitchen when Lou was round. The secrecy was driving Daniel nuts. He'd have made a lousy spy, but it was worth the stress to be doing something special for Beth.

He came back, poured himself a glass of wine, and went to sit down in the garden with Beth, who had been tidying up. It was nice being with her on his own, but he knew she was going to start on at him about Sam.

'I know you and Sam aren't talking at the moment, but can you try and make an effort? Sam didn't mean to hurt you.'

'I know,' said Daniel. 'It's like I said though: it was just that song. I can't understand why Reggie chose it. He must have known it would hurt. I don't know how to explain all that to Sam. He adores Reggie; I don't want to tell him what his grandad is really like.'

'I know Reggie hurt you,' said Beth, 'but he does seem to be a different person now. I don't think he's going to hurt Sam in the same way. Perhaps he saw that song as a way to make amends?'

'I don't think that was the best way to go about it. I just feel so resentful, Beth.'

'Well, don't!' said Beth, exasperated. 'You can't change the past, but Reggie was trying to do a nice thing there and you flung it back in his face. And Sam's.'

'Whose side are you on?'

'Yours, always,' said Beth, softening a bit. 'Even when you're not on your own side.'

Daniel harrumphed a bit, till Beth laughed.

'Honestly, you sound just like Sam,' she said. 'Have you any idea how hard it is to get on with you both? Particularly at the same time. You're like a pair of big kids.'

Daniel grimaced. 'Has it been that bad?'

'Worse,' said Beth firmly. 'And it needs to stop.'

'You're right,' said Daniel, 'as always.' He hugged her hard. 'I promise I'll try harder, and I will do my best to get on with Reggie.'

'Good,' said Beth. 'Now let's have another glass of wine.'

Beth

It's been a lovely evening with Josh and Helen, but I must admit I am enjoying it more now they've gone. I've just signed off the final, *final* proofs of *The Littlest Angel* and am feeling relaxed for the first time in months. I've barely heard from Jack recently, and to be honest, though I can't help feeling a bit disappointed, it's been a relief too. My mad secret crush can be reassigned to the dark recesses of my brain, just where it belongs.

The sun sets over the trees at the end of the garden, and bats are beginning to flit about the sky. It's still and peaceful, and I'm feeling relaxed and happy, my head on Daniel's shoulder. After all the tension of the last few weeks, I am enjoying the two of us spending time together like we used to. I'm just about to pour us both another glass of wine when there's a ring on the doorbell.

We aren't expecting the kids back for a while, so I'm surprised to find Megan on the doorstep.

'Where are your keys?' I say automatically, before realising she's upset. She pushes past me and runs up the stairs in floods of tears.

'Megan, sweetheart, whatever's wrong?' I race up after her.

'Go away. I don't want to talk about it,' she shouts and slams the door.

I pause for five minutes, and then wander in to find her lying on her bed, sobbing furiously.

'Oh darling, what's wrong?'

I put my arms around her and this time she doesn't fight me off. I can't bear her tears: however old she gets I will never stop wanting to keep her from pain.

'It's Jake,' she says through her sobs. Oh. The mysterious Jake. I had a feeling he was trouble. 'He's had sex with Charlie Bennett,' she goes on to say. Trying to ignore the fact that sex and Jake have come up in the same conversation and hoping Megan hasn't succumbed to the lovely Jake's charms, I say lightly, 'Well, he sounds a right tosser then.'

This elicits a small smile.

'But Mum,' she says. 'What's wrong with me? I thought he loved me.'

'Oh Megan,' I say, 'there is absolutely nothing wrong with you. It is a proven fact that all men are idiots.'

'Not all men,' Daniel is standing in the doorway, love

233

and concern in his eyes. 'OK, just fifteen-year-old boys,' I say.

Megan smiles a bit more.

Daniel comes over and sits down beside her. He gives her a hug, squeezing her tightly.

'Any bloke who doesn't know that Megan King is the most gorgeous girl on the planet is an idiot,' he says. I want to hug him in turn for making Megan feel so much better about herself.

'Oh Daddy,' she says. 'Do you think so?'

'I know so,' says Daniel. 'Now dry your eyes and come downstairs and I'll make you pancakes with chocolate sauce.'

Megan pulls herself together, gets into her PJs and is soon in the kitchen happily making pancakes with her dad. I watch them pottering together and try to imagine the situation if I were married to Jack. I can't picture him showing such consideration to his daughter; he'd probably be on the side of the boyfriend. I remember when something similar happened to Gemma. Jack was ostensibly sympathetic, but he couldn't help admiring the way her boyfriend had nearly got away with it. We'd rowed about it at the time. It's a salutary reminder of what Jack can be like. Secret crushes and wishes for a different kind of life are all very well, I think, but this is my life. And I'm happy with it.

Chapter Twenty-Three

Daniel

'Hi, Lou, just checking you've managed to sort out the spa thing.' Daniel was on the phone to his sister-in-law. The plan for the party was to whisk Beth away for the day, while he and the kids got the house ready for her fortieth. Beth had lots of friends locally, so he had plenty of help.

'Yes, it's all planned,' said Lou. 'Rachel and Jo are in on it too. It should be fun.'

'Lucky you, getting the easy bit,' laughed Daniel.

'This was your idea!' said Lou.

'I know, I know,' said Daniel. He was pleased he'd decided to do something nice for Beth's birthday, but it was a bit daunting. He'd managed to work his way through all Beth's contacts, including her college friends, along with her school mum pals, Josh and Helen, and various other people they knew in the area. Thanks to Beth's mate Gemma from college, he'd even tracked down Jack Stevens' email address. He'd been such a help with Beth's book, it only seemed right to invite him, though Jack had been one of a number of people who hadn't responded.

'I'm sure she'll be thrilled, Daniel,' said Lou. 'It's a lovely thing to do.'

Daniel hoped so. Beth deserved it. He knew he hadn't made life easy over the last few weeks.

He sat thinking about what she'd said to him about Sam and Reggie. He was being an idiot, allowing his jealousy of their relationship to ruin the one he had with his son.

Sam was in the garage, playing drums as usual. Daniel went to listen. Loudness aside, Sam was good. Daniel watched him for a while, lost in admiration and pride at his talented, handsome young son. If he wasn't careful, he might lose Sam for ever. It was time to hold out an olive branch. Sam was so lost in concentration, it was a few minutes before he even looked up. When he did, he looked surprised to see his dad standing there.

'How long have you been here?'

'Long enough. Sounds good.'

'Really?' Sam looked shyly pleased, and Daniel had a flashback to when Sam was a little boy and had lapped up praise. When was the last time he had said anything positive to his son?

'Apart from being a bit on the deafening side, yes,' said Daniel.

Sam laughed, which Daniel took as a sign of encouragement.

'Look – about your birthday—'

'What about it?' Sam looked wary, and Daniel felt a pang of regret that he had pushed his son away.

'I'm sorry,' said Daniel. 'I know you didn't mean to upset me. It wasn't your fault. It was mine. Just a lot of old stuff with Reggie that I find difficult to let go of. It was a lovely gesture.'

Sam said nothing, for a moment, and then to Daniel's relief, said, 'That's OK. Reggie told me he made a mistake. He said he wasn't always a good dad to you, and that I should understand that.'

'He did?' Daniel was touched and surprised that Reggie had stood up for him to Sam. It was an odd feeling. In his head, Reggie had been the bad guy for so long, it was strange to feel positive about something he'd done.

'Yeah,' said Sam. 'But you know, I think Reggie's really different now. He feels bad about what happened with you. I think you shouldn't give up on him.'

'I'll think about it,' said Daniel. He took a deep breath and added, 'Listen, I was planning to go for a pint. Do you want to come?'

'Yeah, OK, so long as you're paying.'

'Cheeky sod,' said Daniel. But he was happy too.

Beth

Vanessa has rung to say there's quite a buzz growing round *The Littlest Angel*. Although Vanessa had been reluctant originally when I said I was going back to basics, with a little help from Jack, she finally came on board, and admitted the new direction I had taken was better than the version we'd had. The print run is growing, and my work for the Bologna Book Fair clearly paid off as lots of foreign publishers are getting on board.

'So I was wondering,' she said, 'if you'd be interested in a follow-up?'

'How could I do a follow-up?' I say. 'The Nativity story *is* Christmas. That's it.' I've decided she really is quite bonkers.

'But the Littlest Angel is such an endearing character,' she says. 'I'm sure you can work out a story about what else she does.'

'Start a choir with the Heavenly Host? Play with the baby Jesus?' I say, half joking.

'That's the kind of thing,' says Vanessa briskly. 'How about I book a date in our diaries for a bit of a brainstorm? How about in a month? I'll get Jack involved too.'

'Oh, right,' I say, trying to damp down the tingle of excitement I shouldn't be feeling. What is wrong with me, that the mention of his name is enough to set my pulse racing? Every time I think I've got beyond this, something comes up and I'm back to square one.

I know I shouldn't, but after we've hung up the phone I text Jack.

Have you heard Vanessa's latest idea? She wants me to come up with a sequel to The Littlest Angel. Has she lost the plot?

Ha. Don't think so, Jack texts back. *She's just seeing pound signs.*

But how the hell can I write a sequel? The Nativity's the story. I've done that!

Oh ye of little faith, Jack says. *You'll find a way. You always do.*

I'm glad someone thinks I can.

Of course you can, Beth. Someone as gorgeous and talented as you won't be fazed for long.

He thinks I'm gorgeous. My heart sings treacherously. Even though I'm on dangerous ground, I like the way Jack makes me feel.

Thanks for the support, but from where I'm sitting it looks impossible.

Nothing's impossible, Jack texts. *Especially not for you. xxx*

xxx I text back, then delete all the texts and switch my phone off. What am I doing? I need to pull myself together.

'Right, I'd better get organised,' I say aloud as I stare out into the garden. How on earth am I going to write another story about my angel? I wish Karen would come back from maternity leave, but she's still got a few months to go, so it looks like I'm stuck with Vanessa. I'm going to have to come up with something.

I find myself doodling my angel. She is looking at me quizzically. *You could say no*, she seems to be saying. And I have the feeling she's not just talking about the book. I could, I think. I probably should, but somehow, I don't think I'm going to.

Lou

World War Three has erupted at home, so I'm hiding in my room like a child. Mum has come home from Zumba to discover Dad has been sitting around all day having done nothing, and the house is in total chaos. I've been over at Jo's for the last couple of days, and haven't been there to do anything. The lounge is a tip and the sink is piled high with dirty dishes. I wonder why he hasn't bothered with the dishwasher and then realise it's full.

'I asked you to tidy up,' Mum is saying. 'I ask one little thing and can you do it? No.'

'I'm going to,' says Dad, 'I just haven't got round to it.'

'When are you planning to get round to it?' asks Mum. 'We can't go on living like this.'

'You don't exactly do much these days.'

'Excuse me!' Mum is beside herself with rage. 'One of the reasons I had you back was because you promised to change your ways. And you haven't. You still expect me to run around after you, and I have had enough.' She puts her coat back on. 'I'm going out and I want this mess cleared up for when I'm back.'

I'm open-mouthed. I have never seen my mother like this. It's rather magnificent. I feel as if some power balance has shifted between them, but it worries me too. When she's gone, I can tell Dad is furious. He's banging stuff about in the kitchen. I can't stand it, so I go and help, risking Mum's wrath.

'I don't know what all the fuss is about,' he grumbles. 'It's not as if your mother's ever here any more.'

'You mean she's not at your beck and call,' I say. 'Mum is doing her thing. You could pull your weight a bit more.'

'Do you think so?' Dad looks slightly perplexed, as if the idea hasn't occurred to him before.

'I do actually, Dad,' I say. 'If you don't do it, and Mum doesn't do it, I end up doing it. We're all living here.'

'You're right.' He gives me an awkward pat on the shoulder. 'I probably take you for granted. I know I shouldn't.'

'Yes you do,' I say. 'And it's not fair.' A sense of unease comes over me. Mum and Dad's relationship has always seemed one-sided to me, with Mum making all the effort. Now Mum has changed, and I'm not sure Dad will be able to hack it. What happens then?

'I'm sorry,' he says, 'I promise I'll do better.'

Which is exactly what Jo is always saying to me. I'm beginning to realise that I'm like Mum when it comes to Jo. I let her run rings around me, and I shouldn't. What if I stood up to her, the way Mum is doing to Dad? Dare I risk it? I'm not sure what to do; all I know is I don't need Maria to tell me that I don't want to be like Mum in thirty years' time. The problem is, I don't know how to stop it happening.

Chapter Twenty-Four

Lou

'Is that the lot?' Daniel has come over to get the stuff for the party tonight, which I've been storing for him at Mum and Dad's. He's been making surreptitious trips to Sainsbury's all week, and Mum's fridge is groaning.

'How are you going to get all that in, without Beth finding out?' I ask.

'Aha,' says Daniel. 'I left her in the bath, where I know she'll be for about an hour. And I have Megan and Sam on standby to text me that it's safe to go in. I'll park in the garage, and unload everything when you've gone.'

'What if she comes in the garage?'

'She won't,' says Daniel. 'I've confiscated the keys and told her her presents are in there.'

'You really have thought of everything, haven't you?' I laugh.

'I damned well hope so,' says Daniel. 'Thanks so much for all your help, and for keeping Beth occupied today. I couldn't have done any of this without you.'

'My pleasure,' I say, giving him a hug.

My job today is to whisk Beth away for her pre-birthday spa day. I'm really looking forward to it. The plan is to get her back home for seven, by which time Daniel and the kids should have sorted everything out.

'This is such a great idea, Daniel,' I say. 'She's going to love it.'

'I hope so,' says Daniel.

'She will.' I give him a kiss on the cheek. 'I'll come over in about half an hour and pick her up. Are you sure she doesn't suspect anything?'

'Not a thing,' says Daniel with a grin.

'Perfect,' I say. He's such a star. Beth is so lucky to have him. I can't imagine anyone ever doing anything as thoughtful for me. The thought makes me sad. I know that however well Jo and I are getting on, there's always going to be this big impasse in our expectations of one another. I had asked her to join me, Beth and Rachel today, but she's blown me out. She's promised to come to the party, which is something, but I'm a bit pissed off with her to be honest.

Beth is looking gorgeous as ever when I get her. It's a sunny day, and she's wearing a loose floaty dress, flip-flops and sunglasses. I envy her effortless style. I've always felt slightly clunky next to her. She was always the tall skinny one when we were at school, and I was the slightly dumpy one. That's not the case any longer, I've lost weight since those days, and if I make an effort, I know I can scrub up reasonably well. I'm only five four, but I've worked out what suits me clothes-wise, and I like my hair neat and tidy, in a shortish bob. I used to copy Beth's when I was younger, but I've long since realised that it suits her more than it suits me. I suppose I'm pretty happy with the way I look, but Beth will always outshine me in that department.

When we pick up Rachel, she's fretting as the baby has a slight temperature. Ged has to practically push her out of the house.

'You are going and that is that,' he says firmly. 'Thomas and I will be fine, and you deserve the break.' He really has got it bad. I'm suddenly jealous of Rachel too. Why do I have to be the only one in the family with the knack of choosing selfish partners?

The spa I found is twenty miles away, in a big old country house in the middle of fabulous grounds. It has two saunas, two steam rooms, a Jacuzzi and numerous hot tubs, as well as a lovely pool to swim in. It was a brilliant choice, and we have a great day. We swim, drink Prosecco, have some treatments and swim some more. We're laughing and chatting all day long, particularly when Rachel tells tales about our baby brother. She has him totally wrapped around her little finger.

'I would never have believed it,' I say, wiping tears of laughter away as she tells me how she's managed to persuade Ged to iron his own shirts by promising sex on certain days of the week.

She's lovely and I'm glad Ged's found her. She's done him the power of good. And I can tell she really loves him too, for all her joshing.

We leave around 6 p.m. Unbeknownst to Beth I've been texting Daniel on and off all day and he's just let me know that it's safe to come home.

As I get in the car, my phone vibrates as I get a text from Jo. *Sorry, Lou Lou, something's come up. I won't be able to make it tonight after all.* Bloody great. I am beyond furious but have to keep it in because Beth will be suspicious. Why does Jo always do this to me? I'm getting so fed up with it.

We get back to Beth's to find the house apparently empty. Daniel's done a great job of hiding the guests. I have no idea where they all are.

243

'Hello?' calls Beth, as we walk into the hallway, but there's no answer. I am on tenterhooks, hoping no one will spoil the surprise.

'Where is everyone?' she says, puzzled. 'I thought they were all in tonight.'

'Maybe they've popped out for a bit,' I say, trying not to give the game away.

Beth opens the door to the lounge still looking puzzled, to a huge shout of 'Surprise!' as Daniel and the kids burst from the conservatory, and all three of them throw their arms around her.

'Happy Birthday, Beth,' says Daniel and gives her a kiss.

'Oh,' says Beth. 'Oh!' As the other guests crowd into the room. The look on her face is priceless, and I even forget my irritation with Jo momentarily. I'm so glad that Daniel did this for my sister.

Daniel

Daniel had been getting increasingly nervous as the day wore on. He'd found it a huge struggle making out he was going to spend the day doing DIY while Beth went to the spa. Daniel had forgotten how many lies he'd told in the run-up to the party. He'd hidden food and booze in the garage, and been surreptitiously contacting Beth's mates. More than once she'd nearly caught him in the act and he'd had to make up some spurious story.

By 6.30, the first guests had started arriving: local friends from Beth's school-run days, a couple of Beth's mates from art college and some of their joint friends from Daniel's own college days. Beth's parents were there too, along with Ged and the baby. Ged had been surprisingly helpful –

fatherhood clearly agreed with him. On the other hand, Beth's dad seemed distant and unhappy. Daniel had asked him several times if he was OK, but Fred didn't really respond. He and Mary seemed to be barely speaking to one another. Daniel hoped things weren't going wrong there again. The whole point of this evening was for Beth. He didn't want a scene.

Daniel found himself chatting to Beth's friend Gemma for a while as they waited for Beth to turn up.

'It's great about Beth's new book, isn't it?' he said. 'Apparently they're really pleased with it.'

'That'll be Jack Stevens' influence, no doubt,' said Gemma. 'He was always good at helping Beth find her creative mojo.'

'He was?' Daniel was surprised. 'I didn't think they knew each other all that well.'

'Oh they didn't, not like that,' said Gemma a little too hastily. 'They just had a really good way of working together, and it's clearly paid off with this book.'

'Is Jack here yet?' said Daniel. 'I don't know what he looks like.'

'No,' said Gemma, 'he texted me to say he was running a bit late. I'll introduce him when he arrives.'

'Good,' said Daniel, his curiosity piqued now. He wondered once again, why Beth had been so vague about Jack. Before he could quiz Gemma some more, he got the text from Lou to say they were on their way, and he marshalled sixty or so very excited people into the conservatory, where they waited patiently for the key to go in the lock. Daniel's heart was hammering, and he felt slightly sick. He really hoped Beth would appreciate his gesture.

Beth came into the lounge, at which point Daniel and the kids jumped out and said, 'Surprise!' bursting party poppers into the air. The guests all tumbled into the lounge, where said Beth stood in absolute disbelief.

'Oh, Daniel,' said Beth. 'I had no idea.'

'Your face is a picture,' said Daniel, handing her a glass of bubbly. 'Happy birthday.'

'Thank you so, so much,' Beth kept saying, half laughing, half crying, as she turned to yet another guest and expressed her surprise at seeing them.

'Can I just say something?' Daniel said, tapping a glass to get everyone to listen. 'I'd like us to raise our glasses to my lovely, talented, gorgeous wife, Beth. I don't know why she puts up with a curmudgeonly old sod like me, but I'm very grateful that she does. Happy Birthday, darling.'

Beth

I am overwhelmed by what Daniel has done for me. He's clearly been through my address book, as there are people here I haven't seen in ages. He's made food too, and set the house up with fairy lights. Megan tells me he's had a lot of help, but I don't care. It's such a lovely thing to do. It makes me feel glad and grateful. My family are all here, my friends are here too. My life may not always be perfect, but right now it feels pretty damned good.

There is such a crowd, it's about half an hour before I spot Jack. What the hell? Why on earth did Daniel invite him? I don't know if I can cope with him being here tonight. It feels too much like my fantasy life intruding on reality, and not in a good way.

My heart is thumping as he comes over to me, looking gorgeous as usual. This is horrific. At a moment when I should be concentrating on my family and my husband, my secret crush is standing before me. Fantasies should stay fantasies, not walk into your kitchen looking hot as hell.

'Jack,' I squeak. 'What are you doing here?'

'Daniel invited me,' he says. 'And may I say you look stunning?'

'Thanks,' I say, willing myself not to blush.

'Nice place you have here,' he says, surveying the kitchen. 'You're lucky.'

'I am,' I say. I don't want him standing here, assessing my life. I don't want to feel the uncomfortable things I do when he's around, especially surrounded by my family.

'Have you got a drink?' I ask him, hoping for a distraction.

'Yes, your husband got me one.' I don't like him saying 'your husband', as if it's a kind of dare. I don't like him being here, but I can't help feeling a sense of excitement because he is. What is wrong with me? It's like I've got an itch that I can't resist scratching. No good can come of this. None at all.

The party is spreading out. It's such a lovely evening, most people are in the garden, and it's just Jack and I in the kitchen. I should get out, go and meet my guests. But I'm paralysed to the spot.

'It's great to see you, Beth,' he says. 'It feels like ages.'

Mainly because it is ages. I have deliberately been avoiding him.

'We're meeting soon though, aren't we?' I say hastily. I really don't want to be on my own with him. 'I must go and see my other guests.'

'Beth,' he says suddenly, urgently, holding my arm, 'I know this isn't the right time or place, but there's something I need to say.'

'No, Jack, there isn't,' I begin, but he stops me.

247

'I'm going mad with it,' he says, 'this thing between us. I just can't stop thinking about you. And I know you feel the same.'

'Jack, there is no thing between us,' I say. My heart is hammering. 'We had something years ago. Our lives are different now.'

'I've never forgotten you, you know,' he says softly. Oh God, time to leave.

'Jack,' I say warningly, but he puts his fingers to my lips, and it's such a sensual gesture, I find myself deliciously drawn in.

He leans forward, and I am thinking – nothing – because just then Daniel bursts in saying, 'Beth where's the cork-screw?'

I spring back guiltily, hoping to God he didn't see anything.

'Right here, you numpty,' I say, thanking God that it's lying on the side next to where I'm standing.

'Great party you've laid on for Lizzie,' says Jack to Daniel. He's still standing beside me, a little too close. 'She's a lucky girl.'

'She is indeed,' I say firmly. 'Excuse me for a moment, Jack, there are a few people I haven't seen yet.'

I see Daniel cast Jack a speculative look, and hope that he doesn't suspect anything. I have to get out of here.

I make my way into the garden, and take stock. I'm breathing heavily as I lean against the wall.

What just happened? I am at a party organised by my husband and I nearly kissed another man. What the hell am I doing?

This has to stop. Right now.

Chapter Twenty-Five

Beth

I feel so guilty the day after the party that I refuse to let Daniel do any of the clearing up. This is insane. After all my resolutions to forget Jack and focus on what matters, I nearly let him kiss me in our kitchen. *What is the matter with me?* The trouble is, I can't stop thinking about it. It's as though I've become two people: the one who loves her husband and doesn't want to do anything to disrupt her life, and the one who yearns for something different, who's excited, tantalised, seduced by the idea of the new. I have a feeling I know what my angel would think about the second, but I cannot help dreaming about Jack like a love-struck teenager. It's making me edgy and rattled, so I find myself snapping at Daniel and the kids over the next week. When Daniel queries it, I blame my tension on worrying about Sam's exam results, which are out on Thursday. It's true – I am anxious about them. Sam did precious little work, and has deferred the uni offers he's had for a year. I'm worried he's stuffed up his future, but I still feel bad using it as an excuse for my behaviour.

The night before the results, I am in a particularly foul mood. Jack has texted me to see how I'm doing. I know I shouldn't respond, but I find I can't help myself and in seconds I am sucked into a flirty, bantery conversation, which I delete as soon as it's over. I can't risk Daniel seeing it. I think he might be getting suspicious that something's not right. I can't believe I'm doing this, but I can't seem to stop myself either.

'Why did you change your name from Lizzie to Beth?' he suddenly says out of the blue.

'No particular reason.' (Lie, lie, lie. One very particular reason: Lizzie was Jack's name for me; I couldn't use it once I'd lost him). 'I felt Lizzie sounded a bit young once I left college.' My family had actually always called me Beth; it was only Jack who called me Lizzie, but I don't tell Daniel that.

'According to your mate Gemma, Jack Stevens used to help you out a lot at college.' He says quite casually. 'I didn't think you knew him that well.' Bloody hell, what has Gemma told him? She knows exactly what went on at college, and a little about what has been happening recently, but I swore her to secrecy. Surely she wouldn't have been indiscreet?

'We were quite friendly at the time,' I say hastily. 'He has a really great way of helping me sort out what's really important.'

'Oh right,' says Daniel, sounding unconvinced. 'You never said he was good looking.'

'It didn't seem important,' I say, trying to keep it light. 'To be honest, he was always a bit full of himself at college. He thought he was his God's gift to women.' My heart is hammering erratically, and my palms are sweating. Why is Daniel questioning me like this? Did he see something at the party? Oh please, please make this go away.

'So you were never tempted?' Oh God, he is suspicious. He can't know that not only did I give into temptation then, I am still tempted now.

'Jack was only after himself,' I say. 'He wasn't worth bothering with.' I know deep down inside that still stands true today. He has nothing to lose with having a fling with me, whereas I could lose everything. I doubt Jack is thinking about the hurt we might cause Daniel if anything happens; he wants what he wants, is all. And at the moment, what he seems to want is me.

Guilt propels me to be a bit more emphatic than I need to be.

'Jack was a bastard of the highest order,' I say. 'He treated women appallingly. It's what he does. Which is why I'm so lucky to have you.'

Which is true. In the real world, Daniel trumps Jack every time. He is kind and honourable and loyal. Jack is gorgeous, makes me feel amazing about myself, but isn't to be trusted. That's why he has to stay a fantasy.

I kiss Daniel on the cheek, and hope that I've managed to avert disaster for now. I have to knock this thing with Jack on the head. I have to. Next time I see him, I'll tell him so.

Daniel

Daniel was feeling twitchy. Beth was hiding something from him, he knew it, but he couldn't put his finger on what. It was something to do with Jack. Gemma had seemed to suggest that Beth had been pretty close to Jack at college, and yet Beth had never mentioned it to him. Why had she never told him? Why had she denied it now? He'd taken an instant dislike to Jack. There was something about him that seemed inherently untrustworthy, and Daniel felt uncomfortable about the way he flirted with Beth. She'd seemed to light up in Jack's presence at the party. Could he just be imagining it? Daniel couldn't envisage a situation where Beth cheated on him, but a secret fear of not being good enough was making him worry that she might.

Daniel was up and out early on the day of Sam's results. He had to be in school himself, congratulating and commiserating his own students, so he got up to make Sam and Beth some tea. There was no sign of Sam though, who seemed to be happily sleeping through the most momentous day of his life, having been at a gig the night before.

Tentatively, Daniel knocked on Sam's door, but there was no answer, so he left the mug of tea outside. It was no good; he had to go to school. He'd have to find out about Sam later.

The news eventually came at eleven, when he was in the middle of a tricky conversation with a devastated student who'd just missed his grades. Daniel had just finished advising him about his options, when Beth texted. *Disaster. Failed everything. When can you get home?*

Shit, shit, shit. Daniel wanted to get home immediately. He knew Sam hadn't been doing enough, but to fail everything? Ironically, Jason Leigh had taken Daniel's strictures to heart and was celebrating two As and a B, which was enough to get him to Warwick to study Spanish. Evidently, he'd decided the computer games industry could wait.

By the time Daniel eventually got back, he'd worked himself up into a fury. If only Sam had pulled his finger out. He had so much going for him, and he'd thrown it all away. What was more, thanks to his lack of effort, his school weren't even offering him the option of re-sitting, not that Sam would want to take that path.

'So what are we going to do next?' Daniel said when he got home and he and Beth finally confronted their son in the kitchen. 'I'll look into getting you into a crammer course, Sam, but you need to really knuckle down now.'

'No,' said Sam. 'I don't want to re-sit. I don't want to go to college. I just want to play in a band.'

'That is the most ridiculous thing I have ever heard,' said Daniel. 'You need qualifications.'

'Grandad's done OK without them.' Sam shrugged his shoulders.

'Great, you're taking advice from someone who's bummed his way round the world, never taking any responsibility for his life or those around him. What's Grandad got to bloody do with it?' said Daniel, who was beyond furious now. How dare Reggie get involved? It was none of his business.

'At least he listens to me.'

'What's that supposed to mean?' asked Daniel.

'You and Mum don't care about what I want to do,' shouted Sam, 'All you care about is me not showing you up to your friends.'

'Sam!' said Beth sounding shocked. 'You know that's not true.'

It was a nasty blow, and something inside Daniel snapped.

'How dare you? Your whole life all Mum and I have done is want the best for you. We want the best for you now, and if that means retaking your A Levels, you are going to do it!'

'Stop it! The pair of you,' said Beth. 'This isn't helping.'

'I will not,' said Daniel. 'I've been far too patient for far too long. Sam, you are going to redo your A Levels and that is that.'

'You can't make me,' said Sam.

'Well what else are you going to do?' said Daniel. 'You have no money without us, and no future if you don't re-sit. You have to do as we say.'

'No I don't,' said Sam. 'I'm eighteen, and it's my life, not yours. I don't need this shit. I'm going to do what I want.'

'Which is?'

'Be a musician like Grandad.'

'Not under our roof you're not,' said Daniel.

'Then I won't stay under your roof,' raged Sam. 'I'm going to go and live with Grandad.'

With that, he walked out of the house.

'Well done,' said Beth sarcastically. Daniel put his head in his hands in despair.

Lou

I've been at home for a few days because I'm cross with Jo. I still can't believe that she ditched me at the last moment before Beth's party. Well, I can actually. She used to do this all the time before. I had hoped she'd changed, but clearly she hasn't.

Mum isn't impressed at all.

'You shouldn't let her walk all over you,' she says. 'You should stand up to her.'

'Like you do to Dad?' I say. 'Don't be such a hypocrite.'

Since the dishwasher incident, Dad has been trying a bit harder, and now she's not so tied up with Ged, Rachel and the baby, Mum seems to be letting him off the hook again. She's allowing herself to be sucked back in every bit as much as I am. I've noticed in the last week she's even missed her precious Zumba classes. I hope she's not backsliding. I'd hate for her to just slip back into her old routines. I liked the new, independent Mum.

'That's different,' says Mum. 'We've been married for a long time.'

'How is it different?' I say. 'Dad cheated on you, you've let him come home, and you still run around after him as if he's three.'

'That's enough,' says Mum, who is clearly getting annoyed. 'Your dad and I are working things out. I'm just concerned that this Jo doesn't seem to have your best interests at heart. I think you shouldn't let her push you about, and let her know how you feel about things.'

'You're right, Mum,' I sigh. 'It's not that easy though. I love her. I don't want to lose her again.'

'Oh love,' says Mum, 'I know how you feel, but you have to stand up for yourself, otherwise it'll never work. Believe me.'

I know she's right, and it's what Maria's being saying to me too. I have come to really trust Maria's judgement. I could Skype her now and talk it through, but deep down I know what I need to do. It's so hard though. It's not as if I have the best role model for relationships. For some reason, Beth was able to shake off the way our parents have always been to one another and set up a better dynamic with Daniel. But I'm different. I have always been a people-pleaser; Mum is too. I'm beginning to see it hasn't done either of us much good. If I really want things to work with Jo, something has to change. So I give her a ring.

'Jo,' I say, 'we need to talk.'

Chapter Twenty-Six

Lou

I've arranged to meet Jo in a bar in London. I don't want
to go to her flat, otherwise she'll try to deflect me and I
won't be able to say what I need to say. I really need to say
it; I cannot go on like this. Much as I love Jo, Mum is right;
she pushes me about and I let her. It's no way to live. I
need to put an end to it.

'What's this all about?' says Jo – she turns up looking
absolutely stunning. I swallow hard. This is going to be so
difficult. She's late of course though, which hardens my
heart somewhat. 'You've been dead sulky for the last couple
of weeks.'

'Jo,' I look at her in exasperation. 'Have you really no
idea why?'

'No,' says Jo. 'Have I done something wrong?'

Suddenly as I look at her, it's as if the scales have fallen
from my eyes. Jo is never going to change. And neither am
I. I'm always going to be running after her, expecting her
to be thinking about me the way I do about her, and it's
never going to happen. I either accept that, or I change my
destiny. Love isn't enough after all. I deserve more. I deserve
better.

'Jo,' I say, 'it's not about you doing things wrong, it's about what you *don't* do. You never think of me; you're always letting me down. I can't go on like this.'

'How? How do I let you down?' says Jo. She still doesn't get it.

'By not turning up to my sister's birthday party, by blowing me out constantly when a better offer comes along. Jo, I'm sorry, I can't do this any more.'

'What are you saying?' There's a wobble in her voice, and I am so tempted to put my arms around her and say it's going to be all right, but for my sanity I can't.

'I'm saying it's over,' I say.

Her face crumples, and I realise she's not been expecting this.

'Lou,' she says, 'I need you. I love you so much. I can't cope without you.'

And I know she does. She really does love me. I love her too, but it's not enough. It makes me sad, but I know I'm doing the right thing.

'It's not about how much we love one another,' I say sadly. 'It's about the way we are together. I've let you run rings around me and dominate me for too long. That's my fault, not yours, but I can't live a life like that. I deserve better. We're no good for each other, can't you see?'

'You're wrong,' says Jo. 'We're so right for each other. I've never known anyone like you before.'

'And I've never known anyone like you,' I say, tears in my eyes. 'Jo – you'll always be really special to me, you've made me feel worth loving, but it's not enough.'

'I'm better with you,' says Jo. 'I don't want to be without you.'

I nearly wobble then. She's saying all the things I always wanted her to say, but it's too late.

'But I'm worse with you,' I say gently. 'I'm sorry. It's not going to work, not long term.'

'I can change,' says Jo. 'I promise to change.'

'No,' I say sadly, 'I really don't think you can.'

And that's that. I walk out of the bar with tears in my eyes, but as I walk, I start to feel lighter somehow. I've done the right thing. Time to take charge of the rest of my life.

Daniel

Sam hadn't been in contact since he walked out of the house. The atmosphere at home had been tense and moody. Beth blamed Daniel completely for what had happened. 'If you hadn't gone off on one,' she said, 'we could have talked about it rationally. What if he never comes back?'

They knew he was at Reggie's, because Reggie had let them know, and Megan let slip that Reggie had come round to collect Sam's stuff when Beth and Daniel weren't in. Sam wanted to avoid them that much. Megan was the only other member of the family Sam would countenance seeing, so they had to rely on updates from her as to how he was doing. It was breaking Daniel's heart.

Of all the people for Sam to turn to, why did he have to go to Reggie? Couldn't he have gone to a friend's? It made Daniel feel both enraged and impotent. But most of all, he was angry with himself. He'd done with his son what he'd vowed never to do, and behaved the way Reggie used to with him. He was his father's son after all. Was it any wonder Sam didn't want to see him? He had only himself to blame, as Beth kept reminding him. They were snapping at each other horribly without Sam in the house. Daniel found that the anger and poison that he'd been holding down inside of him was leeching out in waves, and there was nothing he could do to stop it. However hard he tried, it poured out of him, mainly directed at Beth. She only had to load the dishwasher the wrong way and he would shout at her. He knew he wasn't being fair, but he couldn't seem to help himself. All this time he'd worked so hard to be different from Reggie, and it turned out he was exactly the same.

'Is Sam ever coming home?' Megan asked one day over dinner.

'Of course he is,' said Daniel firmly. 'Once he's got over his bad mood, he'll be fine and we can sort all this out. He just needs to take some responsibility for his life.'

Beth looked at him incredulously.

'He needs to take responsibility?' she said. 'He'd still be here if you hadn't been so hard on him.'

'Well your nagging didn't help him, did it?' snapped Daniel. 'We've both done this.'

'No,' said Beth coldly. 'You did this. If you'd only tried to meet your dad halfway, none of this would be happening.' She got up from the table. 'There's no point discussing it any further. I'm going to do some work.'

Megan burst into tears.

'Please don't fight,' she said. 'I hate it when you fight.'

Beth gave her daughter a hug, 'It'll be fine, darling, I promise. We're not fighting.'

But she didn't look at Daniel and he felt a deep sense of dismay. His family was broken and he didn't know how to put it together again.

Beth

It's been two weeks since Sam left home. He finally cracked and texted me to say he was all right, but he refuses to contact

Daniel. I can't say I blame him. I've seen a side of Daniel I really don't like. I know he's under pressure, but he's being an idiot. I have never been so angry with him in our whole married life and I miss Sam so much, it's making me miserable.

I'm rushing out of the house to go to London for a meeting with Vanessa and Jack. I am so unhappy at home that it's actually a huge relief. I haven't thought about Jack much in the last fortnight, I've been so wrapped up in my own unhappiness, but the thought of seeing him today is lightening my mood. Nothing can happen in a meeting. Everything will be fine, but a little light friendly banter won't hurt, and it might just lift my spirits.

Daniel makes a bitchy comment about Jack before I leave, but I let it pass. I don't want to encourage any suspicions he has.

I go to say goodbye to Megan, who is still lying in bed.

'Are you going to be in bed all day?' I say.

She shrugs. This situation is hard on her.

'Are you feeling OK?'

'I'm fine,' she says.

'I've got to dash,' I say, 'I'll see you later.'

'Mum?' Something in her tone catches my attention.

'Is everything all right, Megan?' I say. 'You do know you can talk to me about anything bothering you, don't you?'

'It's just you and Dad,' says Megan. 'You're not going to get a divorce – are you?'

I'm shocked. 'Of course not, sweetheart, whatever gave you that idea?'

'When Amelie's parents divorced they argued all the time too,' she says, and I feel immeasurably guilty.

'Oh darling,' I say. 'Dad and I are grumpy with each other because of Sam. Everything will be fine, I promise.'

'I miss Sam,' says Megan sadly.

'Me too,' I say. I kiss her on the head. 'Why don't you go and see him today? I'm sure he'd like that.'

I leave feeling incredibly guilty that what Daniel and I are doing to each other is having such an effect on Megan. I hope I'm right and that everything really will work out for the best. But despite my worries, I am also getting that familiar pit in my stomach, part anxiety, part anticipation that I am seeing Jack again. What am I doing to all of us? Why can't I focus on what's important?

I try to stop fretting about it on the train, and start going through my ideas for the new book. I feel that familiar sense of excitement I always get when starting a new project, and to my surprise my meeting is actually quite a hoot. Having a brainstorm seems to help exorcise Vanessa's maddest ideas, and a couple of times Jack is really supportive in knocking them on the head for me. In the end, we decide the Littlest Angel saves the baby Jesus from Herod, and leads him, Mary and Joseph into Egypt. Having been unsure about a sequel, I think it could actually work.

Our meeting finishes around 12.30, and Vanessa whisks me round the building to meet people. After all my travails getting my angel off the ground, it's great to see the buzz growing around her.

So it's in a celebratory mood that Vanessa, Jack, the sales director and I pile out of the Smart Books offices, which are positioned quite close to the river, and head towards a posh restaurant by the Thames. I'm flattered; in our previous lunchtime meetings, Vanessa has provided sandwiches. I've clearly gone up in the world as this restaurant oozes money, with its smart maître d' and sleek linen table cloths. It's making me wish I'd dressed up a bit more. It's gone 1.30 when we get there, and Vanessa, who has clearly written off the rest of the day, actually orders some Prosecco.

261

In the past she's always been on water. It's quite a revelation to see Vanessa let her hair down.

We have a great time, the food is exceptional, and the wine is flowing. Jack is flirting lightly with Vanessa, which would make me jealous, but from time to time he plays footsie with me under the table, and I get the idea that he's just putting on a show. It's making me uncomfortable, but at the same time a bit excited too. I hate myself for it, but with the wine and the general bonhomie, I tamp down my conscience. Nothing's going to happen here, we're just having fun. The lunch goes on and on, it's 3.30 by the time we emerge blinking into the sunlight.

'I'm off home,' says Jack. 'I've got an appointment. See you tomorrow, Vanessa.'

Oh. This means we are going to have to walk to the station together. I wonder if I should demur and go another way, but somehow I can't quite bring myself to do so. So I walk to the Tube with Jack. At first we say nothing, but I am acutely aware of his presence by my side. Maybe it's the Prosecco I've had, but this feels heady, dangerous, exciting.

'So,' he says as we get to the Tube. 'About what I said last time I saw you.'

'Jack,' I say warningly, but part of me doesn't want him to stop.

'I know you feel it too, Lizzie,' he says. He leans towards me, and I try to lean away, but somehow I can't. I don't shy away when he kisses me on the mouth.

Chapter Twenty-Seven

Lou

I'm feeling surprisingly calm about Jo. I do miss her, but it feels like a relief to be honest. The more I think about it, the more I realise that our relationship had always been on her terms, but I was too blind to see it. I think that's been the case with nearly every relationship I've ever had. I make a vow that I am never going to let it happen again.

'Good riddance to bad rubbish,' says Mum when I tell her. 'She was taking advantage of you. You ought to get back in contact with that nice Maria girl we met on holiday if you're not already.'

I look at her with renewed respect. She'd picked up I was flirting with Maria in Tenerife? Well I never.

'Er actually, I am,' I say.

'I don't live in the Dark Ages, you know,' she says and smiles. 'Maybe you should go and see her.'

I smile too. And the more I think about it, the more attractive the idea seems. My contract is coming to its end, I have some money saved, maybe I should go over there again. I feel I could have pushed things further with Maria at the time, but I was still in such a mess about Jo

I hadn't wanted to. Just the other day on Skype she suggested I come over there for a holiday. Maybe I should. I decide to Skype her now, and we find ourselves chatting for ages.

'If your job is finishing, you could work here,' Maria says. 'There's an opportunity going in our office. The hours are long, but the pay is good.'

I must admit I'm tempted. I've never exactly been sold on credit control. It's just something I fell into. It might be nice to try something different. I am wary though; I don't want to commit to anything straight away. I barely know Maria, after all.

'I'll come over for a couple of weeks,' I promise. 'Then we'll take it from there.'

So over the next few days I start looking at flights to Tenerife. I'm sitting at work and have just about plumped for one when my phone rings. It's Mum, and she's hysterical.

'Calm down,' I say as she sobs incoherently down the phone at me. 'What's going on?'

'It's your dad, he's in hospital. They think he's had a heart attack.'

My stomach plummets to the floor and I feel cold all over. 'I'm coming right away,' I say.

'That's not the worst of it,' says Mum. 'He was with *her.*'

Daniel

Beth was out in London meeting her publishers. She'd barely spoken to Daniel since their row. All she'd said that morning before he left was that she'd be late back. Daniel was at work, planning for the new school year. He was trying to concentrate as he got through a couple of boring strategy meetings and then tried to iron out problems with the new Year Seven intake, due to start the following week. He also had to have several meetings with students who hadn't got their grades but who wanted to retake the year. He wished that Sam would do that, but it looked like he wasn't even going to consider it. Jim Ferguson was still being difficult, and pretty much contesting every suggestion he made, which was becoming very wearing. On the plus side, the overall fallout from last year's Ofsted hadn't been as bad as Daniel had feared. Although the staff had been disappointed, there was a general feeling that the inspectors had been over-harsh. The governors had accepted that Daniel hadn't been given enough time to bring the school up to scratch, and were happy with the changes he was suggesting to make sure the next inspection went better. With the help of Carrie Woodall, he'd gradually won over more of his staff, so, even if Jim thwarted him at every turn, he felt more positive about school this year. At least something in his life was going right.

However hard he tried though, Daniel couldn't concentrate. His heart wasn't in it, and he found himself unable to focus on the work. The only member of the family still speaking to him was Megan and she was finding the whole situation so distressing it made him feel guiltier still. She'd been crying this morning as he left.

The day went by, long, hectic, and busy enough to stop Daniel thinking too deeply about everything. He had just got back to his office after a tedious meeting about budgets when he picked up some missed calls and a text from Lou. *Ring me as soon as you get this.* That was odd. Lou never normally rang him. Why would she be calling him and not Beth?

He got through after several attempts. 'Hi Lou, is everything OK?'

'Not really,' she said. 'I'm at the hospital with Mum and Dad. They think Dad's had a heart attack.'

'Bloody hell,' said Daniel. 'Have you told Beth?'

'Well that's the weird thing,' said Lou, 'I've been trying her for ages, but her phone seems to be switched off. Have you heard from her?'

'No,' said Daniel, a cold clutch of panic creeping over him. 'She's in London for the day, but I thought she'd be on her way back by now. I'll try and get hold of her, and we'll be at the hospital as soon as we can.'

Daniel rang Beth, but it went to voicemail; he left her a message and then texted her for good measure. Telling his secretary he had to leave because of a family crisis, he set off for the hospital, trying to ignore the nagging worry that something wasn't quite adding up. Where was Beth?

Beth

For a moment, I forget where I am. I shut my eyes, and I am a twenty-year-old girl, standing with the most gorgeous boy I know, and I am kissing him. It's intoxicating and dizzying, and I cannot believe that I am there in his arms. Jack Stevens wants me – he actually wants me. It is all I have dreamed for months. I allow the fantasy I have been living in for so long to temporarily come to life. And then my phone buzzes, and I am pulled abruptly from my dream. Shit, it might be Daniel. I pull back from Jack, even though I want this so much. I know it's wrong and I just can't do it, however much I want to. Things are rubbish with Daniel at the moment, but falling into Jack's arms won't help anything.

'Jack, I'm sorry, this won't work.'

'But why not, Lizzie? Don't you think we owe it to ourselves to be happy?' he says. 'I know we'd be good together.' He pulls me closer towards him.

It's tempting, it really is. I'm fighting so hard not to give in to my emotions, but I know I've just crossed a line, and I can't let this go any further.

'But at the expense of other people,' I say.

'Even if you're miserable?' he says. 'I know you, Lizzie, and I know Daniel doesn't make you happy any more. Not the way I can.'

'That's not true,' I say. 'We're just going through a bad patch.'

'It's like he's squashed all the old vibrancy out of you,' he continues. 'The real Lizzie Holroyd is still in there, I can tell.'

It's so close to what I've been thinking on and off for the last few months, I nearly give in. But is it Daniel who has squashed me, or have I just let life wear me down?

'Don't,' I say. 'I grew up and I've changed. I'm not the girl I once was. I'm not the person you think I am.'

I glance at my watch. It's a lot later than I had realised. I ought to let Daniel know I'm running late – I can't stay here. My phone buzzes again, and I look at it. I have missed calls from both Daniel and Lou. I had it on vibrate in the restaurant, and I can't have heard it over the din. Daniel and Lou *both* calling me. My heart leaps with anxiety. Shit, what's going on?

'Sorry Jack, I have to ring home,' I say, trying to erect a barrier between us.

'Where are you?' Daniel sounds so relieved to hear my voice when he picks up. 'Your dad's at the hospital, they think he's had a heart attack.'

It feels like I've been kicked in the stomach. 'What?' I say. 'Oh God. I'm on my way. I'll be there as soon as I can.'

'What's going on?' says Jack when I hang up. He can see my distress, and he moves to put his arms round me.

'It's my dad.' I blink back tears. Dad's in hospital? He's always been so fit. 'He's had a heart attack.'

'Oh no,' says Jack. 'Is he OK?' He strokes me gently and leans in to kiss me once more, but I push him away. Doesn't he get it? This changes everything.

'Jack, no,' I say. 'This is neither the time nor the place. I have to be with my family. You do understand, don't you?'

'Of course,' he says, 'I'll call you.'

'No, I'll call you,' I say. The last thing I need is him ringing me at the hospital.

'I need you, you know,' he says, a little-boy-lost look in his eyes. Please, don't do this to me.

'I don't think you do, not really,' I say, keeping my voice even, trying to be strong. 'I think you always want what you can't have.'

And with that I walk away.

I'm so churned up. I've allowed another man to kiss me. I've thought about letting him into my bed. And now my dad is ill. Is this some kind of punishment? The journey home is a nightmare; there's a signal failure so my train is slower than ever but I eventually get to the station and order a cab to the hospital.

I rush inside to find Mum, Lou, Ged, Rachel, the baby and Daniel all standing around in the waiting room, talking earnestly. Lou and Mum look like they're about to leave.

'Thank God you're here,' says Daniel. 'Where were you?'

'The meeting went on longer than I thought. How is he?' I hope the guilt isn't obvious in my voice.

'Better than he was,' said Daniel. 'They're doing some tests. Oh – and I should warn you.'

'Warn me what?' But as I push open the double doors to Dad's ward, I see for myself. Dad is lying in the hospital bed, and sitting holding his hand is Lilian Mountjoy.

The Littlest Angel

At last, the Littlest Angel thought her journey was nearly over. She'd heard one of the other angels talking about seeing a donkey, and there was a donkey here, tied up behind a stable door.

'Hello,' said the angel. 'I'm looking for the new baby. Do you know when it's going to be born?'

'Oh,' said the donkey. 'I think it's tonight. I've carried his mother all the way here. He's going to be a very special baby.'

'I know,' said the angel. 'That's why I'm here.'

Vanessa Marlow: Where are Mary and Joseph at this point?

Beth King: I'm imagining inside. Don't ask me awkward questions!

Part Four

The way home

September–December

The Littlest Angel

The angel crept inside. There was no one in the stable but a <u>couple of cows</u>, lowing.

'Where's the baby?' she said. 'Am I too late?'

'Too late?' said the cows. 'No, you're too early.'

Vanessa Marlow: <u>Now this is cute. I hope the cows are going to be cute!!</u>

Beth King: <u>Yes, the cows can be cute.</u>

Chapter Twenty-Eight

Lou

Mum and I have been in A&E for hours. They can't actually decide whether Dad's had a heart attack or not, or whether to admit him. So a very uncomfortable trio of Mum, Lilian and I gather around the bed, while doctors and nurses come to and fro, and strap him up to ECG monitors, take blood samples and attach him to a drip, but no one tells us anything. The atmosphere is tense; Dad looks pale and unwell, and clearly finds it a strain. He seems to be opting out of the whole thing by shutting his eyes as often as possible. He does at least mutter an apology to Mum, but that's all we can get out of him. Lilian was already there when we arrived and we had an awkward few moments before she briefly kissed Dad on the cheek and went out for a coffee. She didn't stay away long though, and now the three of us are awkwardly gathered round the bed. Despite the stress of the situation, I can't help trying to scope her out. Lilian is a tall, willowy woman in her late sixties, and as different to Mum as she could be.

None of us are talking very much and Lilian and Mum have clearly decided that this isn't the place for a public row. They are saying very little to one another, whilst conducting a surreptitious one-upmanship campaign to look after Dad the most, whether it be by bringing him cups of tea or plumping up the pillows. It would be funny if the situation wasn't so bloody awful.

Dad doesn't say a lot. He looks exhausted. I know this situation is his fault, but it's clearly taken its toll. Eventually a doctor comes and tells us that they don't think Dad has had a heart attack, but they are going to keep monitoring the situation, which is a huge relief, but he clearly isn't well. I'd feel sorry for him, but I can't help thinking it serves him right.

One thing is clear to me though: as much as I don't want to admit it, he and Lilian are very much in love. I wonder if Mum can see it. It's the way they look at one another, and the way she places her hand on his or strokes his face. I can't remember Mum and Dad ever being that tactile. Even when we got here, worried as she was, all Mum could do was kiss him stiffly. There was no warmth in it. Understandable in the situation, but Dad could have died.

Ged, Rachel and baby Thomas eventually turn up, followed by Daniel, who still hasn't heard from Beth. We agree to take it in turns to keep Mum and Lilian apart as much as possible. Ged and Rachel offer to take Lilian to the hospital canteen for a coffee to give her a break, while Mum and I stay with Dad. Daniel is off in the corridor trying to track Beth down, so the three of us are left together.

I look at Mum, who is staring at Dad while he sleeps, looking completely shell-shocked.

'What happens now?' I ask.

'This isn't the place,' says Mum.

'I think it is, Mum,' I say. 'He was with Lilian. He wants

278

to be with Lilian. I think we've all been kidding ourselves, like the way I kidded myself with Jo.'

Mum sighs.

'You're right. I thought he'd come to his senses. And now this.' There are tears in her eyes. 'They think he's fine. I don't need to be here any longer, so I'm going to go home now. I'm so tired. If they release him, he can go back to her.' I can see how difficult the words are for her to say. I reach over and squeeze her hand.

'I think that's the right thing to do, Mum. I know how hard it is.'

Ged and the others come back, just as Mum and I get up to go. Lilian takes her place by Dad's bedside, avoiding eye contact with us both. This is beyond weird. At that moment Beth comes flying in too, looking shocked and upset. Daniel clearly hadn't told her everything, because she is horrified to see Dad with Lilian.

'What's going on?' she says. 'Why is *she* here?'

'Long story,' I say. 'But I think Dad's going to be OK. I'm taking Mum home now; it's for the best.'

Ged and Rachel opt to come back with us, bringing the baby, while Beth and Daniel offer to stay.

Mum looks wistfully back at Dad and Lilian, who are holding hands openly now and look very much like the couple they obviously are. They must have decided there's no point pretending any longer, but it makes me cross all over again on Mum's behalf. It's so weird and unnatural to see Dad with another woman, and part of me wants to thump him. But I have to admit they look right together, even if I don't like it. I give Mum a hug.

'If it's any consolation, Mum,' I say. 'I know it won't feel like it right now, but I think you're doing the right thing.'

I'm in bits when I see Dad looking so weak and forlorn, and even more so when I find out what has been happening. How could he do this again? He promised. It's so unfair to Mum, who is being incredibly stoic, despite the effort it's clearly costing her. Lou is being amazing, taking charge and making sure Mum is OK. I am too wrecked to make any kind of coherent decision. Daniel and I promise to go back to see her when we've found out more.

Wound up with my anger is a horrible sense of guilt. I could have lost my dad today. He was in hospital while I was kissing another man. I cannot bear to think about what might have happened if I'd stayed with Jack. What would have happened if I hadn't taken that phone call?

Daniel and I tentatively go in to sit with Dad and Lilian.

'Beth, you know Lilian,' says Dad, 'and this is my son-in-law, Daniel.'

Daniel and I look at one another. There's not much else we can do but go with it.

'Hi,' I say, going to kiss Dad. 'How are you feeling?'

'Pretty rubbish,' says Dad, 'but they seem to think the old ticker's OK.'

'Well that's something.'

I don't know what to say, and neither does Daniel.

Dad clears his throat.

'I'm sorry you all had to find out like this, but Lilian and I—'

'Are clearly not over,' I say. 'Dad, you promised.' As I stare at his face, I imagine Jack leaning forward to kiss me. What have I been doing to Daniel behind his back? I'm no better than my dad. Do I really have a right to judge?

Lilian gets up as if to give us some space, but Dad stops her. 'Beth, I should never have gone back home. It was immensely foolish of me. I should have stuck to my original decision. I kidded myself I was doing the right thing, and I've only made things worse. Please understand though – no matter who I'm with, you are my family, and you mean everything to me.'

'But why did you have to lie about it, Dad? Why did you bother to move in with Mum again? I'm sorry but you and Lilian have made things ten times worse.'

'I know how bad this looks,' says Lilian, 'and your dad has tried very hard to stay away. I kept telling him he had to choose, and I was heartbroken when he chose your mum.' She looks at me nervously but I refuse to meet her eye.

'Bully for you,' I say. I really don't care how heartbroken Lilian was.

'I really was trying to do the best by everyone,' says Dad. 'I know I went about it the wrong way, but I didn't want to hurt anyone – your mum, you children. I feel like I've really stuffed up.'

He looks so sad and forlorn, some of the hardness in me melts.

'Oh Dad,' I say, tears in my eyes. We could have lost him today, and however angry I am with him, I can't bear the thought of a world without him.

'I thought I could make it work, I honestly did. Can you forgive me, Beth?'

I look at him, so small against the hospital pillows. 'I'll try,' I say.

'I know it won't be easy,' he says, 'but I'm going to move in with Lilian. I hope you can all come to terms with that eventually.'

'I don't know,' I say honestly. 'No offence, Lilian, but this isn't the sort of thing that normally happens in our family.'

'None taken,' says Lilian. 'I can understand if you don't want anything to do with me.'

I think about Daniel and his dad, and all the rage and anger he's carried around with him for years. I don't want that to happen to me and Dad. So I take the hand Lilian offers, and say, 'It's not the best introduction, but so long as you make Dad happy, that will do for me.'

Daniel

It had been a surreal evening to say the least. Daniel felt completely overwhelmed by the rapidity with which events had overtaken them, what with Fred announcing his decision to stay with Lilian. Everything was in turmoil. At least the doctors seemed to think Fred would be OK, although they were keeping him in overnight for observations as his blood pressure was still high.

'You OK about all of this?' Daniel asked Beth when they got in the car to go home.

'I have to be, don't I?' said Beth. 'Dad could have died today. I don't want to lose him.'

The subtext being *like you did with your dad*. Maybe he was just being paranoid.

They got in to discover they had a visitor: Sam was in the kitchen, cooking.

'Megan told me about Grandpa and I thought I'd come over and see if I could help out. I thought you might be hungry.'

Daniel stood still in shock, a happy shock that lifted his spirits no end. After the events of the day, the sight of his son back in his kitchen was like balm to his soul.

'Thanks for coming,' he said. 'Food would be great. Are you staying?'

'If you want?' Sam looked nonchalant, but Daniel could see he was nervous. Daniel hated the fact that he had made his son anxious in his company.

'Of course we do,' said Beth, giving Sam a hug. 'And you'll be pleased to know your grandpa is fine. They're keeping him in for observation, but he's going to be OK.'

'Good,' said Sam. 'That's great.' He looked immensely relieved and turned back to the oven, stirring a pot on the stove. Beth went off to find Megan.

'Do you fancy a beer?' said Daniel, going to get one from the fridge.

'Can't – I'm driving,' said Sam. 'I'll just text Grandad to let him know I'm staying a bit longer.'

Daniel raised his eyebrows. Sam never let them know where he was, normally pitching up hours after he was supposed to be home.

'Grandad insists,' said Sam, catching sight of Daniel's face. 'He's quite strict actually. Says he doesn't want a bum for a grandson and I should get my shit together.'

At last. Something he and Reggie agreed on.

'Right,' said Daniel.

'You should – you should try to get to know him,' said Sam. 'I know he'd like that.'

Daniel sighed. 'It's just not that easy for me,' he said. 'When I was growing up—'

'He was a shit dad,' said Sam. 'I know, but he wants to make it up to you.'

Daniel thought about what a hash he and Beth seemed to have made of parenting of late. He'd always been so sure he'd make a better dad than Reggie, and look at him now. Everyone got it wrong occasionally. Maybe it was time to find out why his dad had behaved the way he had.

'I'll think about it,' he said.

Sam gave him a small grin, and Daniel settled down with his beer, feeling happier than he'd done in weeks. Fred's hospitalisation had certainly put things into perspective.

When Beth and Megan came in, they sat down to the first family meal in a long time.

Megan whooped with delight when she saw Sam, although they were soon back to trading light-hearted sibling insults. Everything felt so natural and right, it wasn't till he went to bed that Daniel thought about where Beth had been this afternoon. She'd been out of contact for such a long time. What had she been doing? He thought about asking her, but she looked as though she was already asleep, lying curled up next to him in the bed. It had been such a long day. Perhaps he should just leave it. There'd been enough drama for one night. But as he cuddled up next to his wife, Daniel realised he couldn't leave it indefinitely. He needed to find out.

Chapter Twenty-Nine

Beth

The day after the hospital, I get up late. I've had a sleepless night, tossing and turning, going over the events of the day. I'm still feeling guilty about what happened, but I have decided one thing for certain. Dad's health scare has put everything into perspective: I made a big mistake kissing Jack. I have to put Daniel and my family first. So when Jack texts me to ask how things are, I don't respond.

Instead I go back to the hospital to see Dad, who is looking much better today. After the hustle and bustle of A&E, he's been moved into a proper ward, which feels a lot calmer. He's had his breakfast, and is wearing PJs I don't recognise. I presume Lilian's brought them in, though I don't like to think about that. There's no sign of her, for which I'm immensely grateful.

'How are you doing today?' I say.

'Better,' says Dad. 'They think it might not be my heart now.'

'Oh?'

He looks a little embarrassed.

'Apparently I had a panic attack. Brought on by severe stress.'

He looks so mortified I can't help but laugh. Mental health issues are anathema to my dad. I think he'd probably rather have had a heart attack than admit to suffering from anxiety. I remember all the turmoil I've been through in the last few months. It's made me feel downright panicky at times, so no wonder he's been anxious. Being a philanderer is not in Dad's nature.

'Has it really been that bad?' I say.

'It's been horrendous,' says Dad. 'Knowing that you were all angry with me, and rightly so. I would have been too. Then thinking I should do the right thing and going back to your mum and realising I'd made a huge mistake . . .' He sighs. 'It's hard disentangling your life. You can't just walk away from forty-two years of marriage with no consequences.'

'So you started to see Lilian again? You told me when I saw you in the pub it was all over.'

'I couldn't help myself, I'm sorry,' he says. 'I really meant what I said to you that day, but I was wrong to think I could give Lilian up. I love her. She makes me happy, and I can't make your mum happy any more. Do you understand that at all?'

'Oh I understand more than you think,' I say.

And I do. I can't tell him of course, but I know what it's like to be tempted, to wonder if the person on the other side of the fence might be a better bet than the person you're with. I made a different choice to Dad, but I could easily have taken his path. I'd be a hypocrite to judge him for it.

I take his hand, and say, 'It's not what any of us want, but Dad, we were all so frightened for you yesterday, we're just glad you're still here.'

Mum seems surprisingly chirpy in the morning. I'm amazed. I was prepared for the same sort of reaction she'd had at Christmas. When I quiz her about it, her response isn't what I'd expected.

'I'm sad, Lou, of course I am. But in a way it's a relief. I've been kidding myself for months. I know your dad's not really happy, and the only way it works is if I run around after him. That's no way to live a life.'

'No,' I say, 'no it's not.'

'It was partly seeing the way you and Jo were; it really opened my eyes,' she admits. 'The way that girl had you jumping to her tune, well, it made me see what a mug I've been. Lilian's welcome to him.'

Right. 'Well that's good,' I say. 'I'm glad you're not too upset.'

'It will take time,' Mum says, 'but I'm determined not to waste the rest of my life being unhappy. I deserve better.'

'Yes, Mum, you do,' I say, giving her a hug. I'm actually relieved too. I can see how much better Dad is with Lilian, and if Mum ends up happier too, maybe it's a good thing all round.

To my surprise, Beth has come round to the idea too. I thought she might be angrier with Dad, but she tells me about the chat they had, and says, 'Life's too short to fight, don't you think? People make mistakes.'

'You've changed your tune,' I say. 'I thought he'd be persona non grata for a while.'

'We could have lost him, Lou,' she says, 'and he's OK. That's what counts. I can't help having some sympathy for him. It can't have been easy falling in love at his age. He had so much to lose, and still he went for it.'

I look at her with suspicion.

'Is there something you're not telling me?' I ask, suddenly wary. I really thought she'd be angry with Dad. I'm surprised she's taken it this well.

'No, nothing,' she says quickly. 'I'm just looking at the bigger picture. Maybe this is for the best all round.'

I'm not quite sure I believe her. She's being very cagey about where she was yesterday. She was out of contact for a very long time.

'What happened yesterday?' I say casually. 'Neither Daniel or I could get hold of you.'

Is it my imagination or does Beth look as if she's hiding something?

'I was having a meeting that went on a lot longer than it should have,' she says quickly. 'Then they took me for lunch in a restaurant which had crap reception. I only picked up your messages just as I got to the Tube.'

The answer comes off a bit pat, as if she's rehearsed it. I have a sudden horrible thought. Suppose she's been seeing Jack? Suppose she's having an affair too? I could never have believed it of her before, but then I never could have believed it of Dad. I know how hurt Jack Stevens left her. But I also remember how obsessed she was with him back in college. Is there a part of her that still has feelings for him? I want to ask her some more, but she clams up, so I let it go. Mum and Dad are enough to deal with for now.

Daniel

'Hello, Reggie.' Daniel was actually ringing his dad. He couldn't believe he was doing it, but talking to Sam had given him pause for thought. What had happened to Fred had also given him a shock. What if something happened to Reggie and they were still estranged? In spite of everything, Daniel didn't like to think about that, so he picked up the phone to his father, his nerves jangling.

Reggie's response was cautious but warm.

'I just wondered if you fancied going for a drink,' said Daniel. His words sounded stiff and formal, but at least he'd said them.

'I'd be delighted,' Reggie said, and the pleasure in his voice came as a shock. It pulled Daniel up for a moment. He hadn't quite appreciated that his dad could be that warm.

Beth was pleased when he said he was going out. He knew she would be glad about him meeting Reggie, but his lingering doubts about her whereabouts on the previous day made him suspicious. He felt sure she was hiding something, but he didn't think he was brave enough to find out what.

Daniel got to the bar first. It was rammed, and it took ages to get served, but still he had already had a pint by the time Reggie turned up. Daniel tried not to feel irritated. When he was younger, Reggie has never turned up on time to see him either. He thought back to that ill-fated trip to the States all those years ago. He seemed to remember Reggie leaving him hanging around on his own a lot at that time, and that horrible feeling of rejection when he thought that Reggie's new family was more important then he was. A cold clutch of fear grabbed him. What if Sam had got it wrong, and Reggie was still the same? Part of him did want to see if they could renew their relationship, but the bigger part was afraid that Reggie would reject him all over again.

'Daniel,' Reggie clapped him on the back, and Daniel felt a wave of relief. He had come. 'What can I get you?'

'Another IPA, please.'

They waited awkwardly to be served before finding a quiet corner. There was a pregnant pause, before Reggie said, 'Sorry to hear about your father-in-law.'

'He's on the mend,' said Daniel. 'Luckily it was a false alarm.'

'And what about the – er – other situation?'

Sam had clearly been spilling all the family secrets.

'It seems he's going to leave Mary after all,' said Daniel. 'Which is all rather odd, but she seems to have taken it OK.'

'Always best not to interfere in these matters, I think,' said Reggie. 'My motto is stay friends with everyone and smile.'

'It is?' Daniel realised how little he knew this man. It was exactly how Daniel thought people should behave, and it felt weird to have something in common. He paused and said, 'Why did you come back, Reggie? I mean we haven't seen each other in years, and now you're here.'

'Two things,' said Reggie. 'I had a bit of a health scare a while back.'

'Oh,' Daniel didn't know what to say, Fred being ill had prompted him to this meeting, and now it turned out his own dad might be unwell. He cleared his throat. 'Are you OK now?'

'Yes, fine, fortunately,' said Reggie, 'but it got me thinking about you. You're the main reason I'm here. I want to put things right with you. I should have done it years ago, but I was too ashamed. I know I wasn't the dad I should have been for you. And believe me, I regret that with all my heart. But I never stopped thinking about you.'

'You left us,' said Daniel. 'And you were vile to Mum. I find that hard to forgive.'

'I know,' said Reggie. 'I'm older and wiser now. The situation – well, it wasn't easy. We were very young, on our own in a foreign country, with a child and no support from our families. Your mum had always wanted to be a teacher, but the only job she could get was in a laundrette. I was trying to earn money from my music. It wasn't enough and I had to take horrible temporary jobs to make ends meet. It was a difficult time. I had a temper in those days, one I'm ashamed to say I couldn't control. I'm sorry for the damage it caused you.'

Daniel felt something shift slightly inside him. He had never looked at the situation from Reggie's perspective before.

'I wasn't a good husband to your mum,' said Reggie. 'We got married too young. I was often away from home, and I neglected her. But we were happy for a while. Particularly when you were born.'

'What changed?'

'What do you think?' said Reggie. 'It's the same old story. You neglect someone long enough, and they'll go looking elsewhere.'

'So you had an affair?' It's what Daniel had always suspected. A part of him felt vindicated to finally hear his dad say it.

'Not me,' said Reggie. 'Your mum did.'

Chapter Thirty

Lou

Mum seems to be on fire since she made the decision to chuck Dad out. She's back going to her Zumba classes again, and she's been in touch with James, who seems to have forgiven her for her behaviour at the terrible lunch. She tells me he's invited her to dinner.

'Way to go, Mum,' I say. 'He's quite the silver fox.'

'I don't see why your dad should have all the fun,' says Mum, and I laugh. If you'd have told me this would be happening a year ago, I'd have never believed it. Now it's beginning to seem weirdly normal.

Over the next couple of weeks, James takes to popping over on a regular basis. He doesn't live too far away, on the other side of Wottonleigh, so it's not a schlep for him to come over. He's polite, funny and kind – and what's more, it's great to see that he makes a fuss of Mum in the way Dad never did. I even come home one day to find him cooking.

'Gosh, Mum, you seem to have found yourself a new man here,' I joke.

'We widowers have to learn how to cater for ourselves you know,' says James. 'I'm not entirely useless.'

'I never said you were,' I say. He's far from useless; I'm beginning to think he's the best thing to happen to Mum in a long while. After all the years of fussing over everyone else, it's nice to see her being looked after. Plus she hasn't even mentioned Christmas yet. Which *is* weird. We've normally been discussing the festive season for months by now.

'It's really odd, isn't it?' says Beth. 'I never thought I'd miss the Christmas Conversation, but I can't quite get my head round what's going to happen this year.'

'Best we leave it up to her,' I say. I for one am all for putting it off as long as possible. I'm hoping that if things work out with Maria, I might have plans this Christmas, and for once they don't involve my family.

Maria and I are Skyping even more regularly now. She's thrilled I'm coming back to Tenerife, and having let her know how things stand with Jo, we're having light-hearted but definitely flirty conversations.

'I can say it now,' she teases, 'but I don't think Jo was right for you. I think you need a nice Spanish girl.'

'Maybe I do,' I respond.

'We will have to find out when you come to Tenerife, won't we?' she says, laughing in a way that makes me feel warm all over.

It's easy talking to Maria; she makes me feel good about myself, and doesn't seem to want anything in return. I've never had that before. It's also weird only being able to talk on the internet, as in the past I've always dived straight into the physical side of things first. Maybe that's been my mistake. I'm really getting to know Maria this way, and I'm liking her more and more.

I'm beginning to feel hopeful about my future for the first time in years. Maybe, *finally*, I might be starting to live the life I was meant to live.

Dad has been out of hospital for a couple of weeks, but I've only just plucked up the courage to go and see him and Lilian. They're living together now, and despite what I said in the hospital, I'm feeling nervous and twitchy. While I've accepted the situation has to be this way, I don't have to like it. It's going to be weird to see Dad with Lilian, and I'm not sure if I'll be able to deal with it.

Lilian is as far removed from Mum as could be possible. I hadn't really taken much notice of her in the hospital, but I'm fascinated to see that in her home environment she is very arty-farty, wafting around in a kaftan and big scarves. Her pictures are on the walls, and I have to admit they are rather good. The house is in chaos, in a way Mum would never stand, but seems to suit Dad. She's also very discreet, disappearing into the kitchen as soon as I arrive to give me some time alone with him.

'Are you really OK, Dad?'

He's sitting in the lounge with a blanket over him in the middle of the day. I'm quite shocked; he's normally so active. But now I think about it, Mum would never have allowed him to sit around all day, 'getting under her feet' as she put it.

'Yes, I am,' he says. 'It was just the stress of the situation that got to me.'

'I imagine leading a double life would do that to you,' I say, the words popping out of my mouth before I can think about them. I'm one to talk.

Dad winces.

'Touché, Beth, but I probably deserved that. But you have to understand I never planned any of this. Neither did Lilian. I know you probably think we're a pair of old farts, but you're never too old to fall in love. We can't help the way we feel about one another, and we never set out to hurt anyone. I'm no good to your mum if I resent being with her. Besides, I'm sick of the secrecy. I'm sorry if you don't like it, but that's the way it's going to be.'

I'm saved from replying by Lilian, who comes in bringing tea. I can see she treats him differently to the way Mum always has; she's more gentle with him, but she doesn't take any nonsense either. They have a real sense of mutual respect between them; it shines out of them both. And then it hits me. This is what I have with Daniel. It's what I've always had, and I've nearly risked it on a foolish dream. I put down my tea cup with a clatter. I need to go home to my husband and start putting our relationship right.

Daniel

Over a fortnight later and Daniel was still reeling from Reggie's revelation. His God-fearing, church-going mother had had an affair? It didn't seem possible. Mum who had been so loving, so gentle, so trustworthy. How could she have done that to Reggie, to him? He felt sick. A lifetime of assumptions had just been turned on its head. He had been so shocked at the time that he hadn't thought to ask Reggie any pertinent questions. So one afternoon, when Beth had gone round to see her dad, he popped round to see Reggie. He finally felt ready to deal with the truth.

'I need to know what happened,' he said. 'All of it.'

'I came home one day and found them,' said Reggie. 'I kicked the guy out, we had an enormous row. Your mum begged my forgiveness, and I tried, I really did. But I went a bit crazy to be honest. I'm not proud of the way I behaved, but I couldn't get rid of the jealousy I felt. I was so angry with your mum all the time. I'm sorry that it affected you so badly.'

Daniel felt as though he'd had the wind taken out of him. That explained such a lot. The rows, the bitterness, the anger.

'It did affect me,' he said. 'I'm sorry, but it really did. I was terrified of you.'

'I can see that now,' sighed Reggie. 'I was too lost to see it at the time. I think your generation is better than ours was at dealing with the fallout from these things. If I could turn the clock back I would. I never wanted you to be afraid of me, Daniel. I loved you. I always have.'

For the first time, Daniel started to properly see things from his dad's point of view. How would he feel if Beth ever did that to him? He shivered at the thought. He thought about the way Beth had been with Jack at her birthday party. He wondered if he were right to feel so suspicious. There was definitely a frisson of something there. He knew he wasn't imagining it, and just recently he'd noticed too that Beth was constantly checking her phone. She seemed to send more texts than she used to as well. He couldn't believe she'd ever cheat on him, but he'd never have believed it of his mum. What if Beth *were* doing the same to him?

When Daniel got back to the house, Beth was still out. Idly he noticed that she'd left her mobile, lying on the island in the middle of the kitchen. Daniel swallowed, staring at it. He never normally looked at her phone. Why would he? Most of her messages were about the kids, or to her friends. But for some reason, he felt like checking it now. It would put his mind at rest. He knew he was being stupid, but he couldn't resist it. There was going to be nothing there. It would be fine. Ignoring the guilt in the back of his mind, he scrolled quickly down her messages, looking for the name Jack. He couldn't find him at first, and then he saw a couple of messages under the name 'College Jack'. Heart beating, he clicked on them, but they were all work-related texts, nothing terrible. He breathed a sigh of relief. He was being foolish. And that's when the phone pinged.

Haven't heard from you. Please don't be cross with me. Can't wait to see you. xxx It was from College Jack.

Daniel felt sick. He sat down at the table with a heavy heart. Oh no. Not Beth. He stared at the text message for what seemed like hours. Something was clearly going on, and Beth hadn't told him. His worst fears had come true.

The key turned in the lock, and she came in. Looking beautiful, ethereal, bloody wonderful. But, it seemed, she was in love with someone else.

'Daniel,' said Beth, 'we need to talk.'

'I know we do,' said Daniel, passing over the phone. 'You can begin by explaining this.'

Chapter Thirty-One

Beth

Oh shit. Daniel looks absolutely furious. He's holding my phone and I can only imagine that Jack has been in touch. My heart stops.

'It's not what it looks like.' I swallow nervously.

'What is it like then?' Daniel sounds bitter, and I can't blame him.

'I've – I'm—'

'God, how the pair of you must have been laughing at me behind my back. Were you with him when your dad was ill?'

'Daniel, please, please listen,' I say, beginning to panic. 'Yes, I was attracted to Jack. He turned up out of the blue, and I don't know, it was as though he reconnected me to the person I used to be.'

'I see,' says Daniel coldly. 'So being married to me has suppressed you then, has it?'

'No – it's just that I knew Jack when life was less complicated.'

'Are you in love with him?'

'I was. When I was *twenty*. I thought we were meant for each other and he broke my heart. Daniel, then I met you and I realised Jack meant nothing, and you were the real deal. You were kind and considerate and made me feel good about myself. Jack never did that. I fell in love with *you*, Daniel, I *am* in love with you.'

'If that's the case, what is this text about? Why have you even been going near him?'

Oh God, how can I explain it to him, when I can barely explain to myself the way I've been behaving for the last few months?

'Stupidity?' I say weakly. 'Jack burst back into my life unexpectedly, and I've allowed myself to be momentarily dazzled. I'm not proud of myself, but it's you I love. It's always been you.'

'How can I believe a word you say?' says Daniel. 'You always said Jack Stevens meant nothing to you. Have you slept with him?'

'When I was a student, yes. But now, no, of course not. I'm not in love with Jack, Daniel. I think I fell in love with a fantasy. He's always been a bit of a shit, and he hasn't changed. I'm sorry I haven't been honest with you. I should have told you when I met you. But he made me so unhappy, and I was so ashamed of how pathetic I was around him, I just wanted that part of my life behind me.'

'You could have told me,' says Daniel.

'I know, I should have,' I say. 'I can see that now. I'm so sorry that this happened. I never wanted to hurt you, I just got a bit lost back there for a while, and we've not been getting on well and . . .'

'This isn't my fault,' says Daniel, looking incredulous. 'Don't you dare lay it on me.'

'No, I know,' I say, 'but you have your secrets too, and it doesn't help.'

'What's that supposed to mean?'

'Your dad. You've been so secretive about him. I know you've told me some things, but you push me away when I try to talk to you.'

'That's different,' says Daniel angrily.

'Is it?' I say. 'If my behaviour has caused problems, yours has driven our son away. We need to be open with one another. I'm trying to tell you the truth. I've been tempted by Jack, I'll admit it, but I haven't been unfaithful to you.'

'Have you kissed him?'

I can't look at him. I want to deny it, to put it behind me, but I know I have to 'fess up or it will never go away.

'Yes, just once. I'm not proud of myself. We'd been rowing such a lot, and I was confused, and—'

'This is not my fault,' says Daniel again, throwing his hands up into the air. 'I have never so much as looked at another woman since we've been together. I can't believe you would do this to me.'

'Daniel,' I say, 'I made a foolish mistake and I'm profoundly sorry. But I chose you. I will always choose you.'

'Maybe that's not enough any more,' says Daniel. 'I'm going out.'

Tears are forming in my eyes, threatening to overflow. 'Where?' I ask.

'I have no idea,' says Daniel.

'Daniel, don't go,' I beg, reaching out to grab his arm. He shakes me off angrily.

'I can't stay here,' he says. 'Don't wait up.'

Lou

Beth is hysterical when she rings me. She and Daniel have had a major row and it sounds serious. I pop in the car and go right over. It's so unusual for my together sister to be crying on my shoulder; it's always been the other way around.

'What the hell's going on?' I demand. 'Please don't tell me this is something to do with Jack?'

'Yes,' says Beth. 'Daniel found a text from him on my phone and he's got the wrong idea.'

'But you haven't done anything, right?' Surely she wouldn't have been so stupid?

'I kissed him,' she admits, looking distraught.

'Oh Beth, you idiot.'

'You don't have to tell me,' says Beth. 'It was the day of Dad's panic attack. That's why I was late to the hospital. I pulled back and told him it couldn't happen again. I haven't seen him since.'

She pours the whole story out. How ever since she met Jack again she hasn't been able to stop thinking about him. How she kept thinking of the life she never had. I can scarcely believe it. I never imagined that Beth could have done something so foolish, especially after the conversation we'd had.

'I think I was in love with a fantasy as much as anything else,' she says. 'When I think about it logically, there's no way I could ever choose Jack over Daniel. That's why I put him behind me in the first place.'

'You can't blame Daniel for being angry,' I say.

'I know,' says Beth. 'This is all my fault. I got carried away. I can't believe I've been so stupid.'

'Oh Beth, you'll work it out. You've been together such a long time. This is a blip, surely? Daniel will calm down, and realise that it's not such a big deal.'

'You didn't see the way he looked at me,' said Beth. She's so distraught. Her eyes are red-rimmed from crying and lack of sleep. 'I don't know if we can ever get through this.'

301

'You can't believe that, surely?' I am so shocked. Daniel and Beth can't split up, they just can't. 'It will blow over in time. In a few months you'll be looking back and wondering what the fuss has been about.'

'I hope so,' says Beth. 'I really hope so.'

Daniel

Daniel drove and drove. He couldn't make sense of what had happened. Beth had nearly had an affair. His mum *had* had an affair. The two women he loved most in the world had lied to him. He couldn't take it in. It was as if the edifice on which he had built his whole life was crumbling away. He had clung to the idea that Reggie was a nasty bastard for so long, and the break-up was all his fault, it was a shock to discover it wasn't as clear-cut as that. And then Beth. The way she had made him feel tonight . . . he had never felt so angry in his life. Is that what it had been like for Reggie? No wonder he had sought solace in drink. The temptation to do the same was immense. Although what good would that do?

Eventually, after hours on the road, he turned around and went home. This wasn't solving anything.

He got back to a house in darkness. Beth had clearly gone to bed. He wondered uneasily if Megan had heard anything of their row. He'd seen enough kids at school with family problems to know how much damage they caused, and she'd been upset enough recently. But he needed to process this, and he couldn't yet find it in him to forgive Beth. He just didn't know what he was going to do. He was so angry with her, and so hurt that he couldn't see his way clearly. He couldn't see how they were ever going to be able to move on from this. The thought of her kissing Jack made him feel physically sick.

He went into their room to find Beth lying in the dark, staring miserably at the ceiling.

'Thank God,' she said, sitting up as he walked in. 'Are you OK? You didn't answer any of my texts. I was starting to worry.'

'Really?' Daniel's answer was more sarcastic then he'd intended.

'Daniel, please,' said Beth. 'Can't we try to work it out?'

'I can't,' said Daniel. 'Not now. I'm going to sleep in the spare room, and tomorrow I'll go and stay with Josh and Helen for a bit.'

'Daniel—'

'Don't,' said Daniel. 'We've both said enough for one night.' He turned away, trying not to see the distress in Beth's eyes. He couldn't afford to. He went down the hallway and lay in the spare room, staring into the darkness, wondering how on earth his life had gone so spectacularly wrong.

Chapter Thirty-Two

Lou

I am brimming over with excitement for the future. I've booked my flight to Tenerife and Maria is meeting me at the airport. For the first time in a long while, I feel my life is full of possibilities. My contract is coming to an end, and I've decided to take some time out before doing anything new. The one benefit of living at home all these months is that I've actually been able to save. I think Mum's quite glad to see the back of me. I suspect she has some dinners à deux planned for her and James, who she seems to be getting on with better and better. I think I cramp her style. Dad, meanwhile, seems to have his feet firmly under the table at Lilian's. I'm glad now. I think both he and Mum are happier apart. I just wish they'd found the courage to do it when they were younger.

The only blot on the horizon is Beth and Daniel. Daniel has moved out and refuses to speak to Beth, who is distraught. I cannot believe the perfect life I thought she had has imploded in such a spectacular way. Beth is literally falling apart in front of my eyes. I've never seen her like this before. I've spent nearly every day of the last week at her house, talking in whispers so Megan doesn't hear. Though of course she knows something horrible is happening.

'I know they always tell you to be honest with your children,' says Beth, 'but I can't tell her the truth, I can't. What will she think of me? She'll hate me. And I can't bear to think of her hating me too.'

'Daniel doesn't hate you.'

'Oh no?' says Beth. 'I think he does right now.'

I offer to take her to Tenerife, but she says she can't leave Megan in term time, and I can tell she doesn't want to come anyway.

I'm so worried about her; she's lost a lot of weight. Seeing strong, dependable Beth in such a state is something I never expected. It seems weird too, that this is happening to her just when my life is suddenly improving. I'm feeling guilty about leaving her, but she's insisting I go.

She takes me to the airport to see me off, and we go for a cup of coffee before I get my flight.

'Thanks so much for the lift,' I say.

'It gives me something to do,' she says. 'Less time to mope around.'

'Oh, Beth,' I say. 'I feel bad about leaving you at a time like this.'

'Don't be silly,' she says. 'You deserve this. Really Lou, I'm genuinely happy for you.'

She's so generous. I know she's been stupid, but it's awful seeing her suffer like this.

I reach out and give her a hug. 'I wish things weren't so awful for you at the moment.'

Beth smiles weakly, 'It can only get better, right?'

'Will you be OK?' I ask.

'Eventually,' she says. 'Now please, don't worry about me. I want you to go off and have a fabulous time. And I want to hear all about it.'

'I wish you were coming with me,' I say. And I mean it. For so many years I have envied my big sister, and now I can see she's struggled as much as I have, just in different ways.

'Maybe next time,' she says. 'Now, go on, woman. Or you'll miss your plane.'

I hug her again, and set off through customs with a tingling sense of anticipation. I'm taking charge of my destiny. Life, here I come.

Daniel

Daniel's day was not going well. He had a crick in his neck from lying on Josh's sofa for the seventh night in a row and had barely slept. Two of his teaching staff had just announced they were pregnant, and a third had had to be disciplined for speaking inappropriately to a Year Ten boy. Normally he'd brush it off as part of the job, but right now, it felt like he couldn't cope with the burden of running a school. He almost wished he was a junior teacher again, with a fraction of the responsibility. He hadn't confided in any of his colleagues either, though Carrie Woodall was looking at him in a worried kind of way. Turning up at work looking exhausted with bloodshot eyes every day was a bit of a giveaway that something was wrong. But he couldn't bring himself to tell anyone. He felt too much of a failure. He dreaded to think what Jim Ferguson would have to say if he found out the Head's home life was in such a catastrophic situation.

As for Beth, he was doing his best not to think about her. It was easier that way. If he let his thoughts dwell on her he just kept picturing her with Jack, and it was too much to handle. She'd said nothing had happened beyond a kiss, but that was bad enough. She'd clearly been lying to him about Jack all along. How could he trust that what she said now was true?

He and Josh had been for a couple of beery, lads-only bonding sessions, and ended up mainly talking about work. On the one occasion they had discussed the burning issue of the day, they hadn't solved anything. Josh was very straightforward.

'If it were Helen, I'd ditch her,' he said.

'Really?' Daniel saw where he was coming from, but it seemed a bit of a drastic route to take. He needed time to think about it. 'I think it's more complicated than that.'

'No, it's not,' said Josh. 'She lied to you. How can you trust her now?'

And that was Daniel's problem: he couldn't, but he also couldn't imagine a life without Beth in it. She had been his world for so long, and he didn't want to lose her. He just couldn't see a way forward, and confiding in Josh about it wasn't helping.

So he'd stopped talking about it and got drunk instead. It was one way of easing the pain, but Daniel knew that it wasn't the answer. Nor was staying on Josh's sofa. He had to pull himself together, make an effort to focus at work and figure out where he was going to live in the long term. He couldn't stay with Josh permanently. It wasn't fair on him, Helen and the children – they might be enjoying the novelty of having Uncle Daniel in the house for now, but he knew they would soon get fed up of it. And he was conscious he was getting under Helen's feet. But could he go back home? Beth kept asking, but he wasn't ready for that yet. He just didn't know what to do.

So it was with some relief that he received a text from Reggie at the end of the day. *Hear things are rocky at home? You're always welcome here.* They'd only spoken a couple of times since the last time they'd met, but Sam had clearly filled him in on what was happening.

Daniel paused. Maybe that's what he should do. Beth had always accused him of not giving his dad a chance. In light of everything, Reggie was the only person right now who might actually understand what he was going through, which felt ironic to say the least. *Ok*, he texted cautiously. *And thank you.*

Beth

I have drawn two spreads of my new book. My little angel is staring out of the page at me in an accusing fashion. As well she might. I feel so ashamed of myself. Not only did I basically cheat on my husband, but my fifteen-year-old daughter is a mess because of it. She keeps asking why Daniel and Sam have both left us, and I have no answers. I can't bring myself to tell her the truth. How has it come to this? I feel like my family has fractured. I cannot see how we will ever heal.

The only thing going right is my work. *The Littlest Angel* has sold really well into the bookshops, and Vanessa tells me there's a great buzz around it. I should be thrilled. Any other time I would be. But without being able to share it with Daniel, my success feels hollow.

More and more now, I look at my infatuation with Jack in utter disbelief. I cannot believe I fell under his spell again so easily. He hasn't changed. He's never really cared about me. He just likes the chase. Now that I've made it clear that he really has overstepped the mark, he's stopped texting me. I don't even miss him. What does that say about me? I put my marriage in jeopardy for a dream. How could I have been so stupid?

I've heard on the grapevine that he's seeing one of the girls in marketing at Smart Books. Well, good luck to her. I've blocked him from my phone and email – something I should have done weeks ago.

Daniel has been home once to pick up some things. He's staying with Reggie, which is something, I suppose. At least he might be able to repair their relationship, and he's with Sam. But he doesn't want to see me, and it's a bitter pill to swallow. Once, I'd have said nothing could tear us apart. Now, Christmas is nearly here and it's making me sad. I love this time of year, all the build-up and expectation, even with the fact that we're going to Mum and Dad's. Christmas is such a special time in our family, and I can't bear the thought of trying to get through it without Daniel.

Normally by now I would be buying cards and wrapping paper, and even starting to look out for presents. I would be looking forward to carol concerts at school, and planning a few social evenings with mulled wine and mince pies. But this year I am all at sea. My family is broken and I don't know how to put it back together. I've managed to destroy all the trust that was between us, and I've only myself to blame.

Chapter Thirty-Three

Daniel

Life at Reggie's was odd. He and Sam were obviously in a good routine, and Daniel envied their easy banter. They joshed endlessly about music, Reggie being of the opinion that anything after 1975 wasn't worth listening to, Sam teasing him by telling him the lyrics of the rap artists he loved.

'That's downright disgusting,' Reggie would tell Sam, while Sam would laugh and say, 'It's better than your old-man music.'

Daniel listened to them jamming together with renewed respect for his son's musical abilities. Sam had taken to joining Reggie on stage occasionally for his gigs, but the rest of the time he was working behind the bar in the local pub, Reggie having insisted on him getting some sort of job. Daniel wished he could join in with their friendship, but he felt like a stiff and awkward outsider. Sam had tried to find out what was going on with his parents, but Daniel felt unable to tell him. It was all such a mess.

Work was the only thing that was keeping him going. He was focussing as hard as he could on doing his job, to shut out the pain of what was happening at home. Most of the time it worked. Although there had been a day when he'd ended up bawling out a bunch of Year Sevens for being in the wrong place, and then felt awful for not having dealt with the situation more gently. Carrie Woodall had found him sitting in his office with his head in his hands, and he'd ended up confiding in her. She was discreetly supportive, and had advised him not to make any rash decisions.

She was right, Daniel knew that. For all that he was angry with Beth, he knew at least some of the situation was down to him. He'd made a mess of all the most important relationships in his life; all of them apart from Megan. Thank God for Megan. She tried to see him most days, and if she didn't she would send him funny Snapchat stories. He loved her for it. He hadn't explained to either Sam or Megan why he'd moved out yet; however angry he was with Beth, he didn't want them judging her. So Megan was puzzled about why he wasn't coming home.

'But what about Christmas?' she kept saying. 'You have to be home for Christmas.'

Christmas? The thought of Christmas made him want to cry. It had always been such a happy family time, all his married life – until last year. The idea of not spending Christmas with Beth or the children was horrific. He couldn't even bear to think about it. Christmas was a vast, unknowable distance away. Who knew what would have happened by then?

He missed Beth badly but couldn't bring himself to talk to her. His pride wouldn't allow it. Whatever he did, he couldn't get beyond the thought of her kissing Jack and the thought of what might have happened if it had gone further. He worried constantly that she hadn't told him the whole truth and even now was seeing Jack behind his back. He felt sick to the stomach every time he thought about it

After a week, Reggie insisted on taking Daniel for a drink. Daniel hadn't told him what had happened; he was too embarrassed by the position he found himself in.

'So are you going to tell me what's going on with you and that lovely lady of yours?' said Reggie the moment they'd sat down.

Direct hit, Reggie. Well done.

Daniel sighed.

'Like you said. The same old story. She cheated on me. Well, I think she did.'

When he actually started to talk about it, Daniel began to wonder if he was being a tad overdramatic. Beth had confessed to kissing Jack. That was all. She said she'd been tempted but hadn't followed it through. That counted for something, didn't it? If he could trust her, that is.

'And why do you think she did it?' Reggie probed.

'I have no idea,' said Daniel. 'She said something about feeling trapped by domesticity. I don't know, I thought we were happy.'

'But something must have gone wrong,' Reggie said gently. 'Beth doesn't strike me as the kind to be unfaithful. She must have had her reasons.'

'I guess she wasn't happy with me,' Daniel said. It hit him dull and squarely in the chest. That old feeling of not being good enough.

'You know, son,' said Reggie. 'There are two people in every marriage. Had you been paying her enough attention?'

Daniel bristled. 'Of course I had. I adore Beth. All I've ever wanted to do was make her happy.'

'So none of this is your fault?' Reggie was remorseless.

'She lied to me, Reggie,' said Daniel. 'She kept things from me.'

'And you've never kept things from her?'

'This isn't like you and Mum,' Daniel said coldly. 'I've been a good husband and I don't deserve this.'

'Maybe not,' said Reggie. 'But what are you going to do about it?'

Beth

The days rumble on and still Daniel doesn't come home. Megan reports that he looks tired and Reggie's house is in squalor.

'I think you should go round and sort them out,' she says. 'Honestly, they live like pigs.'

I smile wanly at her not-so-subtle attempt to get me to see Daniel, but the next day I decide to take matters into my own hands, pluck up my courage and go to Reggie's house.

I arrive before Daniel gets home from work. Walking up the path I can hear Sam playing with his grandad. Well, whatever else is going on in our lives right now, I'm grateful for this relationship. I'm glad Reggie is helping Sam. They sound great together.

I knock on the door tentatively and Reggie lets me in, giving me a great big bear hug, followed by Sam. God, how I miss my boys.

'Music sounds great,' I say. I follow them into the lounge, where last night's pizza boxes litter the floor, along with coffee cups and beer cans.

Why oh why can't men living together be tidy?

'Anyone caught anything yet?' I ask as I gingerly lift a mouldy mug away from me. I'm not sure I want to sit down. The sofa is horribly sticky.

Reggie laughs. 'If I'd known you were coming I'd have cleared up.'

'Yeah, I bet.'

'Tea?' he asks.

I don't really want one judging by the state of the mugs, but it seems impolite to refuse. I follow Sam into the kitchen, which is barely better than the lounge. The sink is piled high with plates and the oven looks like it was cleaned some time in the last century.

'Honestly, Sam, how can you live like this? If you're going to sponge off your grandad, the least you can do is keep the place clean. Right – gloves and cleaning materials out, now.'

It's been a point of pride to me to make both my kids responsible and tidy, and Sam seems to be sliding backwards. He grumbles a bit but gets down to it.

'You don't have to do this,' says Reggie.

'Take it as a thank you for looking after this lazy lump here,' I say. It's a good way to soothe my nerves. I'm so anxious about seeing Daniel again, my heart is hammering in my chest. Maybe I'm getting panic attacks, too.

By the time he gets in, the flat is in some semblance of decent shape. Daniel doesn't realise I'm there at first, because I'm still in the kitchen.

'Have the fairies been?' he asks.

'Only this one,' I say, appearing at the door.

'Oh,' says Daniel. I have no idea what that means. Reggie and Sam make themselves scarce and I follow Daniel into the lounge.

'Daniel,' I say, deciding to get straight to the point, 'Christmas is coming. And our family feels like it's been ripped apart. Can we fix this?'

'I don't know,' says Daniel. He looks exhausted and sad. I go over to him and tentatively put my hand on his shoulder. He doesn't pull away.

'Please,' I say, 'come home for Christmas. I miss you.'

Daniel rubs his eyes. 'I'll see.' He stares at me. 'Every time I think of you, all I can see is him. Jack. I can't stand it, and I don't know if I can get over it.'

I feel so terrible when I see the hurt in his eyes. I did this to him. *I* did. I have never felt so bad about myself in my life.

'We've both kept things from each other, Daniel,' I say. 'It would have been better if we'd been honest from the start. Maybe now everything's out in the open we . . . we can move on?'

I say this more with hope than expectation. It sounds lame. Why should Daniel agree with me? He looks at me with tears in his eyes, and I feel another wave of guilt. I have ruined everything between us, and for what? A hopeless dream that could never have been reality.

'I'm sorry, Beth, I'm not ready to do that yet.'

It's what I've expected him to say, but still, I feel a dull thud of pain as I realise he means it. What if he never comes back, what do I do then?

'Daniel—' I say.

'Beth, please go,' says Daniel. 'I'll think about Christmas. But I'm not ready to come home.'

Chapter Thirty-Four

Lou

I arrive back home after my fortnight in Tenerife full of *joie de vivre*. Being with Maria has opened my eyes up to what relationships should be like. We've had so much fun together. We took a trip up to Mount Teide, with her driving – it was so lovely and restful. We went swimming every day, and she even took me fishing on her uncle's boat.

'You are a natural,' she teased me when more by luck than judgement I managed to make my first catch.

'I have a great teacher,' I responded, and kissed her.

It all felt so natural and right. I'm not on edge with Maria, in the way I often was with Jo. I don't have to pretend to be something I'm not.

Maria gets me totally. She gives me space. She laughs at my jokes. I loved every minute of being with her. As soon as I waved her goodbye I had an aching hole of missing her. I've never ever felt like this in a relationship before, and I've made an important decision. The more I think about it, the more I want to go back to join her in Tenerife. Maria wanted me to stay longer, but I've decided to come home and sort my life out first. Then I'm going to fly back before Christmas and move in with Maria. In one way it feels risky; everything has happened so fast. In another, it somehow feels like the perfect thing to do.

So I'm feeling chirpy when I get back to Mum's at 9 a.m. I didn't ask Beth to pick me up because my flight landed at seven, so I got myself a cab instead.

I hear voices in the kitchen as I open the front door.

Beth is here. She's in pieces.

She hasn't been in contact much since I've been away, I think she didn't want me worrying about her, but I know that Daniel hasn't budged an inch.

'Love, you need to give him time,' Mum is saying. 'He's stubborn and you've hurt his pride. Men hate that. But he'll come round. You'll see.'

I wonder if she's right. The sulk Daniel has been in has gone on for several weeks now.

I give Beth a hug.

'Welcome home, Lou,' she says, holding onto me tightly. 'How was it?'

'Fantastic,' I say, 'but we're not talking about me. We need to sort you and Daniel out. Mum's right. You two are made for each other.'

Beth gives me a watery smile.

'I used to think so,' she says wistfully. 'But that's before I cocked things up so spectacularly. He won't speak to me at all. I don't know what to do.'

'Oh Beth,' I give her another hug. I had hoped Daniel would have come round by now.

'What about Christmas?' I say. 'Surely he's going to come home for Christmas.'

Beth gives a helpless little shrug, 'I honestly don't know, Lou.'

Christmas is fast approaching. I cannot imagine how it's going to be this year. Different, that's for sure.

'Talking of Christmas, what is happening this year?' I need to get my two pennyworth in about my own plans. I'm not sure how Mum will take the news that I'm not planning to be there.

Mum has been strangely quiet on the subject. But it's been a strange year.

'I want to spend it with James,' says Mum. 'And I don't want to be in charge.'

Crikey. Words I never thought I'd hear my mum say.

'You're welcome to come to us,' says Beth. She looks defeated. 'I know it won't be the same, but at least I'll have Megan and Sam there. You and James could come too.'

The thought of a new and different family Christmas with all those exposed emotions fills me with horror, and it confirms the decision I've already made.

'Actually, I've been meaning to talk to you,' I say. I take a deep breath, crossing my fingers that no one will get upset. 'This might come as a bit of a shock, but Maria wants me to go and live with her in Tenerife – permanently. I've just come home to sort a few things out and then I'm going back. So I won't be here at Christmas.'

I await the inevitable *how can you leave your family at Christmas?* response from Mum. She's going to be so cross with me, but it's time I lived the life I want to live. But to my surprise the anger doesn't come.

'Oh Lou,' she says, 'that's wonderful. I'm so happy for you.'

And with that she envelops me in a warm and heartfelt hug.

Beth

With everything that's been going on, I've been putting Christmas on the back-burner. I am dimly aware that the festive season is starting to get underway, and I haven't even started shopping yet. But Mum's got me thinking. I can't sit and feel sorry for myself forever. Megan and Sam deserve better. Even though Lou can't come, I press Mum to see if she and James will come over for lunch at least.

'As long as it's not too early,' she says, which is a bit rich considering how early she always makes us come to her.

I've asked Rachel, Ged and the baby too. I need a crowd to hide the emptiness I'm feeling. I even ask Dad and Lilian. Well, in for a penny in for a pound. It's going to be weird enough anyway. I text Reggie to ask him too. Maybe if he comes, Daniel will join us. But I haven't had an answer yet.

On a cold, grey day in late November, I set off for the shopping centre in Wottonleigh. Everywhere is looking festive, and carols are playing in all the shops. Santa's grotto has been set up in the centre of the shopping mall, and a queue of excited children has formed to go and meet him. I feel a pang, remembering the times I used to take Sam and Megan to see Santa when they were small. Sam once had a huge paddy because he got a Transformer toy when he wanted Spiderman. I was mortified, and thought I had reached the nadir of horrible parenting moments. Little did I know.

Lights are twinkling on and off in the shops, and the mall is heaving with people carrying bags crammed full of presents and wrapping paper. Normally I throw myself into the Christmas shopping, but I have no appetite for it this year. There are copies of *The Littlest Angel* everywhere, and a proud display from our local bookshop for a signing session I agreed to do months ago but I now wish I could avoid. The book is doing so well, but not being able to share the moment with Daniel is breaking my heart. Megan is very enthusiastic about it, but it's not the same.

I am mooching around the shops, utterly uninspired

319

about presents, listening to the Christmas tunes belting out and wishing I were feeling more festive, when I catch sight of Daniel. My heart stops for a moment. He is standing staring into a window display and he looks so lost and lonely that I want to go and hug him, but I daren't. I'm so nervous. What if he ignores me? I don't think I could bear it. To my huge relief, he doesn't. He gives me a faint smile, so I seize the moment and ask if he wants a Starbucks Caramel Brûlée. It's always our thing when we come Christmas shopping.

'OK,' he says, and we go to queue up inside.

'How's everything?' I try to remain polite, neutral.

'Fine. I'm getting on better with Reggie, you'll be pleased to know.'

I am. At least one good thing has come out of this mess.

We sit down in a corner of Starbucks, and neither of us say a word. Daniel is avoiding my eye. He sips his drink fast, and looks like he's dying to go. How has it come to this? We've been together for so long, and we were so happy. I think back to when the children were born, and Daniel brought me flowers in the hospital. He was so thrilled to be a dad. We made a great team; has that really all gone because of one stupid kiss?

'Daniel, I'm so sorry,' I say. I lean over to reach for his hand, but he withdraws it, and I feel a little lurch of hurt.

'I'm sorry too. But I'm not sure it's enough.'

'Daniel, please.' I want him to say it's all right, I want him to say we can get through this, but he doesn't. He doesn't say anything. Oh God. I've made such a terrible mistake and I've driven him away.

'I'm sorry,' I say again. I don't know what else to say. Tears are filling my eyes, threatening to splash into my drink. 'If I could take it back I would.'

320

'I know,' he says, but his eyes are sad, and my heart drops to the floor. I've been kidding myself. I thought we could get over this, but it's clear that I've hurt Daniel too badly. He obviously doesn't want me back any more. I have to face it. I have to let him go.

Daniel

Daniel saw Beth before she saw him. He'd been thinking long and hard since their last meeting. Christmas alone with Reggie didn't seem very appealing; he wondered whether he should at least go home for Christmas Day. A year ago he couldn't have imagined being in this situation, but here they were.

He walked over to Beth, not sure if she'd reject him. He'd hardly been welcoming the last time he saw her. He was relieved that she didn't brush him off and eagerly accepted her offer of coffee.

The Christmas musak played incessantly, causing a dull throb in Daniel's head. Normally he loved the magic of Christmas. As a small child many of his Christmases had been sad and lonely, despite his Mum's efforts. But once he had been part of Beth's clan, it had all changed. He was welcomed into her family and loved the ritual of the season, the time spent together, the sharing of presents. Once the children came along it only got better. He had loved the years of pretending to be Santa, putting out mince pies and carrots for Rudolph, filling up their stockings in secret. He hadn't even minded being woken early; it had all been worth it to see the joy on the kids' faces. He couldn't bear the thought of not being with his family on Christmas Day.

Beth seemed nervous, as if there was something on her mind. Daniel tried to pluck up the courage to say he was sorry, but found he couldn't, so he sat in silence, brooding. Beth kept apologising to him, tears in her eyes, and he knew he should say something, but he didn't know how. Daniel wanted so badly to tell her that he forgave her, but somehow the words stuck in his throat. He could hardly bear to look at the disappointment in her eyes, so he focussed on his drink instead. Why couldn't he open his heart to her? What was wrong with him?

Belatedly Daniel tuned in to hear Beth asking a question.

'So will you come?' she asked. 'You and Reggie? For Christmas Day? It would mean such a lot to the children.'

He wished she'd said it would mean something to her as well. Had he pushed her away? What if he'd sent Beth straight back to Jack? He wanted to ask her how she felt, but couldn't find the words.

'You don't have to stay, and I understand that after Christmas we need to sort things out properly, but can we at least be civilised about it?'

What?

'Beth, what are you saying?' Daniel stuttered. He was stunned. Of all things, he hadn't expected this.

'I'm giving you an opt-out,' she said. 'After Christmas I imagine you'll want to move out permanently. But please, let's keep it civil for the kids. It's the least we can do.'

What? Daniel hadn't expected that at all. He felt sick. Surely this couldn't really be happening? Thanks to his own stubbornness, had he lost his wife?

Chapter Thirty-Five

Beth

'You said *what* to Daniel?' Mum is appalled when I tell her my decision. 'What on earth were you thinking of saying that?'

'I was thinking about you and Dad,' I say. 'You couldn't make it work after all the time you spent together, so what chance do Daniel and I have?'

'A much better one than your father and I had,' says Mum firmly. 'You and Daniel have something we never did: a loving, respectful, equal relationship. Your dad and I, well, we just rubbed along together because that's what we were used to. Now I've found James, I can see how wrong we were together. But you and Daniel – you already have that. Don't throw it away.'

'What if he doesn't love me any more?' I say.

'And what makes you think that?' says Mum. 'That boy worships the ground you walk on. I saw it in his eyes the first time you brought him home. He adores you and that hasn't stopped just because you hurt him. I was prepared to forgive your dad for much worse. Daniel will come round in time, you'll see. But you need to be careful not to push him away.'

I think about what Mum says when I get back home. It's a frosty, bleak day in early December. The days feels so grey and cold, the house is freezing, and it seems so empty. Normally we'd have all the decorations up by now, the lights would be sparkling in the conservatory, making me feel festive. Daniel and the others would have been off to get the tree, and they'd have decorated it while I cooked the Sunday roast. I haven't had the heart to do it on my own. Which I know is ridiculous, and not at all fair on Megan.

When she gets in from school, I drag her off to the local garden centre to get a tree. I might not be feeling festive, but I should make the effort for her sake. She's thrilled and texts Sam to come over so they can put the decorations up together; half of them are things they made at nursery and infant school but so much a part of our family tradition now that I can't bear to let them go. It's lovely to have them both here, and we put some Christmas carols on while we decorate. Megan and Sam have always been such good friends. I'm glad what's been happening hasn't altered that.

I sit down to start planning the Christmas lunch. I haven't even ordered a turkey yet. I swear Mum always puts an order in to her butchers in September. I hope I haven't left it too late. If they haven't got any left in our local butchers, I'll have to risk Mum's disapproval and get one from Sainsbury's. I've definitely left it too late to make a pudding. Oh well, I can pick one up in Waitrose if necessary. Mum normally has hers all done in October, but I suspect she's had other fish to fry this year. She and James seem to be getting closer and closer, and she seems quite happy to leave Christmas up to me. I would have been delighted in the past; now I just wonder how I'm going to get through the day.

When I've finished sorting out my Christmas lists, I pick

up the latest spread I've been working on, to see if it's exactly as I want it. Misery seems to be firing my imagination, and unlike the previous book this one is almost drawing itself. The pages I'm looking at come at the end of the book, when my angel leads Jesus, Mary and Joseph to safety. It's such a lovely, cosy, safe scene. It makes me long for the security I had such a short time ago. I look at my angel and she looks back at me compassionately. 'Oh angel,' I whisper, 'I wish you could lead me safely home.'

Lou

I'm having a blast back here in Tenerife. Maria and I get on so well. We might not have known each other very long, but I quickly realise that she's the total opposite of Jo – in a good way. She's kind and caring, and living together is great; we share domestic tasks equally. She's from a large family, who all welcome me with open arms. And unlike Jo, she's interested in my family, and asks frequently about what is happening at home. Finally I feel like I've found my soulmate. Took me long enough.

It's great being in the warm, knowing that life in England is so grey and miserable. Although it's going to be strange to be away for Christmas, I am enjoying the adventure.

Maria introduced me to her family over a long Sunday lunch. We're going to spend Christmas Day with them – though weirdly in Spain they celebrate on the sixth of January, and Maria tells me we'll be working on the twenty-fifth of December. She's sorting out the paperwork for me to join her firm. I can't wait.

Beth Skypes me frequently. She and Daniel still seem to be at odds, and she's made what I think is a calamitous decision to let him have a divorce if he wants one. I think she's pushing him away, and punishing herself for what happened.

'You should fight harder for him,' I tell her. 'You have so much going for you.'

'I don't think he sees it like that,' she says sadly. 'He didn't say anything when I suggested it. I think I've hurt him too much.'

'But, Beth! You can't give up that easily, you just can't.' I so want her and Daniel to be happy again.

'I think I have to face facts, Lou,' she says. 'Daniel just can't get over this, we're not going to be able to make it work.'

I know she's wrong, but she won't be budged, and I am in despair when I tell Maria about it.

'I can't bear to see her so unhappy,' I say, 'and I bet Daniel is too.'

'You should help them,' she says.

'But what can I do?'

'You talk to your brother-in-law, no?'

'Yes, I do,' I say, 'I'm not sure he'll listen to me though.'

'It's worth a try, don't you think?'

I agree with her – it is.

I decide to take matters into my own hands. I am very fond of my brother-in-law, but Daniel can be both stubborn and stupid.

Sorry to hear the love nest (my joke from when they were first married) *is still in disarray. Any chance of a Christmas reconciliation?*

Daniel's response is surprisingly swift.

I'm not sure she wants me back. I've been such a dickhead to her, and she's made it pretty clear she wants to move on after Christmas.

I smile wryly. They are both being such idiots. I could bang their heads together.

Daniel, you muppet, she thinks you want to move on.

She does?

Daniel, darling. Go and get your wife back. She's miserable without you.

He sends me a smiley face in return.

I'm not usually one to play Cupid, but I can't help hoping I've succeeded this time.

Daniel

After the texts Lou sent him, Daniel began to have a small flickering of hope. Christmas was almost upon them, but Daniel had been too miserable to take much notice. Now though, he tried to be more positive. Maybe all was not lost after all. There was a definite happy vibe in school, with everyone winding down for the Christmas break. Even Jim Ferguson was being friendly, which was surprising. Daniel did his best to join in with the overall festive spirit. The school was full of excited students, and there was the usual round of end-of-term concerts, fairs and services, which somehow Daniel got through. It at least meant he was too busy to dwell too much on his unhappiness, or work out what he should do to get Beth back, but with the prospect of school finishing, Daniel knew he was going to have to face up to the reality of his personal life pretty soon. There wasn't much time left to bury his head in the sand.

On the day term broke up, Megan gave him another boost.

'You do know Mum's doing a signing in Waterstone's on Saturday, don't you?'

Daniel smiled at her lack of subtlety. He had seen the posters all round town last time he'd been in Wottonleigh, but had deliberately blanked them.

'I'd forgotten,' he admitted.

'You should go,' urged Megan, giving him that sweet smile that reminded him so much of her mother.

'What if she doesn't want me there?'

'You won't know unless you turn up,' said Megan with a grin.

Which was true, but Daniel wasn't sure he'd be able to stand it if Beth rejected him.

He was still fretting about whether or not to go on the Friday night. Reggie and Sam were performing at their local, so he went down to join them. The pub was teeming with cheerful revellers, and a roaring fire by the tree gave the place a cosy Christmas feel. Reggie's band completed the effect by churning out renditions of all the Christmas songs in their catalogue. It was a fun night, and Daniel actually enjoyed himself. He could see more and more the good Reggie had done Sam; he'd brought him out of his shell, and didn't let him get away with any nonsense. By the end of the evening, Sam had been worked to the bone. If he had any illusions before how hard a career in music was going to be, Reggie had clearly shattered them.

Daniel could see clearly now how much his anger had poisoned his feelings about Reggie. Since he'd left Beth, he could see the bigger picture. Much as he adored his mum, she had hurt Reggie badly. He had had to adjust his view on her, but he realised now that he hadn't actually listened to what she'd said about Reggie, assuming that her anger matched his. Now he could see there was guilt mixed up in her emotions towards her husband. He remembered how insistent she had always been that he shouldn't cut his dad out completely. It was the only reason he had stayed vaguely in touch over the years. He wished he'd known the truth earlier. So much wasted time. He knew a lot of the fault was Reggie's, but some of it was Mum's too. Thank God, he'd had this second chance with Reggie. Thank God Sam had pushed him into it. His son had forced him to go to a place he had been running from his whole life, and thanks to Sam, he was on the way to having his dad back. And in doing so, he'd got his son back too.

'Well done, mate,' Daniel said, when Sam had finished and was coming for a well-deserved pint.

'Thanks,' said Sam, looking pleased. 'Dad, erm, I've been doing some thinking. Grandad thinks I should go back to college and retake my A Levels.'

'What do you think?' said Daniel cautiously.

'I don't want to work in a pub for the rest of my life, and if I want to be a musician I think I need to know more about it. So I'd like to do a musical arts course at uni.'

'That's great!' said Daniel. 'I'm really pleased. Have you told Mum?'

'Yeah, she's happy about it too.'

Sam looked a bit abashed. 'I think I maybe didn't listen to you both enough at the time.'

Daniel laughed. 'No one ever listens to their parents enough. And to be fair, maybe I didn't go about saying things in the right way. I'm really sorry.'

Sam grinned. 'I think I may have been a bit of a knob at times,' he said.

'You may have been,' agreed Daniel. 'But that's all in the past. I'm just pleased you have a plan. Come here, you idiot.'

He pulled his son into his arms, and they hugged tightly. All the hurt and pain that had been between them slipped away. At least one thing had come right in his life – his son had come back to him.

'So does that mean you're coming home?' Daniel asked, feeling a bit nervous. 'I don't think living with Reggie will be exactly conducive to study.'

'Yeah, I might,' he said. Then he looked at Daniel slyly. 'What about you? When are you coming home?'

Daniel sighed. 'That depends on your mum.'

Reggie came over; he'd overheard the last part of their conversation.

'I'm not about to interfere in your life, son,' he said. 'I know that I don't have the right. All I'd say is, don't make the mistakes I made. I have regretted the way I treated your mum for my whole life, and I have suffered for it. I'd hate to see you throw your marriage away. Beth's lovely. I think she deserves another chance.'

'I'll think about it,' said Daniel, sipping his pint.

Maybe they were both right. Maybe it was time to go home.

Chapter Thirty-Six

Lou

'So, Louisa,' Maria wakes me up as the sun streams through the windows. 'It's time to come and watch me in the day job. No more holiday for you. We have a lot of Christmas guests flying in.'

I've been back here for a week, and am still absolutely loving it. I've left a lot of stuff at home, but I've arranged for some crates to come over from England. It feels crazy, and daring, and so *right* to be leaving my old life behind. I can't wait to get started on my new one. It's weird having Christmas in the sunshine, but I like it.

I give Maria a mock groan, but I'm pleased really. I like the idea of us working together.

We go to her office, and she gives me a list of guests and which villas and apartments we need to inspect before they arrive. Maria is meticulous as we check over the properties, calling the cleaners back if she doesn't think they've done a good enough job, making a note of what needs repairing. We have a fun morning, and I particularly enjoy handing over keys to the couples and families who've just arrived, loaded with Christmas presents, for some longed-for winter sun. It's actually a lovely thing to see people arriving for their holidays.

It's a long day, but by the end of it, I feel more satisfied than I have at work in a long time.

'So what do you think?' Maria wants to know.

'I love it,' I say. 'Thanks for the opportunity.'

'You are good with people,' Maria says. 'And it's great to have an English person to help out.'

'It's great to have a job that for once I think I'm going to enjoy,' I say. 'I've never really enjoyed work, and I think I like the lifestyle here. It's much more laid-back than in England.'

'Good,' says Maria. 'I hoped you would say that.'

'Best I start taking Spanish lessons, then.'

Maria laughs and I kiss her softly on the lips. I feel so lucky to have found her.

'Thanks for everything, Maria,' I say. 'You've turned my life around.'

'And you mine,' says Maria with a smile. I feel a warm, comfortable glow. I know this time it's going to work out.

We clink glasses as we sit on the little balcony of Maria's apartment, watching the setting sun.

'Do you think you'd like to stay a while?' she asks.

'Oh yes,' I say, 'I think I'd like to stay a very long while . . .'

Daniel

It was eleven in the morning and Daniel still hadn't left the house. He knew he should. He knew what he wanted to do, but somehow inertia kept him on the sofa. It was one of those bright, cold, sharp days in December that make you feel alive. He should really at least get outdoors.

It was Megan who made up his mind. *So RU coming or what?* she texted.

He was still worried that Lou might have got it wrong and Beth didn't want him any more, but it seemed churlish not to be there for such a special moment. *The Littlest Angel* was riding high in the bestseller charts, and there was already talk of them making a children's film. Beth deserved it after all her hard work. He was still her husband. He should support her.

He made his way through the humming throng of shoppers on a last-minute dash to finish their present-buying. Everyone seemed so happy and vibrant, and looking forward to the big day. It made him feel hopeful for the future, and even though he was nervous as hell, today the Christmas music cheered him up. It was a special time of year after all; maybe miracles really did happen.

There was a long queue at the bookshop, and Beth was so busy she didn't see him. He decided to queue up and surprise her, waiting patiently in line with the mums, dads, grandparents and small children, all thrilled to meet Beth. His wife. *His* Beth. It made him feel unbearably proud.

It was while he was waiting that he suddenly clocked there were a couple of people with Beth, one he didn't recognise, but the other – what the hell was Jack Stevens doing there? He was overcome with a sense of fury. How dare he turn up now? Did it mean he was with Beth? Daniel's heart was hammering. Please, not that, not now. Not after everything.

He tried to gauge Beth's reaction to Jack, but from this distance he couldn't. At one point Jack leaned down towards her and Beth looked as if she were trying to get rid of him, but he couldn't be sure. Then Jack left. Good. Daniel hoped he'd gone for good. Anxiety gnawed at him. What if he'd pushed Beth straight back into Jack's arms?

There was still no sign of Jack by the time he got to the front of the queue, which made him feel marginally better, but he still felt nervous. There was so much riding on this. What would he do if Beth told him to piss right off?

She still hadn't spotted him. Stepping forward, he pushed his copy of the book in front of her, and said, 'Any chance of a special message from my favourite author?'

Beth looked up, her face lighting up to see him. Daniel's heart leapt. That was a good reaction. A better one than he'd hoped.

'I think there's every chance,' said Beth softly. 'Every chance indeed.'

Beth

I am gobsmacked when Daniel turns up. I hadn't even told him about the signing. Then I see Megan, who has popped in to wish me luck, and I twig from her slight smirk that she's responsible for Daniel's presence. She gives me a thumbs up, and then leaves to finish her Christmas shopping. My heart is pounding, but in a good way. This has to be a step forward, doesn't it? Daniel has come, he's actually come to see me. Perhaps I dare hope. I'm anxious too though – of all the staff at my publishers, why did Jack have to come down to support me? Vanessa was supposed to come but had pulled out at the last minute. I felt sick to the stomach when he arrived. I'd rather have had no representative at all. Any feelings I had for him have long gone. I cannot imagine why I let my fantasies about Jack ruin my marriage. I've sent him off to get coffee and get him out of my hair. I really hope he doesn't come back before Daniel goes.

Which is why, of course, he turns up two minutes later.

'I got you a latte the way you like it,' he says, and then, 'Oh,' when he sees Daniel.

'Oh, indeed,' says Daniel.

They glare at each other like a pair of marauding bulldogs. *Please don't let them cause a scene here*, I think. There are still people queuing up.

'Guys, can you please just keep hold of your testosterone levels till we're done?' I hiss.

They reluctantly move away from the table, and stand glowering at one another from opposite corners of the room.

After half an hour I'm done and I say my goodbyes and thank yous to the people in the bookshop. Jack makes a beeline for me, reaching me before Daniel does. He deliberately kisses me on the cheek and hugs me. I stiffen.

'Lizzie, you were fabulous. I insist on taking you out for lunch.'

I bristle at this. Who does he think he is?

'I rather think that's my job,' says Daniel, appearing by my side looking bullish, which makes me feel much better.

'I believe Lizzie is a free agent now,' says Jack. 'She doesn't have to put up with this middle-class bag of shit any more. Honestly, Lizzie, I can't believe you've stood this small-town living for so long. You're a city girl at heart.'

What the hell is Jack playing at? I've had no contact with him for months, and now he's behaving like a jealous terrier. He's going to make Daniel think something's still going on. Oh, right. I suddenly clock it: that's exactly what he wants Daniel to think. I'm not going to play his stupid manipulative games.

Daniel moves towards him menacingly. Oh no. I've never seen him hit someone, but I think he might be getting close to it now.

'Beth can make her own decision about lunch,' I say firmly, 'and this "small-town living" happens to be my life, Jack, and I love it. Now can you please go?'

Jack looks at me sorrowfully, 'You can't mean that.'

I look at him with distaste. What does this man know about me, really? In his head I am still the twenty-something girl he knew, who would do anything for him; he knows nothing of my life now.

'I do,' I say. 'I don't know why you've come today, Jack. I made it clear I didn't want to see you again. I made a mistake over you, and I don't intend to repeat it.'

'But we could be good together,' Jack urges. 'I know we could.'

'Like we were twenty years ago?' I say. 'Jack, it's over. You have to believe me when I say that. I was infatuated by you for a little while, but I love Daniel.'

'But I love you—' Jack starts.

Suddenly I am furious with him. He doesn't love me, he never has loved me, I was just a game to him. He still has no idea of the hell he's put me and Daniel through.

'No you don't,' I say. 'You've never loved me, you just love the *idea* of me being at your beck and call. It's over, Jack. I want you to leave right now.'

'I think the lady asked you to leave,' Daniel steps closer to him, in a slightly threatening manner that is most un-Daniel like. Jack flinches. For a terrible moment I really think Daniel is going to hit him, and part of me rather wishes he would. But then he says, 'Nah you're not worth it, but if you don't go now I'll call security to get rid of you.'

And with that Jack is gone.

I turn to look at Daniel.

'My hero,' I say. 'I thought you were going to hit him.'

'I'd never do that,' he says, smiling at me.

'So are you coming home or what?' I ask.

'What do *you* think?' he says, as he leans over to kiss me.

In the end, it's as easy as that.

The Littlest Angel

The Littlest Angel crept forward.

'Would you like to see the baby?' Mary called her over.

'Oh, yes,' said the Angel. She flew down to look at the special new baby. He was sleeping and looked so calm.

'What is his name?'

'His name is Jesus,' said Mary. 'And he's the <u>most important baby in the world</u>.'

Vanessa Marlow: <u>Oh this is lovely. Really cute ending. I can picture the final scene!</u>

Beth King: Thanks.

Epilogue

'Sam and Megan, are you *ever* going to get up? There's stuff to do!'

I got up early this morning to start getting everything ready. I refused to get up at six though, and have told everyone to come for 2 p.m. I'm determined there are going to be no rules today, and definitely no charades. Everyone is going to have as relaxed a time as possible. So far it's been great. Old as they are, Sam and Megan insisted on coming in at 7 a.m. to show us what they'd got in their stockings, a tradition instigated by Sam aged four. We went through the stockings and then they both shuffled off back to bed, bleary-eyed but happy. Daniel got up to make me tea in bed, and we'd had lovely Christmas sex to celebrate the festive season properly. It's been the best thing about us breaking up. We've had a lot of making-up sex in the last week.

I went downstairs at eight and put the turkey on (Sainsbury's finest, I'm hoping Mum won't notice) and Daniel came down looking deliciously sexy in his dressing gown. We peeled the veggies together, singing tunelessly to old Christmas records. Well, I was tuneless. Daniel has, as I say, got a rather wonderful baritone.

I've finally persuaded Megan and Sam to get up properly and help tidy the house. They keep nudging each other and giggling, and then giving Daniel pointed looks. I'm sure it's to do with my Christmas present, so I'm doing my best to ignore them. Sam and Daniel make a makeshift table out of bits of plywood, and attach it to the end of our table. There are going to be eleven of us for dinner, plus baby Thomas, and our own table isn't big enough. I smile fondly as they wrestle with the wood; it's lovely to have my boys back together, working as a team. They're getting on well at the moment; Sam has enrolled at the local college to re-sit his exams and Daniel is being supportive of his music as well.

Megan has spent hours over the last few days making table decorations of Santas and snowmen. She lays them out carefully, one at each place setting. By the time she's finished, the table looks very festive.

I hug her and Sam. I'm so glad my family is whole once more.

'Get off,' says Sam, when I say so. 'I am eighteen you know.'

'You'll always be my little Sammywam,' I tease, and he rolls his eyes.

I am about to ask Daniel if he can help me transfer the enormous turkey onto a roasting dish, when I realise I haven't seen him for about half an hour.

'Where's your dad?' I ask. The kids just shrug their shoulders.

'I think he's popped out,' Megan offers helpfully.

'Popped out? Popped out where? People are going to be here any moment.'

'It's OK,' says Sam, glancing out of the window, 'I think he's back.'

Daniel walks into the kitchen holding something under

his coat. I'm so preoccupied with the turkey that I don't clock it at first.

'Where on earth have you been?' I start, and then look at what he's holding. 'Daniel, you didn't?'

Daniel breaks into a huge grin, 'I did. Happy Christmas, Beth,' he says and hands me over a wriggly, licky, adorable Labrador puppy.

I am speechless, 'But you said—'

'I said a lot of things, Beth. I know how much you've wanted a dog. Your mum's been looking after him for the last couple of days.'

'Oh Daniel, you big idiot,' I say, and give him a fat soppy kiss. I am overwhelmed. I can't believe he's done this for me. I fuss over the gorgeous puppy for a few minutes before setting him down for Megan and Sam to take over.

At 12.30 the doorbell rings and Rachel, Ged and Thomas arrive. Thomas is sitting up now, playing with his toys, and Megan is immediately down on the floor trying to make him laugh. I've invited Rachel and Ged to stay over so they can both have a drink, and they happily join us in a toast.

The atmosphere is light, so different from last year.

'Which of the parents is going to arrive first, do you think?' says Ged.

'Mum,' I say. 'Dad's always late. So long as they don't arrive together . . .'

Sure enough Mum and James arrive first, followed by Reggie, who hits it off with James straight away. Luckily he also seems to get on well with Dad when he and Lilian eventually turn up, which makes life a lot easier.

Everyone seems to be getting on in a civilised manner, and I'm hoping it will stay that way.

I needn't have worried. Both couples seem to be on their best behaviour, and it turns out that Reggie has a great talent for bringing people together. He and Daniel are more relaxed now in each other's company, and I'm noticing how alike they actually are. They both care about other people, and want to put them at their ease. It's lovely to watch them together.

Everyone loves the puppy too, and all the fussing over it breaks the tension nicely. So by the time we sit down to lunch the atmosphere is quite riotous, with James joshing Dad about whether cricket is more important than golf, and Lilian complimenting Mum on how well she looks. It's going better than I could have ever imagined.

I am stressed up to the eyeballs about the turkey, but Daniel takes over the last bit of cooking for me so that I can enjoy myself a bit more. Ged and Rachel are really helpful when it comes to serving up, so I don't feel as if the whole day is on my shoulders.

As we sit and raise a Christmas toast, I'm just so glad to be with my family, patchwork and all as it is. I cannot think of anyone I'd rather spend Christmas with. It would be lovely to have Lou here, but she's so happy with Maria, I can't begrudge her this time. And there's always next year.

After lunch there's an orgy of present opening. Thomas inevitably ends up chewing most of the paper along with the new puppy. Thomas has been given an inordinate amount of noisy things, and Ged doesn't look impressed. He rolls his eyes at Rachel, who kisses him on the cheek.

'Never mind,' she says, 'perhaps we can hide them.'

'I can see myself losing the batteries on a few of these,' Ged says.

'Don't worry, they run out pretty quickly,' I laugh. 'Most of the toys will probably be broken by New Year's Day.'

The puppy is happily bouncing about the room, and

we're all trying to think of names for him when we remember that we've promised to Skype Lou and Maria.

It takes a while to set up, but thanks to the young techie bods in the house we finally get it to work. We all crowd round the screen, waving and shouting 'Happy Christmas!' while Lou and Maria beam wildly back at us. They look so happy together, it's really lovely to see.

'While I've got you all here,' Ged suddenly says, sounding a little self-conscious, 'I thought it would be a good moment to tell you – I am proud to announce that Rachel has agreed to become my wife. We want to get married in July next year, and I really hope you'll all be able to come.'

Wow. I give Ged a huge hug, beaming at him. I'm so proud of him for changing his womanising ways.

'You keep us away!' shrieks Lou. 'That's so exciting.'

There's a blur of raised glasses and toasts, and then Reggie says, 'How about we have some music?'

We wave goodbye to Lou and Maria, and Reggie gets out his guitar and starts strumming, 'Simply Having a Wonderful Christmas Time' on his guitar. We're all a bit drunk by now and the atmosphere is getting raucous. Amazingly Thomas manages to sleep right through it.

'You having a good time?' says Daniel.

'Yup,' I say. 'Happy Christmas, darling.'

'Happy Christmas, and here's to a better year next year.' I smile at him. The puppy wanders over and licks my hand.

Daniel stands up and shushes everyone.

'This has been a momentous year for our family in many ways. But I think we can all say we've come out of it stronger, better and with a few new members. To the Holroyd family in all its forms. Happy Christmas.'

'Happy Christmas!' Everyone raises their glasses.

'Look,' said Megan. 'It's snowing!'

We all go to look out of the window as the snow falls softly down. I look out at the dark sky, and see the festive lights from our neighbours' houses twinkling in the distance. I can almost imagine my little angel up there, helping other people out the way she's helped me.

Happy Christmas, little angel, I say to myself, *and thank you*.

I pull myself closer to Daniel.

'You're the best Christmas present I could possibly have,' I say. 'Welcome home.'

The Littlest Angel Saves the Day

So the Littlest Angel led Jesus, Mary and Joseph over the border from Israel into Egypt.

There she took them to a place where they would be safe, and she looked over them all until it was <u>time to go home.</u>

<u>**Vanessa Marlow:** Lovely! I can really see us making a series out of this. Have you any ideas for the next book?</u>
<u>**Beth King:** Erm. NO.</u>

Beth

It's funny how sometimes you have to take the long way round. I thought my life was going nowhere. I thought it could be better. And then I learnt the hard way that the life I already had was the one I wanted and needed. If my little angel has taught me anything, it's this: be content with your life. It's the only one you've got. Whichever way you look at it, there are parts which are always going to be pretty wonderful.

Acknowledgements

As ever, a massive thank you has to go out to the amazing team at Avon who have been very supportive. Particular thanks go to Phoebe Morgan, Natasha Harding and Eloise Wood. A big thank you to my agent Oli Munson for his support.

When writing this book I asked a lot of people for help on a variety of matters, so I would also like to thank: Anne Booth, Deirdre Cleary, Peter Graham, Catherine Johnson, Lucy Pepper and Nina Wadcock for answering a lot of my questions.

Finally a big thank you to my twin sister, Virginia Moffatt who as always was my first cheerleader and gave me useful feedback.

The Littlest Angel

By Beth King

The Littlest Angel was very excited. The whole Heavenly Host were preparing for a Big Event.

'*The* Big Event,' Gabriel said.

There had already been a buzz around a baby born a few months earlier, but Gabriel said this baby was going to be even more important. *This* baby was going to save the world.

The Heavenly Host were going to go and tell people, and for the first time the Littlest Angel was going to be allowed to come too.

'Is it today?' the Angel asked her mother.

'Not today,' said her mother.

'Is it today?' asked the Angel.

'Not today,' said her mother, 'but soon.'

The days went by and still it wasn't the right day, until finally the Littlest Angel asked, 'Is it *today*?'

And her mother said, 'Yes, it's today.'

'Yippee!' cried the Littlest Angel. And she got ready to go.

*

The Littlest Angel was so excited she flew straight to her room to pick up her trumpet. But she couldn't find it anywhere.

'Hurry!' said her mother, 'Or we'll leave without you.'

The Littlest Angel searched high and low, but it was nowhere to be seen.

'I can't find it!' she said to her mother, who was busy gathering together the other little angels by the Pearly Gates as the Heavenly Host got ready to leave.

'Go and look again,' said the Angel's mother, 'but be quick!'

The Littlest Angel had just found her trumpet under the bed when she heard a huge flurry, the blowing of trumpets and a chorus of Hallelujahs.

Oh no! The Heavenly Host were about to set off on their journey.

'Wait for me!' cried the Littlest Angel, but it was too late; by the time she'd got to the Pearly Gates, the Heavenly Host had left in a blaze of glory.

The Littlest Angel flew after them with all her might, but she was too little and they were too fast. They swirled in a huge golden mass far ahead of her in the dark of night. She flew and flew but as hard as she tried she couldn't catch up with them. Before long the Littlest Angel was all alone and very lost.

The Littlest Angel flew this way and that, but it was no good, she couldn't see the Heavenly Host anywhere. How would she find the new baby now? Sadly, she flew down to earth to take a rest. She landed on a hillside, overlooking a large plain. In the distance she could see lights sparkling from some far off town. Was that where the baby was going to be born? Without the Heavenly Host to guide her, how would she ever know?

The Littlest Angel started to cry. She didn't know where she was, or what to do.

'Are you all right, little angel?' A small boy who was cradling a lamb in his arms came shyly up to meet her. 'You seem sad.'

'I am sad,' said the Angel. 'I'm looking for the new baby who is going to be born on this special night, but I've lost the other angels and I'll never find him now.'

'But the angels were here!' said the boy. 'They came singing songs of praise, and asked the other shepherds to go and worship at the baby's feet.'

'Where did they go?' said the Littlest Angel.

'They went that way,' said the little boy, pointing in the direction of the faraway town.

He looked a little sad too.

'Didn't you go with them?' said the Angel.

'No,' said the boy, 'I must stay and guard the sheep. Will you come back and tell me about the baby?'

'Of course I will,' said the Littlest Angel. 'But now I must go. I'm to sing at the baby's cradle and I mustn't be late.'

'The angels told the shepherds to follow that star,' said the shepherd boy, pointing to the brightest star in the sky. 'You will find the baby where the star rests.'

Of course! The star. The Littlest Angel had forgotten that the star would lead them to where the baby lay. She could see it shining bright far away in the distance.

'Thank you,' said the Littlest Angel, and she went on her way.

*

The Littlest Angel set off feeling much happier. She knew which way to go, and soon she would find the baby. She flew into the night sky, but still she could see no sign of the Heavenly Host. The star looked very far away, and she wondered if she would ever reach it. Then below her, she spotted a camel train riding across. Maybe they had seen the Heavenly Host.

The Littlest Angel flew down to the ground and landed beside a grumpy-looking camel.

'Have you seen the Heavenly Host?' she asked.

The camel stared at her in disdain.

'I don't know,' said the camel. 'I think they went that way.'

'I saw them,' said a page boy who was walking behind the camel. He was holding a precious looking box.

'What have you got there?' she said.

'Gold for the new king,' said the page.

'Do you mean the baby who is going to be born tonight?' asked the Littlest Angel.

'Yes,' said the page boy. 'My masters are looking for a king. The angels told them to follow a star, and it would lead us to him.'

'Oh,' said the Littlest Angel. 'I think you're going the wrong way.'

'I'll tell them,' said the page boy, and the angel went on her way.

The Littlest Angel was growing excited. She couldn't be too far behind the Heavenly Host now. The star was growing brighter in the sky, yet somehow the further she flew, the further away it seemed. Sometimes the Littlest Angel thought she would never get there. But she couldn't give up. She had to be at the new baby's birth.

*

At last, the Littlest Angel could see the lights of the town she had seen from the hill so many hours ago. To her surprise, the star seemed to have stopped over a small building. Maybe that was where the new baby was going to be born. Her journey was nearly over!

But the star had stopped above a stable. The Littlest Angel was puzzled. Surely the special baby wouldn't be born in a stable?

She flew down to the ground, and saw a donkey tethered against the stable door.

'Hello,' said the Littlest Angel. 'I'm looking for the new baby. Do you know when it's going to be born?'

'Oh,' said the donkey. 'I think it's tonight. I've carried his mother all the way here. He's going to be a very special baby.'

'I know,' said the angel. 'That's why I'm here.'

The Littlest Angel pushed open the door of the stable and crept forward.

There she saw a lady and a man. The lady was holding a baby, and laying it in a cradle. The Littlest Angel's heart was filled with joy. Here at last was the special new baby. And she was the first to see him.

'Would you like to see the baby?' Mary called her over.

'Oh, yes,' said the Angel. She flew over to look at the baby. He was sleeping and looked so calm.

'What is his name?'

'His name is Jesus,' said Mary. 'And he's the most important baby in the world.'

Just then there was the sound of trumpets, and the most beautiful singing. The Heavenly Host had arrived! The Littlest Angel flew to greet them, and together they sang songs of praise for the baby who would save the world.

A hilarious and just a little bit heart-breaking festive treat for anyone who's looking for a dash of magic this Christmas time . . .

The perfect read for fans of Carole Matthews, Trisha Ashley and Jenny Colgan.

The course of true love never did
run smooth!

If you like Katie Fforde and Veronica
Henry, you'll love this!

For anyone who's wondered
whether Christmas is over-priced
hype, think again . . .

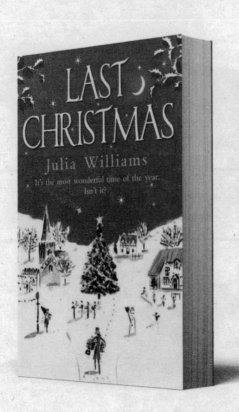

Discover the true spirit of Christmas
with this seasonal treat for fans of
Love Actually and *The Holiday*.